Deadly Mates

DEADLY MATES

Deadly Trilogy Book 2

Ashley Stoyanoff

Ashley Stoyanoff Books

London, Ontario

Also by Ashley Stoyanoff

Dedication

For my husband, Jordan, because you have always
believed in me.

CHAPTER 1

JADE

I shuddered as flares of hot adrenaline shot through my limbs. My legs crunched and snapped, a hollow, echoing sound as they twisted and reformed. It was weird shifting; I could feel each bone in my body bend and break, but it was also a rush — electric. My face was numb and tingly as my snout became a nose. I still expected it to hurt. It sure sounded painful. But it wasn't. The adrenaline that came with the shift was invigorating, coursing through my blood and sending each nerve ending into a breathtaking current of delirious heat. *God, how I love this feeling.*

The cool fall breeze prickled along my bare skin, littering it with goosebumps, but I hardly noticed. My heart was thrumming against my ribs, and my breath, short and fast. I lay on my back, the cold grass tickling my sensitive skin, as I gazed up at the canopy of trees overhead, catching my breath. The leaves danced in the wind, a mixture of pumpkin and cherry and lemon. A few fell from the branches, floating to the ground around me.

The sound of a wolf's whimper and grunt flitted through the air, and with a groan, I pushed myself up

1

to my feet, feeling each achy muscle in my body as I rose. I pivoted in place, scanning the small clearing for the wolves I knew were close by, keeping my muscles tight and ready.

A rumbling growl filled the air, and I swiveled to the right. There wasn't much light in the small clearing. The sun was just starting to rise; peeking through the trees, the sky was a deep denim blue with soft veins of gold. I strained my eyes and senses, keeping my stance ready. It took me a moment to find the wolves, but when my eyes landed on them, I couldn't stop the burst of laughter that erupted from me.

Jared and Beck were heaped together in a tangled mess of paws and legs, nestled at the base of a thick oak tree in a pile of leaves. I may not have been physically stronger than they were, but I was by far faster. I laughed again. I just couldn't help it. I'd only been a werewolf for a week, and already, I'd managed to outsmart and outmaneuver the big, bad enforcers.

Beck poked his gray snout out from underneath one of Jared's paws. His eyes shimmered with flecks of gold, and he gave me a big doggy smile and let out a playful yip before squirming out from underneath Jared. They both managed to get back on their feet, and as soon as they did, Jared's deep brown coat started to ripple as he began to shift.

I shook my head and smirked, swallowing the giggle that bubbled up in my throat and darted into the trees to fetch my clothes before Jared could finish his shift. It was one thing to stand stark naked in front of them as wolves, but I still wasn't all that comfortable doing it while they were human. Well, okay, to be honest, it was more that I wasn't comfortable standing in front of Jared naked. I didn't trust my inner-wolf to behave. She was pulled to Jared, enthralled by his dominant scent more than I liked or cared to admit.

I had just made it behind the broad pine where my clothes were stashed when Jared called, "Where are you running off to, kitten?" The huskiness of his voice made my inner-wolf squirm and my spine straighten. I sucked in a breath, trying to calm the beast within me. *Darn it!* I loathed the effect he had on her. Even the sound of his voice made her perk up, sending excited shivers along my skin.

"To get clothes on," I called, snagging my underwear and bra from the pile and yanking them on hastily.

"We've seen you naked before," Jared said, chuckling.

I bristled, seriously not needing the reminder of Jared seeing me naked. It had happened yesterday after seeing Aidan for the first time in two days. My inner-wolf had been crazy worked up. She'd been furious at me for walking away from him — her mate — and when training started, Beck and Jared had gotten the brunt of her fury. I'd had them both cowering at my feet within five minutes. When I'd shifted, my stomach was growling. I couldn't get the food-like clouds that Aidan had pointed out, out of my mind. And my inner-wolf couldn't let go of the way rubbing against his hand made her feel. The contentment, the tingling skin, the frantic need to get closer to him, to have him.

After we'd shifted, Jared had tried to use his scent to soothe her. It didn't work. She'd gone wild, taking me over. If it weren't for Beck, I would probably be mated right now, and it wouldn't be with the wolf that I knew, without a doubt, was mine. No matter how pissed I was at Aidan, my inner-wolf and I both knew that he was my mate. It was a feeling, something deep within my bones. My inner-wolf recognized him as hers — as mine — even if I wasn't ready (didn't want) to claim him.

Jared's chuckles echoed in my ears, and I felt my

heart beat a bit faster. I huffed and shouted, "Doesn't mean I have to stand there and let you gawk." I didn't mean to shout it, he probably would have heard me at even a whisper, but right then, I couldn't control my tone. A blush flared along my skin; it started at my toes and spread all the way to my cheeks.

"I don't gawk, little girl," Jared growled. He was trying to sound fierce, but I caught the humor and something that sounded a whole lot like longing in his tone.

I rolled my eyes. Jared didn't exactly gawk, but he also didn't hide the fact that he looked. And that appraising gaze he gave me after I shifted yesterday, well, it made my inner-wolf shudder. But the thing was, Jared was a dick, plain and simple. Other than his enthralling scent and the undeniable strength he had within the pack, there was nothing about him that I really liked, well, at least nothing that would make me want to take the mating jump with him. He was friend material, loyal beyond sanity, but nothing more, and each moment that passed, I regretted it a little bit more that I hadn't asked Beck to pretend to be my mate. Beck was hot, but nothing about him made me, or my inner-wolf, sing. It would have been a safer choice.

"Uh, yeah, you kind of do," Beck said, laughing. "Why'd you shift, Jade? It was just getting fun."

I grabbed my jeans, tugged them on, and grinned. *Fun.* I had to admit, learning to use my scent and manipulate them with it was kind of fun, but no matter how much fun it was, I was exhausted and achy, and I'd had enough for the day. "Because I'm freakin' tired, is why," I said, as I buttoned up my jeans. "We've been at it for hours already, and besides, I have school." *And you guys haven't let me get a full night of sleep since I became alpha female,* I thought, not bothering to remind them. They only insisted that it was all part of my training each time I did.

"Your dad's coming home tomorrow, and you're going to school?" Beck asked, amusement clear in his timbre.

I cringed a little at the mention of my dad. I wasn't ready to see him or talk to him. I sucked at lying to him, and I had no clue how I would act as if nothing was wrong. I still didn't want to believe the video Erika showed me. I had watched it at least fifty times since the first time I saw it, and each time I watched it, I wanted to throw up. How didn't I know he was a shifter? How didn't I notice that he was like an evil spawn of Satan? I sighed and said, "Yep, Aidan said ..."

"When were you talking to Aidan?" Jared's breath was hot against my neck, and his voice was a low growl. I stiffened, and my breath caught in my throat. He pressed against me, his skin warm against my bare back, and I cursed myself. I needed to pay more attention. I couldn't let them sneak up on me like this. I couldn't let down my guard.

"He sent me a text message last night when you were in the shower," I said, hating how raw my voice sounded and how crazy guilty I felt all of a sudden. I cleared my throat. "We are the alpha pair. It's not like I can ignore him forever." Except, I had kind of planned on doing just that. Well, at least until the whole werecougar mess was dealt with. He didn't need the complication, and honestly, I already had enough to deal with. The last thing I wanted to think about was whether or not I could get over all of his lies. He may feel like home to my inner-wolf and me, but I just wasn't ready to forgive and forget.

Jared placed a hand on my bare shoulder, letting his fingers trail down my arm. My inner-wolf stirred restlessly as his heady scent engulfed me. "Stay home with me. I promise it'll be a hell of a lot more fun."

"Why in the world would I want to do that?" I asked sweetly, stepping away from him and yanking my T-shirt over my head. I didn't give him time to snap out a response before I started to walk away. The hot, salty scent of sweat and anger spiked in the air, and my inner-wolf fought me with each step I took away from him, trying to force me to stay. I didn't think I would ever understand that part of me. Why my inner-wolf reacted to him so strongly, I still didn't know. Sure, Erika had said it was because she recognized a dominant male — a potential mate — but as far as I was concerned, Jared had no potential, not as my mate at least. And my inner-wolf had already picked her mate; we just hadn't claimed him yet. Shouldn't knowing that her mate was close by change her reaction to other males?

I'd only made it a few steps before Beck's rumbling warning reached my ears. "She's his, Jared. She has been from the day they met. You've got to back off. Let all this shit go before you have both of them out for you, man."

For about half a second, I thought about spinning around and telling them that I wasn't *his*, that I didn't belong to anyone, but I didn't. The truth was I belonged to Aidan just as much as he belonged to me.

Jared and Beck followed me, keeping their distance, but I still caught their murmurs as they discussed the plan for tomorrow when Dad got home. I was dreading it. Dreading all of it, I hated how glad I was that Jared would be with me, staying in the house, helping me deal with it all.

When I stepped out of the forest into my backyard, the scent of Belgian waffles and bacon frying drifted around me, and my stomach growled. Mom hadn't been working since Jared moved in, and to my dismay, I really didn't think his presence bothered her much. She doted on him like crazy, always cooking for him and cleaning up after him. They chilled out, watched movies together, and joked around — a lot. I knew the mouthwatering scent wasn't for me. It was for him. Not that it really bothered me. It was just something I noticed. If I knew anything about my mom, she loved to take care of people.

But Jared, on the other hand ... He'd only been living with me for three days now, but he was already getting on my last nerve. He was taking our little act way too seriously, and he was enjoying it far too much. Especially when Aidan was watching. I didn't know how Aidan could stand to watch Jared and me together. I was certain that I wouldn't be able to do it. And God help the wolf or human that tried to move in on him. Yes, it had been my idea to make the act look real. Yes, I knew that we needed to successfully fool the pack and the town to actually fool my dad. The more people who knew it was an act, the more chance my dad would catch wind of it. It had been Dad's idea to mate me to an enforcer when he thought I'd lost the games, and if we had any chance of figuring out exactly what he was doing, playing along with his suggestion seemed like the best way to do it. But honestly, I was beginning to think that Jared believed I was, or soon would be, his mate.

"Mmmm, she made me waffles again," Jared said, coming up beside me and draping a loose arm over my shoulder.

"And bacon," Beck added.

"That's what it smells like," I said dryly, shrugging off Jared's arm. "Way to point out the obvious, guys."

I rounded the house, and I wasn't surprised to see the driveway full. The team hadn't missed a mealtime since Jared had moved in. I climbed the porch steps and reached for the doorknob, my arm stiff and heavy, my muscles screaming at me to rest. I clenched my hand around it and yanked the door open. And then I heard it, a light, bubbly laugh that really shouldn't have been coming from within my house.

Marcy was here.

For about half a second, I stood in the doorway, frozen, before forcing myself to follow the sound. I didn't know whether to be thrilled because, well, I'd been missing my best friend like crazy or pissed off because she'd actually come by. She might be like a sister to me, but she had gone too far. I couldn't help but wonder if things might have played out differently between Aidan and me if she'd just stayed out of it all.

"Jade, look who finally came home," Mom said, waving a hand toward Marcy as I padded into the kitchen. By the look of her, it was a cleaning day. Her thick, dark hair was tied up in a messy knot at the top of her head, and she was wearing faded jeans and a bleach-stained T-shirt.

The team, plus Erika and Marcy, gathered around the table. Landon looked well, hungry, but then he usually did. His tall and lean frame was hunched over the table, his chin resting in his hands. His bleach blond hair was gelled and spiked, and his baby blue eyes met mine for a brief second, and he winked. Beside him was Mark, the youngest member of our team, only seventeen. He was leaning back, slouching in his chair, a thick arm draped over the back. He had on a light grey hoodie, the hood pulled up, covering his mop of curls. A few of them were poking out, framing the hard lines of his face. And then there was Craig with his soft features. Out of all of them, he looked the most unthreatening, sweet even, but his smaller size and warm smile were deceiving. When he was on, he was deadly, but right then, he was too involved with trying to get Erika's attention to even notice we had come in.

Over the last few days, mealtimes had become a bit of a circus with them all here. Our house wasn't really small, but it wasn't big enough for this many people. We bought another table, a bigger one that barely fit within the kitchen, but at least it was big enough for us all to sit down at.

I finally let my gaze drift to Marcy. "Hey," I said, giving her a little nod. She looked awkward sitting with the team. Her cheeks were flushed, and deep crevasses marred her forehead.

"What are you doing here?" Jared questioned, stepping past me. He hadn't bothered putting on his shirt, instead draping it over his shoulders. He gave Marcy a bored once over before sliding into his chair.

"Jared! Marcy lives here, too." Mom scolded, cutting him a disappointed look. It didn't even faze him.

"I thought maybe we could walk to school together," Marcy said, or I guess croaked would be more like it. "Aidan said you were going back today." She made sure to keep her eyes on me as if she were trying to imagine that it was only us and that she wasn't really sitting at a table with the pack enforcers.

I didn't get a chance to answer before Jared said *No*, as if he actually had the right to answer for me.

I pursed my lips and rolled my eyes at him. "Oh, shut up, Jared." I didn't care what *game* we were playing. I was still one of his alphas, even if he didn't want to acknowledge it.

"Now, kitten." Jared's voice was a low growl. He didn't bother looking at me, but his shoulders tensed, and I was sure his eyes were a nice shade of gold right then. "Is that any way to talk to your mate?"

"Will you shut up, please?" I said through gritted

teeth, biting back the reminder that I wanted to spit out. I wasn't his mate — never would be — no matter how much my inner-wolf craved him. This was an act. Something to fool my dad. Nothing more.

My response earned me a few chuckles from around the table, a long, drawn-out groan from Erika, and an annoyed huff from Mom. She pursed her lips and cut me a dirty look.

I rolled my eyes. Mom had always wanted me to hook up with one of the pack members, and to say she disapproved of the way I spoke to Jared was definitely an understatement.

Jared looked up, meeting my eyes. His flared brighter, and he said, "No, I don't think I will. You're not walking to school." And then, as if it were settled, he grinned at my mom and said, "Breakfast smells delicious, Pam."

I watched him in stunned silence for a moment, my jaw dropping a little. My blood was boiling. It was a serious effort to calm down and not blurt out all the nasty things I wanted to say, but after a few deep breaths, I managed to simmer down.

I glanced at the table; Jared and the team were already digging in, and although my stomach was rumbling, I turned, heading out of the room. Right then, the last thing I wanted to do was sit down with my *so-called* mate and play the sweet girlfriend part. "Come on, Mac," I said, waving a hand.

I hadn't even made it to the doorway when Jared's growled command reached my ears. "Jade, sit down and eat."

"I want to talk to her," I said, turning toward him like an obedient mate would do, loathing myself for doing it, and if Mom hadn't been there watching us, I wouldn't have, or at least that's what I tried to tell myself.

Jared dropped his fork, letting it clatter to his plate, and pushed his chair back. His expression was lethal. "I don't like the idea of you walking alone." There was an underlying threat to his tone.

"I won't be alone," I said. "And besides, we're just going up to my room for now."

He opened his mouth to say something else, but I didn't want to hear it. I channeled my scent, feeling the burn of my imprint as it heated beneath my top, sending out a clear warning for him to back the hell off. He stiffened, and his jaw started to tick. He tried to hold my glare, but he couldn't, and I watched as his eyes began to drop.

Marcy didn't miss what was happening. She scrambled from her chair and darted over to me. "Come on, Jade," she said, nudging me with her elbow, "let's go."

CHAPTER 2

AIDAN

It took five minutes for my head to clear enough to realize that the insistent knocking sound was actually someone at the door, and by that time, the knocking had turned into a head-splitting thud, thud, thud. And even then, I stayed in bed, staring up at the ceiling.

Slivers of light streamed through the cracks along the edges of my blackout blinds as the sun began to rise. I shifted my pounding head; the glowing red numbers on my alarm clock read 6:05. I knew I should probably get up, see who the hell thought banging on my door at sunrise was a good idea, but honestly, right then, I didn't really care.

I felt like hell. My head was throbbing as if it had its own pulse, and my eyelids were sore, heavy. I'd only been asleep for about fifteen minutes, and that fifteen minutes had been the longest I'd managed to sleep at once in the last three days. Between the pack, the threat of the werecougars, and the constant, relentless urge to run out, find Jade, and drag her — kicking and screaming, if needed — away from that damn enforcer, sleep had become a luxury; a luxury that I was seriously craving.

I groaned and snagged a pillow, putting it over my head, hoping to drown out the banging. Maybe if I ignored it, whoever it was would just go away.

It didn't work.

The thudding came again, loud enough that it felt as if it were shaking the entire house. Where the hell was Dominic? He was supposed to be dealing with the pack and their petty issues. He was supposed to be giving me time to sleep.

I heaved myself out of bed, stumbled over a pile of clothes, and banged into my dresser. "Dammit!" I growled, kicking the pile of laundry out of my way. The room I now called my bedroom was small cluttered, with a king-size bed and a worn mahogany dresser taking up most of the space.

I sucked in a deep breath, trying to calm my sour mood. It helped — a little. Gritting my teeth, I headed downstairs, not bothering to get dressed. Whoever it was wasn't staying.

The banging came again, hard enough to make the windows rattle. I took the last few steps two at a time and crossed to the door in a few long strides, throwing it open. "What the hell do you want?" I growled before it was even fully opened.

"Missed you, too, pup." The deep, rumbling voice made my entire body stiffen, and the temperature around me rocketed up at least twenty degrees. My inner-wolf woke up, clawing at my chest, itching to break free, and I swallowed hard, fighting him back.

I looked up slowly. I didn't want to. I wanted to slam the door shut, but I couldn't make myself do it. The two men standing on the deck were people I had wished to never have to see again. Chris and Tommy, my dad's most trusted enforcers, the ones that had helped Dad teach — torture — me as a kid, looked almost bored standing in front of me. My eyes swept over them. They looked the same as I remembered: Chris, tall and thick, chiseled face and goatee, and Tommy, short, stocky, and bald. They were twice my age and had been with my dad since I was born.

"Get the hell off my deck." My tone was calm and controlled, masking the blazing anger that filled my core. I moved forward, filling the doorframe, rolling my shoulders back, lifting my head, keeping my hard glare fixed on them. My nerves were already fried, my patience at a breaking point and this unwelcome visit only managed to send my stress level sky-rocketing.

Tommy smirked. "Your parents sent us." He held out a hand, a folded piece of paper clasped between his fingers.

I narrowed my eyes, glancing down at the paper, and my skin shuddered as my inner-wolf tried to push free. It took a moment for my groggy, pounding head to catch up, but when it did, I groaned. *Mom.* I knew I shouldn't have called her yesterday. And I sure as hell shouldn't have told her where I was or about the pack I had taken over, but after seeing Jade, the way Jared touched her, the way she smiled, that damn kiss ... I'd caved. I needed advice. I needed ...

Tommy waved the paper in front of me, waiting for me to take it. "You going to just stand there, or let us in, kid?"

"Haven't decided yet," I said, snagging the paper and unfolding it. I scanned the simple note, my jaw tightening with each word I read. *Your mother filled me in. Use Tommy and Chris however you see fit. They are there to help, and they will stay as long as you need them. I know I haven't said this enough, but I'm proud of you, son.*

It wasn't signed, but I would have known my father's sloppy scrawl anywhere. I read the note twice before crumpling it, balling it in my hands. Proud of me. What a joke. My father didn't even know the meaning of that word. I was sure of it. I lifted my glare back up to theirs. "Turns out I don't need you guys. Go home." It was a command. They heard it. They felt it. For a quick second, I saw surprise pass across their faces, but then their wolf nature took over. Their shoulders started to sag, and their gazes began to drop. I channeled my scent, giving the command a bit more punch, and as I did, their eyes fell to the deck.

"Your mom filled us in," Chris said, his voice hoarse, strained. "We're here to help, kid."

I didn't budge from the doorway. It wasn't that I didn't need the help because I did; it was the principle. My father had absolutely no right to send anyone from his team. Not without speaking to me first. I hadn't asked for his help, and the last thing I wanted was to owe him anything. My jaw clenched, and my face heated. *This is my pack — my territory.*

Chris snuck a quick look at me and jammed his hands in his pockets. "Come on, Aidan. We've been driving all night, and I'm starved. At least let us eat and grab some sleep before you throw us out."

I wanted to stand firm, slam the door, and kick them out of town. But even if I wanted to, I couldn't bring myself to do it. Guilt wormed its way through my stomach. I knew it was stupid. I shouldn't have felt guilty about sending them away. It wasn't as if I'd ever been close with either of them; my feelings for them had always been a tossup between sparks of admiration and all-out hatred. And the last thing the pack needed right now was two more hard-headed enforcers hanging around. As it was, I was already struggling to keep control of the fragile balance I had attempted to create here. But even if I knew that having them stay, even for a quick bite, wasn't a good thing, I still felt my resolve slipping. The idea of having someone that I knew, really knew, close by, even for a short time, started to eat at me. I was pretty sure I would regret it, but I stepped back from the door, letting them in. Really, what harm could a little food and sleep do?

They stepped into my house, keeping their gazes tight to the floor. "I'm going to take a shower," I grunted, shutting the door and nodding towards the kitchen. "Food's in there. Don't leave the house."

I didn't wait for a response before heading upstairs, taking the steps two at a time. I went straight for my bedroom, grabbed my cell phone from the dresser, and fired off a quick message to Dominic telling him to get here, now, and then I scrolled through my contacts. When I found the number I was looking for, I started to pace the narrow length of my room, glaring at the phone in my hand. I attempted to rack my thoughts, organize them, sort them, and line them up, but it was a useless effort. The only thing that kept surfacing in my exhausted brain was that my father had no right to send anyone to me. This was my pack, not his. My territory, not his. My life. I let out a frustrated growl. I knew part of the anger that was building in my chest was from a lack of sleep, but I couldn't seem to stop it. I glared at his name again, and the anger burned red-hot. I sucked in another breath, let out another growl, and scrolled down a few more names. I found the one I wanted, tapped on it, and brought the phone to my ear.

She answered on the first ring, most likely waiting for my call. "Hi, sugar." Her voice was soothing and warm, so warm that I could actually hear her smile.

"Is there something you forgot to tell me, Mom?" I asked. I tried to sound firm, but I couldn't, and before the full question was out of my mouth, I felt a grin tugging at my lips. Being annoyed at her was impossible, even if she was out of line. I dropped down, taking a hard seat on the edge of my bed.

"I'm going to assume my gifts showed up this morning," she said with a wicked giggle.

"Gifts?" I chuckled, but there was no humor in the sound; it was more stunned than anything. "On what planet are Chris and Tommy considered gifts?"

She laughed at that, the throaty sound rupturing through the speaker. "Be nice, Aidan. They volunteered. Believe it or not, I think they missed you."

For a second, I was taken aback. I couldn't imagine Chris and Tommy volunteering for anything that involved me. "Yeah, sure they did," I said, disbelief thick in my voice. I paused for a second, pulling in a deep breath, trying to pick my words carefully. Letting the breath out with a long sigh, I said, "Look, I know you mean well, but you can't just send me your enforcers. I'm an alpha now, Mom. I have my own pack, my own team. You and Dad need to respect that. You can't just butt in, trying to fix everything."

She made a *tsk* sound. "Oh, Aidan, I think you're forgetting that you're also my son."

"They can't stay," I said adamantly. "I'm feeding them, letting them sleep, and then they're leaving."

"You can't send them back," she countered, her voice losing all motherly compassion, taking on the firm tone of an alpha. "Trust me. Chris and Tommy are exactly what you need to fix that pack of yours." She paused for a second, inhaling a deep breath that sounded like static in my ear. "And they're what you need to get that mate of yours back."

My grip on the phone tightened, the casing digging into my palm. "She's not my mate." I felt myself say it, except I couldn't hear my voice. The words sounded like a wave crashing in my ears — reality trying to drown me in my own stupidity.

Mom sighed a gusty sound. "She'll come around. I don't know a single female that can run from her mate. Believe me, I tried to run from your dad. I couldn't run from him any more than I could run from the alpha in me."

I swallowed hard, trying to fight the uneasiness that squirmed within me. I wasn't so much worried that Jade would run from anything. It was more that she would do something stupid just to spite me — to get even. If I knew anything about her, it was that she was the kind of person that held a grudge.

The thing was, most alphas never found their true mate, or if they did, they couldn't act on it. My parents were one of the few. I had always believed that my mom won the games simply because she couldn't walk away from Dad. Her inner-wolf wouldn't let her.

And I knew — my inner-wolf knew — Jade was my mate. The feeling was profound, unexplainable, and undeniable. I felt it with every fiber of my body. I hadn't truly understood the feeling until she walked away. I'd known I liked her; hell, I'd even known that I could love her, but I didn't understand how much, how deep the feelings ran until I'd stupidly pushed her to the point that she turned her back on me. I knew she felt it, too, even if she was hell-bent on fighting it. And just like that, another piece of my resolve snapped and broke.

"You couldn't have sent Lance with them, could you?" I asked, hating how bitter I sounded. *Damn, was I really even considering this?*

That earned me another laugh. "If you needed a father figure, I would have. It sounds to me like you need brute strength and discipline with that pack of yours."

"Yeah, you're probably right," I said, running a hand through my hair. I hated to admit it, but maybe, just maybe, having some help wouldn't be the worst thing ever. Surely it would give me a bit more time to try and fix things with my mate, if nothing else.

"So you'll be letting them stay." It wasn't a question. The certainty of the statement was as if she knew she had already won.

Shit! If Jade was pissed at me now, what would she be like with Chris and Tommy here? But even though I knew she would probably kill me for bringing new members into the team without asking her first, I found myself relenting, and I said, "For now."

CHAPTER 3

JADE

Marcy sat on my unmade bed cross-legged, hugging one of my pillows to her chest. The crisp white comforter was balled up beside her, twisted around the emerald sheets, and she nudged at them absently, as if she were trying to push the mess of blankets out of her way. She looked a bit tired and a lot flustered, but then, that wasn't really anything new for her. Her long blond hair was down, hanging around her shoulders, and she was in black leggings and an off-white sweater dress. She wasn't looking at me; instead, her stare was fixed on a strand of photo booth pictures that was wedged in the dresser mirror. They were of us, four silly photos from a shopping trip last summer.

On the floor beside my bed was another pile of blankets — Jared's makeshift bed — a telltale sign that we weren't actually sleeping together. It was a serious effort not to rush over and pick up the pillows and blankets. But if Marcy had noticed them, she wasn't letting on, and the last thing I wanted to do was draw attention to them. My dresser was scattered with his things — deodorant, cologne, cell phone, wallet, keys. His clothes were strewn all over the place, and I found myself hoping she'd chalk up what looked like a bed on the floor to Jared being a slob and not see it for what it really was.

I leaned against the closed door to my bedroom, gazing out the window at the forest, listening to the sounds of the team joking around and eating downstairs. I didn't really know what to say, and by Marcy's silence, I figured she felt the same. I opened my mouth and then closed it. Each time I tried to say something, it just felt ... wrong. It wasn't that I didn't have anything to say, because I did. Loads. I just didn't know how to say everything or even if I should.

I sighed, a heavy sigh, and asked, "Why are you here, Mac?"

Marcy shifted her gaze, focusing somewhere around my belly. "I ... Jade ..." She huffed and started twirling a long strand of hair around her finger. "Wow, I didn't think this would be so awkward." She huffed again, letting it draw out until she'd expelled every drop of air from her lungs.

"Did Aidan send you?" I asked cautiously, folding my arms over my chest, more to stop the chill that slid through me than anything else, as I braced myself for the answer.

My question caught her full attention. She screwed up her face, still staring at my belly, and blurted, "Really? You think I'm here because of Aidan? God, Jade, I can't believe you'd even ask me that."

She was lying. I heard it in her outburst, the way her voice rose and fell and trembled. I could smell it in the air, the salt, the thickness, the staleness. And it stung. Bad. Worse than I really thought it should. "Mac, please don't be like him." My voice was soft, filled with the sting piercing my heart. "Don't lie to me."

"Dom sent me, okay?" She met my eyes then, hers

were rimmed with glossy tears, and she squeezed the pillow tighter. "Maybe it was Aidan's idea, maybe it wasn't. I really don't know whose idea it was. But I swear that's not the only reason I'm here. I miss you. So much crap is happening. Trev hasn't been home in two days now, and I think Dom is going out today, too, and Aidan has been a moody prick since you left with Jared and ... and ... I need someone to talk to. I need my sister back."

For a moment, I forgot to breathe as I watched her bottom lip tremble. I didn't need an awesome sense of smell to know everything she'd said was true; it was written clearly in that quivering lip. I pushed off the door and stepped over to her, perching on the edge of my bed. "Where's Trevor been?"

She looked at me as if I should already know the answer, and I figured she was probably right. "Aidan has him and some of the others searching for the cougars. They keep finding tracks around town, coming closer and closer. Trevor said that they lead to the mountain, but once they get to the base of it, the tracks just vanish."

"What?" I asked. "How don't I know they're trying to track them?" I didn't expect an answer, and I was sure Marcy knew that, but it didn't stop her from snapping one out even if she did.

"Because you've been ignoring the pack. You've been ignoring Aidan." She tossed the pillow at me, smacking me in the chest with it, and yelled, "Jeez, Jade, you've been blowing off everyone except that team of yours, and as far as I can see, they aren't in any rush to find your dad or those nasty beasts."

"What's that supposed to mean?" I asked, keeping my voice just above a whisper, "and keep your voice down." I was sure the whole team could hear her, and I knew they had to be listening. The house was quiet, so quiet it was as if the house itself were holding its breath.

She didn't keep her voice down; instead, she let it rise higher. "You know exactly what it means. You and those enforcers haven't even tried to help find them. Do any of you even care that they're actually coming into town? I woke up this morning to find tracks all over my yard. The pack is supposed to keep our town safe. You and those enforcers are supposed to keep us safe."

"Shut up, Mac," I hissed, squeezing my eyes shut, listening. It felt like an eternally long moment before I heard chairs scraping along the floor, shuffling footsteps, and the round of *thank-yous* for breakfast. And then, just as I was about to let out my pent-up breath, my bedroom door swung open, and Jared walked in.

He didn't say anything as he padded across the room, snagging his phone and stuffing his wallet into his back pocket. Taut, strained muscles lined his neck and shoulders. He opened the closet, reached in, tugged a black long-sleeved T-shirt off a hanger, and then pulled it on.

Marcy kept her head ducked, but I could see her watching him from the corner of her eye, and when he turned to face us, her complexion paled just a little.

He didn't seem to notice. He was giving me an expectant kind of look, although I really didn't know what it was he was expecting, so I said, "I take it you're going out?"

"Yep." A cocky smirk twitched at his lips. He crossed the room in two long strides and reached out, running a finger along my cheek, before wrapping his hand around the back of my neck, pulling me to him. His lips were on mine, hot and rough before I had a chance to even register what he was doing. Thankfully the kiss ended just as quickly as it started. He feathered a light peck on the tip of my nose and then let his hand drop from my neck. "You better hurry up, kitten. You're going to be late," he said before turning away and leaving the room.

I sat in stunned silence, staring at the empty doorway. I had expected him to growl something at Marcy, to defend his team, even defend himself, or at the very least tell her to keep her nose out of enforcer business. I had figured he would give me a lecture about walking to school or snap at me for the way I had spoken to him downstairs, but he hadn't done any of that. Actually, he had acted normal, and that normalcy kind of freaked me out.

"Well, that was um ... interesting," Marcy squawked at the sound of the front door slamming. She cleared her throat. "What's going on with you and Jared? He hasn't given you the time of day since we were in seventh grade, and you had that crush. And even then, he wasn't interested, and you know it."

I hesitated, wanting to tell her the truth, but not sure if I could trust her to keep it to herself. I had never been away from Marcy for this long, and right then, seeing her sitting there, I wanted to blurt out everything. I knew it was a bit hypocritical of me. I had told her I didn't want to see her for a while. It was my fault she hadn't been here, but really, she was practically my sister. And it had been three days already. Three long days of having no one to talk to about the mess I had gotten myself into with Jared.

Sure, there was Erika, and theoretically, I should have been able to talk to her, but I just couldn't. She didn't get it. Anytime I tried, she was all like, *It's not about your feelings, Jade, it's about the pack*, or, *You're the alpha, suck it up*. In all fairness, Erika didn't know the truth. She really thought Jared and I were together mainly because I didn't trust her enough to tell her any different, and thanks to the way my inner-wolf reacted to him, she believed the lie. Yeah, I had named her as my beta, but that had been a heat of the moment kind of decision, and as the days slipped by, I realized how little I knew about her and how much I just didn't like her. It wasn't that she was completely awful. We just didn't click. She wasn't Marcy.

The thing was, even if I was sure that what I was doing with Jared was right, it felt sickeningly wrong. It felt wrong to have him sleep at my house, let alone in my room. And honestly, I hated having to lie to the pack, letting them, and everyone else, think we were together. But I didn't know what else to do. We had all agreed that my dad couldn't know that I'd become the pack's alpha female, and pretending to be with an enforcer seemed like the best cover-up. Really, until we had a clear picture of exactly what my dad's plans were, it didn't seem like I had much of a choice.

Maybe that wasn't entirely true. There was a choice, but I knew one thing for sure: choosing Aidan right now had to be the worst of two bad choices.

Marcy nudged me. "Talk to me, Jade. What's going on?"

"It's complicated," I said, glancing at the clock. It was already 7:30, and I still needed a shower. I got up and trudged over to the closet, riffling through the hangers. My mind was reeling. I couldn't understand why Aidan would send anyone out searching without talking to me about it. Didn't I have a say in what the pack did now? And he knew the team was working on it, kind of, well, okay, maybe not really. Most of their time was taken up on working with me. But they had been spending at least an hour a day looking. That was something, wasn't it?

"Well, un-complicate it," she snapped, following me

to the closet. She reached in and snagged my plum hoodie, tossing it on the bed. "Because you're going to end up regretting this. He's playing with you. I know it, and I know you know it, too. There's something else behind this." A thought dawned on her then; I saw it pass across her eyes a moment before she visibly shuddered, and when she continued, her voice was whisper quiet. "You haven't slept with him yet, right? Please tell me you haven't because I did with Trevor and well ..."

I yanked a pair of jeans off a hanger and grabbed a white tank from the shelf before turning to look her straight on. "I know, Mac. You're mated. I can smell it. You have two distinct scents, yours and Trevor's. It's weird, though. I thought you had to be a werewolf for that."

"Um, yeah, well, you and me both." She blushed, a light pink, dropped her eyes and smiled — a little. "I just ... you can't, not with Jared. You don't even like him and Aidan ..."

"My inner-wolf likes him," I said, cutting her short, not wanting to hear anymore. "And really, who I end up mating with isn't important." I grabbed the hoodie she had tossed on the bed and started for the door. "I need to take a shower. You can wait or go, whatever."

"This wasn't Aidan's fault," Marcy blurted. "It's all on Dom and me. If you have to hate someone, then hate us. Don't take our bad advice out on him."

I didn't turn around. I couldn't. I was sure my face was crumbling just like my heart, and I didn't want her to see it. I kept my hand on the doorknob, but I couldn't bring myself to twist. "You didn't make him lie, Mac." I swallowed hard, hating how raw my voice sounded. "You didn't make him manipulate me. You didn't force him to put me in danger. He was the one stupid enough to follow through with it all."

"We just wanted you to be happy," she pleaded, coming up behind me. She squeezed my shoulder. "You can fool everyone else, but not me. I see through you. I always have. Aidan's the cheese to your macaroni, and you know it."

"The cheese to my macaroni?" I asked as I dropped my grip on the doorknob and turned around. I arched a brow and pursed my lips.

She grinned, wrapping me in a too-tight hug. "I've missed you, Jade. Three days is way too long."

CHAPTER 4

Dominic looked uncomfortable. He leaned against the kitchen counter, watching Tommy fry up some bacon and scrambled eggs. His blond hair was gelled, but that was pretty much the only thing he'd bothered to do before coming over. His jeans were stained with dirt, and his olive hoodie looked as if he'd been wearing it for weeks. His eyes were bruised veined red. It was clear that he'd been sleeping just as well as me.

My unwelcome guests had made themselves at home while I'd taken a shower and gotten dressed. They had raided my fridge and cooked up the last breakfast food I had. A heavy layer of greasy smoke filled the room, and the small, dusty-gray countertop was covered with pots and dishes.

Chris drummed his fingertips on the table, watching the coffee pot as it gurgled and dripped. "Your dad was telling me your beta is in high school and the head enforcer is about your age."

A strained tension shifted through the cramped space. For the last five minutes, Chris and Tommy had been chatting with me as if Dominic weren't there, and Dominic looked as if he were about ready to snap.

I scrubbed at my face and leaned back in my chair, stretching my legs out in front of me. "Yep, Dominic's graduating this year, and Jared's a year older than me."

Tommy grunted. "He looks like a pup." He cut a quick look at Dominic. "How long have you been in the pack, kid?"

"Two years," Dominic said, his tone more hostile than I would have liked, but I guessed I couldn't really blame him. They were being dicks. He pushed off of the counter and headed to the cupboard, pulled it open, and grabbed four mugs, setting them on the table before pulling out a chair and taking a seat.

"And Jade, the alpha female, she's only eighteen?" Tommy asked, his tone calm, friendly even as if we were old friends just catching up. He switched off the burners and began dishing out scrambled eggs onto the plates lining the counter.

"She is," I said, keeping my tone just as friendly. I knew what they were doing. Trying to loosen me up. Looking for the foothold. They were under orders to stay and help me out, and they were looking for a reason to do just that. I probably should have told them that they would be sticking around for a bit, but honestly, I was kind of enjoying watching them sweat a little.

"So every pack member in a position of real power is under twenty-one." The coffee pot rumbled and spat out the last of the brew. Chris reached for it, pouring himself a cup. He took a deep drink before glancing over his shoulder. "You ever heard of anything like this before, Tommy? Because I sure as hell haven't."

"Nope," Tommy said as he made his way over to the table, juggling the heaping plates of eggs and bacon, and passed them out.

"Ray replaced all the enforcers with newly turned werewolves," Dominic offered. "He ran his last beta out of town, too, when I was turned. He wanted people he could mold, ones that didn't know any different, didn't know pack law."

"Huh." Tommy sat down, grabbed his fork, and shoveled in a large mouthful of eggs. His forehead creased, a sharp V forming in between his eyes, as he tried to make sense out of what Dominic said. We ate in silence for a long moment before he said, "And you've let your head enforcer move in with your mate."

"She's not my mate." The words felt like gravel on my tongue. I hated how screwed up this whole situation was. I figured I deserved it all, but really, Jade was taking this too far. Yeah, I'd hid things from her and lied to her, but right now, she was screwing with the delicate balance that I'd created within the pack, and whether she knew it or not, she was on the verge of shattering it completely. We were supposed to be a team, and her ignoring me wasn't showing a united front. It made the pack nervous, and a nervous pack of werewolves was really not something either of us needed.

Tommy waved a fork at me. "She's the alpha female, which makes her your mate."

I rolled my eyes and let out a long, windy sigh. "According to her, it doesn't."

"You know what I'd do?" Chris said casually as if he were just making small talk and not giving me advice. "If I was the alpha, I'd force that enforcer out of her house. You said they aren't mated. There's really no reason why they should be living together."

"I don't know about that," Tommy said. "If she's as hard-headed as I hear, she'd probably just follow him. I'd send him out of town; get him away from her altogether."

I groaned. I was way too tired to play this friendly chat game. "Guys, I know what you're doing. I've watched you work with Dad long enough to know what this is, so cut the small talk crap." I snagged the coffee pot and poured myself a cup, thinking. They knew damn well they were gaining ground with me, but then I was sure that they'd both known they weren't going anywhere the moment I let them in the door. After a long moment, I said, "I can't send Jared anywhere. Jade's dad is coming home tomorrow, and I need every pack member I have to deal with the cougars."

Dominic's eyes flared, and a spasm worked its way along his jaw. "You should send him out hunting them." His voice was growled, and an angry red flush settled over his face. "The team has barely spent any time looking for them. He's been too busy with Beck, teaching Jade how to fight."

Chris chuckled and leaned forward, resting his elbows on the table. He looked Dominic over, a flash of curiosity passing across his face, before he asked, "What's the deal with these cougars, anyway?"

I almost told him it was none of his business. The words were right there, on the tip of my tongue, but the truth was, I wanted to hear someone else's thoughts. Dominic was too close to the issue, too close to Jade, and well, the pack didn't have much of a clue about what was really going on. Before I knew it, I was telling them everything. I told them about the video of Jade's dad and about how the cougars used women. I explained the town's dynamics, and I even talked about Jade, telling them about the games, about the lies, about tricking her into competing.

And just like they did with my father, Chris and Tommy listened, throwing in their thoughts and pulling apart the problems, separating them and categorizing them. Breakfast turned into lunch, and lunch turned into early afternoon, but we actually had a plan by the time we were done. A real, solid plan. It was too bad it was a plan involving Jade and Jared staying together.

JADE

School was well ... it was school. Nothing spectacular. I knew I was supposed to be learning something, but I couldn't focus. All I could think about was that Aidan had been sending *our* wolves out to track the cougars — to track my dad. I should have been okay with it all. Clearly, my dad was evil. He'd even said that he would be using me at some point. But even if I knew all that, there was this little nagging voice in the back of my head that kept reminding me he was still my dad, and no matter what I tried, I couldn't shake it.

The walk to school with Marcy had been insightful, if nothing else. She'd warned me that most of the pack members that should be in school wouldn't be. Aidan had them all running on fumes. From what she'd said, he'd turned into a bit of a slave driver over the last few days, but the pack had really warmed up to him. They respected him trusted his judgment. Although, she also let me know that even if they respected him, they were also getting fed up with his short fuse, especially the females. Personally, I couldn't picture Aidan with a short fuse. He'd always been so laid back and carefree. Well, at least most of the time, he was.

Marcy spent most of the walk and all of lunch trying to convince me that I needed to talk to Aidan. Really talk to him. I hated to admit it, but she was right. The thing was, yesterday hadn't gone so well when I saw him. Just thinking about the broken look on his face when I walked away with Jared made my chest squeeze and my breath shorten.

And that feeling led me to another issue. The one I'd been trying to pretend didn't exist. Was I lying to Aidan about Jared because it was needed? Or was my subconscious trying to inflict some kind of petty revenge for all the lies he'd told me?

Yep, the whole situation really sucked.

Word had spread about me joining the enforcers, and as the day went on, I heard a few whispers about Jared and me. Really, I should have been happy that people were buying it, but I wasn't.

Instead, it only made me feel sick. God, I hated lying. Nothing, *nothing*, good ever came from a lie.

Dominic hadn't shown up yet. But then, I guess I'd never really believed he would. I knew he would be with Aidan, but still, I'd hoped to see him nevertheless. I'd fought with Dominic before. Hell, I'd even shunned him for two years. But still, after patching things up with Marcy, I wanted to see him, too. I wanted to make sure he was okay.

I shifted in my chair and glanced at the clock: 1:49. Six more minutes until gym, until laps. Oddly enough, I was looking forward to running for the first time in my life. I felt restless, confined, and running would help — hopefully.

And after gym, I would go see Aidan.

I hadn't quite figured out what I would say when I got there, but I knew, just knew, that I needed to tell him how I was feeling about the whole dad situation, if nothing else.

The six minutes dragged. When the bell finally sounded, I hastily shoved my books into my backpack. I was just about to stand when the classroom door opened. My senses came alive as an aroma assaulted my nose. It was musky and woodsy and sharp, and on top of that, I could smell the wolf. A wolf that I was sure I didn't know. My inner-wolf perked up, and my heartbeat doubled.

I slid out of my chair, a soft flare of adrenaline pushed through my veins. Unease started to claw in my chest like an animal trying to break free, and a slow growl started at the base of my throat, working its way up. The room fell silent, completely silent. I breathed in the scent again, and I caught something else. Dominic.

But there was something ... off. I could feel it, knotted and tangled in my gut. My classmates rushed into the hallway, most likely to get out of my way. My skin was crawling with shivers. I didn't wait for everyone to clear out. I couldn't. My inner-wolf pushed me, begged me to move. I quickly shouldered my bag and headed out the door.

Dominic stood beside a man who was casually leaning against the lockers. I would have said he was in his early forties if I had to guess. He was short, an inch or two shorter than my five-foot-six, but he was thickset — sturdy looking. His head was clean-shaven, and as he looked at me, I caught a fleck of gold in his eyes.

"Dom, who's your friend?" I asked, eyeing him closely. He didn't answer, didn't even bother to acknowledge that he'd heard my question. Instead, he just kept that infuriating expressionless mask of his in place.

I took a step toward him, and as I did, the man's nostrils flared, and then he smiled a surprisingly friendly smile. "You." His voice was raspy, and he was pointing a stubby finger at me. "You're coming with me." He didn't take the chance that I might not agree. Within a second, he was across the hall, grabbing my wrist and yanking me forward.

"Let go of me," I growled. A fast shiver cut across

my skin, and my inner-wolf brushed against my chest as if she were asking if she could come out and play. I pushed the sensation back and pulled on my alpha scent, focusing on everything Jared had taught me. I imagined it thick and heavy and suffocating, and as I did, my imprint began to heat up like a flare of a match tip.

He shuddered, only slightly, and the friendly smile melted away. "That's really not a nice way to greet a guest."

"Wasn't meant to be," I said and yanked hard, pulling my wrist from his grasp.

The man chuckled, not a nice sound. "Apparently." He snatched my hand again, yanking me forward as he started down the hallway. Students jumped out of the way, pressing against the lockers and trying darn hard to pretend they didn't notice us. "The alpha asked me to retrieve you, but he didn't tell me how to do it. Rein in that scent of yours, kid, or I'll drag you out of here and tie you up in the back of my truck."

I tried to yank free again and snapped, "I'd like to see you try it."

"Jade, Aidan sent us to get you," Dominic growled. "Give it a rest." He wouldn't look at me as he fell into step beside us. He was nervous — I could smell it — but I couldn't tell if it was because of me or the dumbass holding onto me.

I gritted my teeth. I was pretty sure it was true. Dominic wouldn't have been there if it weren't. Obviously, he wasn't being forced into helping, but really, wasn't the dragging thing a little extreme?

"Who the hell are you?" I demanded, letting my scent fade a little, as he pulled me through the doors into the harsh sunlight. A cool breeze cut through my hoodie as he tugged me toward the parking lot.

"That doesn't really matter," he said. It wasn't

unkind, just cool and brisk as if he'd written me off as a low-ranking pack member (although clearly from the way he'd shuddered under my alpha scent, he knew I wasn't).

"You do know who I am, though, right?" I asked, a little baffled.

He chuckled, stopping beside a steel gray pick-up truck. "Sure do," he said and winked. "You're the alpha's mate."

I laughed. Hard. I didn't mean to, but it bubbled up and out before I could stop it. "Clearly, you have no clue who I am." I poked him in the chest with my free hand. "I'm the mate of an enforcer. The head enforcer, actually. And I'm also the alpha female of the pack in town."

The man was totally unfazed. He pulled the door open, and Dominic jumped into the back of the extended cab before he finally let go of my wrist, gesturing for me to get in. "Exactly what I said. You're the alpha's mate."

A growl rattled around in my chest. I opened my mouth, ready to tell him again, when Dominic said, "Jade, get in the damn truck. Don't make me call him. Trust me, right now, this is the better option."

I snapped my gaze to him, taking in the hard lines on his brow and the bruises under his eyes. He looked like crap. He held my glare, unrelenting. I was tempted to tell him to make the call for about half a second, but I didn't. Right then, I didn't think I could handle talking to Aidan in a civil way, so I bit my tongue and hopped into the truck.

The man slammed the door as soon as I was in and then made his way around to the driver's side. When he was in the truck, and his door was shut, I swiveled, looking him straight on, and asked, "Where are you taking me?"

"Home," he grunted, starting up the truck and shifting it into gear.

Home, I thought. Relief swelled in my chest. At that moment, home was exactly where I wanted to be. I would take a hot shower, calm down, and then go and see the jackass who had me pulled from school. Yep, home was perfect.

The drive took less than five minutes, and for those five minutes, I sat rigid in my seat, my gaze fixed to the floorboards. Dominic didn't try to talk to me, and neither did the man driving, and I was seriously glad for it. The last thing I wanted was to have to talk. Frankly, I was just too busy stewing over being dragged out of school.

I didn't look up until the truck came to a stop in the driveway, and when I did, my jaw clenched tight. As it turned out, the bald man did take me home; it just really wasn't the home I wanted to go to.

CHAPTER 5

AIDAN

Jade was, to put it mildly, pissed off.

I was sitting on the couch, my legs stretched out and arms folded behind my head, trying to stay awake as I waited for the inevitable when she burst through the door. She looked like she was ready to punch someone, most likely me. She stalked toward me, Tommy and Dominic trailing along behind her, neither of them looking impressed.

I had kind of hoped she would have calmed down a little by the time she got here, but by the look of her, she hadn't. I'd known she would be fuming. I'd expected it. But the thing I hadn't expected was that even though she was furious, her skin didn't shudder, her eyes didn't flare. She was in control of her inner wolf. Completely in control. I hated to think it, but whatever Jared had been doing with her was helping. And that thought made my blood boil. I knew a lack of sleep and stress made me so edgy, but knowing it didn't make the thought of Jared helping her any easier to swallow. *It should have been me.*

She stopped a few paces away from me, and as her

eyes swept over me, a layer of ice settled in her glare. "You ever hear of a phone, jackass?"

I kept my expression blank, which was harder than I thought it would be. *Home.* The word filled my mind, my body, as I took her in. Her long, brown hair was loose, hanging around her shoulders. As my eyes raked over her, my skin warmed, my heart raced. She was in jeans and that plum hoodie she always wore, nothing out of the ordinary, but on her, well, everything looked good on her. Her scent, fruits mixed with almonds, made my inner-wolf stir, and a deep-seated craving spread through me. She was mine. My inner-wolf agreed, echoing my thoughts, *Mine.*

I pulled in a deep breath, letting her scent reach every nerve within my body, and then I met her cold gaze. "Jade, sit down. We need to talk."

Jade's jaw dropped a little, and the layer of frost that had settled over her eyes thawed slightly. Her nostrils flared. She was breathing me in. Her inner-wolf heard the command in my tone — in my scent — even if she didn't want her to.

Dominic made a sound. It wasn't quite a laugh, but I was pretty sure that's what it was supposed to be. It was choked, gurgled as if he had tried to swallow it.

Jade ignored him, but his laugh seemed to clear her head a little. She swallowed hard and fixed a lukewarm glare back in place. "Talk," she said, putting her hands on her hips, drumming her fingertips impatiently. "Come on, I'm dying to hear what reason you could possibly have for sending Dom with a complete stranger to drag me out of class — literally drag me — when it was your idea for me to go in the first place."

I smirked. I couldn't help it. Jade was just so damn cute when she was pissed off. Her peach complexion was slowly turning to an adorable shade of pink. "Actually, that was Dom's idea, not mine."

I held her glare in total silence until Chris shattered it by clearing his throat. Jade shifted her fuming gaze to him. She started to vibrate a little. Adrenaline, most likely. Her fingers stopped drumming; instead, they trembled slightly as she pressed them against her hip bones.

"So this is the girl," Chris said, bemused. "This is your mate? Really?" He folded his arms over his chest and chuckled, leaning against the doorframe to the kitchen.

"I'm not his mate!" Jade pivoted, and I caught another shudder of her skin as she faced Chris head-on. "Who the hell are you?"

I chuckled softly. I knew it was completely horrible, but part of me was seriously glad that she wasn't as in control as I initially thought she'd been.

The glad feeling was short-lived. Her scent flared, and I almost flinched — almost. I glanced around the room, taking in the smirks from Tommy and Chris and Dominic's scowl. Suddenly, my stomach twisted and sank. Maybe having them all here wasn't such a great idea. She looked as if she were ready to launch herself at Chris. But I knew that Chris and Tommy needed to see what I was dealing with if they were going to help at all, and as for Dominic, well, if I was being honest, I had kind of hoped having him here might chill her out a little. I knew she was mad at him, but they had a history. One that I had really hoped would bring her down a notch or two. And, yeah, I probably should have called her instead of sending Tommy, but I knew she wouldn't have answered. I'd barely gotten a response when I told her to go to school, and she hadn't answered a single one of my calls since she became alpha female.

"Jade." I said her name carefully, keeping my voice firm, forceful, hoping it would speak to her inner-wolf, if nothing else. "These are the newest members of Jared's team. The guy you're thinking about attacking is Chris," I said and then nodded toward Tommy, "and you've already met Tommy."

"We aren't looking for new members." Her voice was growled, harsh, and when she looked back at me, her eyes flared with a challenge. "You have no right to ..."

"Stop," I said, raising a hand in warning. "I have every right. This is my pack. I've made my decision."

"It's our pack," she said, throwing up her hands. "You just can't ..."

"No," I said, cutting her off. I stood up and stepped toward her, closing the distance until we were so close that if one of us pulled in a deep breath, our chests would touch. I glanced down at her, and she met my gaze with something that looked a hell of a lot like hatred, but underneath that hatred, I swore I saw a lick of fire just waiting to ignite. I swallowed down the urge to take her into my arms and said, "It's not ours. It's mine. Until you decide to step up and get involved with the pack, you don't get to make decisions involving them."

"Screw you, Aidan," she said, exhaling the words on a breath. She closed her eyes, squeezing them tight, and then blinked a few times before meeting my gaze again. She opened her mouth as if she would say more, closed it, and then turned her back on me — again.

It wasn't the first time she had turned away from me, and knowing her, it wouldn't be the last. But still, it burned. I reached out without thinking, wrapping my arms around her waist, and pulled her back flush against me. Leaning forward, brushing my lips against her ear, I said, "Don't walk away from me, Jade."

JADE

Aidan's breath brushing against the back of my neck — warm and sweet — sent a hot chill careening through me. My breath hitched. I could feel every ripple of his abs and chest against my back as he held me close. His strong arms tightened around my waist, pulling me closer still, and darn it, but I leaned into him.

His command and this show of dominance should have bothered me, but it didn't. I felt delicate, like a flower, with his arms around me, surrounding me with his power. My inner-wolf lapped it up as if hearing him, feeling him, having him so close was the best treat she could have asked for, and even though I hated it, I completely agreed with her. The last thing I actually wanted to do was walk away from him. Doing it once was pretty much all I had in me. Right then, I was sure of it.

I could feel the others watching us. Their breathing, their heartbeats, whispered around me like a breeze rustling through the forest, but at that moment, I didn't care.

Aidan's steady heartbeat thrummed against my back, and his heady scent ... I licked my lips and took a deep breath. *Home. I was home.* His betrayal had hurt. I was sure that I would never be able to trust him again, and yet, as I stood there incased in his arms, I knew that I would never be able to stay away from him either.

And then, my phone rang a sharp pitch, sharp enough to clear my head.

I wrapped my hand around Aidan's wrist, pulling his arm from my waist. He didn't stop me. Instead, he let his arm fall, then the other, and then the warmth of his body pressed against mine was gone. I felt the separation like losing a limb, and I almost turned into him. God, I wanted those arms back around me, but then my phone rang again, and I hastily fished it out of my pocket, glancing at the screen.

Jared.

Guilt pooled in my stomach, which was completely asinine. I had no reason to feel guilty. It wasn't like Jared, and I were really an item, but I felt it, like searing hot water pouring over my skin. I forced a smile, took a breath, and tapped the screen as I brought the phone to my ear.

"Hey, baby," I said. My voice was raw as if I'd swallowed a handful of tacks, and I swallowed hard, trying to clear the lump from my throat.

"Where the hell are you, Jade?" he yelled.

I cringed from the blast of his voice piercing my ear, and I almost glanced around to see if anyone noticed, but thankfully I caught myself. I forced my smile wider, hoping it would ease the rockiness of my voice. "I'm at Aidan's. You should probably get over here."

"You're supposed to be in school," he barked.

I could feel Aidan's eyes on my back, and I found myself hoping that he couldn't hear Jared. I didn't want Aidan to hear the possessive edge in my *so-called* mate's voice. I didn't even want to hear it myself.

"I didn't have much of a choice," I said. Was my tone sweet enough? I didn't know. I wanted to walk outside. I wanted to tell Jared off, but I couldn't. Not with everyone watching. Darn it! I hated having to play the sweet girlfriend. I wasn't even sweet on a good day. I sighed and felt my forced smile stretching further. "Can you find Erika and bring her with you? Oh, and maybe call the team. I want them all here."

"I'm not your damn secretary, Jade," he growled. "Call them yourself if you want them. Better yet, get your ass home."

I sucked in a deep breath. I was vibrating all over, and I felt the twitch in my jaw as I bit down, swallowing the urge to rip into him. "Jared, I'm not asking."

Aidan stepped into my line of vision and tapped my chin, forcing me to look up. He smirked, a knowing kind of smirk, and reached out, taking the phone from me before I could stop him and bringing it to his ear. He chuckled, and an amused grin curved his lips. "Jared. Come. Now." He barked out the order, grinning the entire time, and then thumbed the screen, disconnecting the call. His grin spread wider, and he winked at me, tossing the phone back.

I caught it easily and jammed it in my pocket. "You look a little too proud of yourself there," I snapped, glowering at him.

"Yeah?" he asked, chuckling. "Well, I kind of am."

CHAPTER 6

Aidan's house was comfy. I was pretty sure it had belonged to one of the previous alphas of the Dog Mountain pack, but I had never been inside before. It wasn't much, a living room done in browns and greens, soothing just like the woods, with a smallish kitchen off to the side and a set of stairs leading up to the second floor. The carpet was kind of gross, and the paint was chipped and peeling in spots, but other than that, it was cozy. And it smelled like him. Strong, a little sweet, and green. It was a peaceful scent, one that I was pretty sure I would never get enough of. Every few minutes, it would get stronger and then fade, as if he were using it, trying to stir a reaction from me, and it was a crazy hard effort to keep the stoic expression on my face and not let him see how much he was affecting me. I had already slipped up once since I walked through the door, and there was no way I was going to do it again.

I sat on the couch, my feet pulled up underneath me, waiting for Jared and the team to show up. Aidan sat across from me in a big, beat-up leather chair, with Chris and Tommy standing behind him. His light brown hair was askew, and his jawline was rough with a couple days' growth. His brown eyes were tired but alert, and he wore an easy smile as if the five of us together weren't awkward at all.

Dominic paced the small space, five steps one way, five steps back. His calm mask was starting to splinter. Every few minutes, he would steal a glimpse at me, and when he did, I caught the slivers of pain and regret spreading through his eyes like ice cracking under pressure.

While I waited for Jared, Aidan filled me in on why he had me pulled from class. He had a plan. As far as I could see, though, it wasn't much of a plan, and I was eighty-nine percent sure there was more to it than he wasn't telling me. The gist: he was calling the team together, and tomorrow, once Dad got back and I played up my relationship with Jared a little, they were going into the mountain to hunt the werecougars.

But my doubts about his plan could have also had something to do with the new additions to our pack. Aidan said they were temporary, help sent from his parents, and I really didn't know what to make of that. I hadn't thought about Aidan belonging to another pack before now. I guessed it made sense; he had been a werewolf before he'd shown up in Dog Mountain, but the information only managed to fill me with questions and reaffirm the fact that I really knew nothing about him. Another item to add to the growing list of things he hadn't told me.

Chris and Tommy were like statues behind him as he spoke. Seriously, it was as if they weren't even breathing. The only thing that moved on them was their eyes, constantly sweeping the room and windows, alert and ready. Was this how enforcers were supposed to act? If it was, then our pack was more screwed up than I had thought.

"Don't think you've actually thought this one out," I cut in when Aidan paused to yawn for at least the twentieth time. "Have you considered that Dad's going to notice Tiff isn't around? If you're not here, who's going to stop him from trying to seek her out to get the wolves she promised him?"

Tiffany had won by default when I refused to fight for alpha female, accepting the role and technically becoming Aidan's mate. Her reign hadn't lasted long. She had been the star of the video Erika had gotten, her leading man, my dad. She had conspired with him for reasons none of us knew, agreeing to send some female wolves to the cougars because, as my dad put it, his boys liked some fight in their women, and the werewolves would heal faster. Once I saw that video, everything changed. I hadn't been able to not fight. I couldn't stand back and do nothing. Not when *my* wolves were in danger. So I fought. And I won. I killed her.

I shuddered at the memory. There were times when I swore I could still taste her blood on my tongue. I knew I should have felt sick over the whole thing, but I didn't. Really, the only thing that got to me was that for a short time, Aidan had belonged to someone else. I couldn't feel bad for taking the life of someone that would willingly risk the lives of my pack members. My inner-wolf wouldn't let me hold onto the feeling even if I had wanted to.

"Yeah, I thought about it," Aidan said and yawned again. "That's why I'm going with the team. It would make sense that Tiff would be with me since she's supposed to be the alpha female, my partner."

A pang of jealousy worked its way through my chest. *Partner.* I guessed I should have been thankful he didn't call her his mate, but nope, I wasn't. *Partner* was just as bad. I swallowed down a growl. "And me?"

I asked and winced inwardly at the bitter tone in my voice. I swallowed hard. "What am I supposed to do?"

He arched a brow, and a crooked smirk appeared. "You're part of the team now, aren't you?"

"Hold up," I said. A shocked laugh worked its way out of my throat, and my eyes widened. He couldn't be serious. He just couldn't. I fixed him with what I was sure was a stunned glare. "You really think going with Jared and me to hunt them down is a good idea? 'Cause, it's not."

God, it really wasn't.

How was I supposed to spend that much time with him and not let my struggle show? How was I supposed to pretend that Jared was the one I really wanted? Even sitting here in the same room as Aidan was a challenge. My inner-wolf was restless; I was restless. I could still feel his arms around me, the heat of his body pressed against me. And I couldn't believe the way my body was responding to his scent as if it belonged to me and no one else as if I had to have it or die trying to get it. It was crazy but as crazy as it was, I found myself drawing in another deep breath, letting the sweetness and the greens and the power of his aroma fill my lungs.

I trembled, and my inner-wolf stirred, swirling my own scent around me. *I need to tell him the truth,* I thought, as I watched him close his eyes. His nostrils flared, and then he winced as if I had just hurt him. Really not the reaction I had wanted, that was for sure, and just like that, my confessions died on the tip of my tongue.

Aidan shook himself, readjusting in his chair, and his smirk turned into a full smile. He chuckled. "Jade, whatever it is that you think is happening here, it isn't." The smile died, and his lips thinned. "My pack is being threatened. Like you just said, Tiff would give some of *my* wolves to them, and your dad is still expecting that to happen. You can hate me all you want later. Right now, the pack is more important."

That hurt and I groaned, trying to hide the pain his words were causing. It wasn't that I hated him. I just didn't trust him. "Get over yourself, Aidan," I said with as much snark as I could muster. *This was your choice*, I reminded myself sternly. *You're the one that walked away.* But even if I knew that it didn't lessen the pain, it didn't change how I really felt. I tried to spit out the truth, but the confession was stuck in my throat. I swallowed a few quick swallows, then I sighed. "We don't even know why she was going to do it. What was she getting out of it? We need to be here. We need to try and get the information out of him."

"No, we don't," Aidan said. He held my eyes for a long moment and let out a windy breath. "This really isn't up for discussion."

The rumble of a diesel engine pulling into the driveway caught my attention, stopping me from snapping out something that most likely wouldn't have helped. I glanced over my shoulder to the window. Jared. His truck was a monster, diesel with dual back tires. He killed the engine, and the team slowly piled out.

Jared didn't bother to knock, instead just barging in as if it were his house. The team hung back as he walked in the door, kicking off his shoes. His gaze swept the room before settling on me. He looked calm enough, although I could see he was pissed. It was in his eyes, the flecks of gold, the hard edges. I grinned at him, hopping off the couch. "Hey, baby, what took you so long?"

Jared watched me closely as I made my way across the room. He was in black jeans and a black, form-fitting tee. His fists clenched at his sides, the muscles in his forearms roped and straining. I stopped in front of him, overly aware of everyone watching us, specifically Aidan. My inner-wolf bucked and fought me, begging me to back up walk away. But I didn't.

Jared stared down at me, unblinking and unmoving, for a moment longer, and at that moment, he was impossible to read. His face was a mask, his scent calm-ish. His arm snaked out, wrapping around my waist, pulling me against him, and I squealed in surprise. "Couldn't find Erika," he said, finally. He leaned down, pressing his lips to mine. His lips were warm and moist, his kiss was rough and demanding.

Something dark and wild, and frantic surged through me. I stood rigid in his arms. I knew what he was doing, marking his territory. Showing Aidan I was taken. My inner-wolf bucked some more, furious with me. The only thought I had as I fought against her protests was that Jared was so not the cheese to my macaroni. *Darn you, Mac, for putting that thought in there!*

I sighed when he broke away, and he grinned, clearly taking the sigh as something more than just relief that the kiss was over. He winked and then let go. As he stepped past me, he asked, "What's my girl doing here?"

"She's my partner," Aidan replied coolly. "We had some business to deal with."

I cringed. I couldn't stop it. And I couldn't turn around. I felt dirty, filthy, letting him kiss me like that, mark me as his, but I didn't know what else to do. As far as everyone else was concerned, I was with Jared. Beck was the only one who knew the full truth, and he was keeping it quiet, just as Jared and I had planned.

The guys stood just outside the door, grinning at me as if they actually thought this was funny. Landon leaned into Beck and whispered something that I was glad I couldn't hear because I was sure I would want to deck him if I had. He was grinning at me, a grin that was both knowing and condemning. Whatever he had said, it made Beck laugh hard.

I was about to tell them to shut up and get inside when Jared said, "Jade, come here."

I cut a dirty look at the team before turning around. I mustered up the sweetest smile I could and started toward him. "What do you mean you can't find Erika?"

Jared was already sitting on the couch, his arms draping over the back, and his glare was fixed on Aidan. "Exactly what it sounds like," he said without looking in my direction. "I don't know where she is."

I sat down beside him, pressing close, and nudged him with my shoulder, trying to pull his death stare off of Aidan. He didn't respond, so I nudged him again and wiggled against his side.

I risked a look at Aidan. His glare was fixed on me. His jaw ticked. His nostrils flared. His hands gripped the armrests, his fingers turning white. The butterflies in my stomach made themselves known, flapping and fluttering. The jealousy that flashed in his eyes stole my breath, and a hot blush streaked to my cheeks.

"Who are the statues?" Jared asked, tensing further. I knew he could smell the spike in my scent and hear my frantic heartbeat, but I couldn't make myself calm down.

I shifted my focus to Jared, snuggling a bit closer. "They're friends of Aidan's." My voice squeaked a little, and I cleared it. "Um, they're kind of joining your team."

"Your idea?" he asked, glancing down at me. The warning in his eyes was clear, and again I tried to tone my scent down.

I shook my head. "No. But we could use the help, don't you think?"

For an incredibly tense moment, Jared didn't say a word. The team crowded around us, along the back of the couch, and Beck, Landon, Mark, and Craig touched me one by one. Whether the hands were there for support or to show Aidan they'd staked a claim to me, I didn't know.

"Anything you want, kitten," Jared finally said. His arm draped around me then, pushing off all the hands that had found their way to my shoulders, and his body relaxed as he pulled me into his side. He kissed the top of my head, breathing me in, and then asked, "So what's this business about that was so important that you forgot to call me before ditching school and rushing over here?"

CHAPTER 7

AIDAN

I was sweating. My boxers, yeah, were soaked. I felt as if I were sitting in a puddle. No, it was more like a lake. Had the team agreed? Had Jared agreed? I scrubbed at my face. I felt as if I were losing my mind. Her scent worked through my system, screwing with my brain. I didn't know if the constant flares of her scent were for him or for me. Damn, it almost seemed as if the fragrance was spiking for both of us. My biceps flexed. My inner-wolf shifted. I started to get up, but my legs wouldn't move. This was a nightmare. It had to be. The kind where I knew I needed to run, but my legs wouldn't obey. Did any of that just happen?

Jade smiled. She waved. Jared wrapped an arm over her shoulder and kissed her lightly. He winked at me; clearly, he knew this was torture for me, and I was sure he loved every second of it. I was living in a damn nightmare. The door shut. The truck started. And I sat there watching as my mate left me again with Jared.

"Well, that was ... interesting," Tommy said, running a rough hand over his clean, hairless head. He paced a few steps, tugged at the collar of his polo shirt, and then dropped onto the couch.

"He sure has some hold on her," Chris added with a long whistle. He was sitting on the arm of the couch, his arms crossed over his chest and legs stretched out, folded at the ankles. "I've never seen an alpha female or any female fight so hard to ignore the call of her mate." His chiseled face looked harder under all the creases lining his narrowed eyes.

I swallowed hard. Her scent lingered. Fruits and almonds. My muscles flexed again. *Shit!* "She's not ..."

"Yeah, she is," Tommy said, cutting me off. "It's pretty obvious, kid. She feels it. Jared sees it, too. Her inner-wolf may want him, but she sure as hell doesn't."

What the hell just happened? I took another breath. I shifted in my chair. No one had argued. No one had challenged my decision. Jade agreed to everything. She even told Jared she wanted Chris and Tommy on the team, that she wanted me with them on the hunt. Where was the fight she had before Jared showed up? How the hell had he calmed her into a docile, obedient ... *Shit!*

For a second, I'd thought I still had a chance. A real chance. She'd melted against me like putty. I had smelled it. Her desire. Her need. But then he showed up. He calmed her. Her inner-wolf wanted him. The scent was there. She had been throwing it off like crazy when he had walked through that door. He possessed her in a way that I'd dreamed of having her since the moment I had met her.

I shifted again, sweating even more. "Dom?"

He looked just as confused as me. He sat on the couch beside Tommy, one arm over the back, staring at the door with a big question mark on his forehead. His brow furrowed, and he shook his head from side to side a few times before his hazel eyes finally focused on me. He shrugged. "I told you before she's stubborn, but if I had to guess, this whole Jared thing really has nothing to do with you. Jade might hold a grudge, but she wouldn't do this just to hurt you. She's not that much of a bitch. My best guess is she actually likes him. It's obvious her inner-wolf does." His tone was dry as if his throat had closed up, and the look he shot me said he didn't really believe what he was saying, but that didn't matter. All I heard was *likes him.*

"Likes him," I echoed. My jaw ticked. My eyes flared. *Get it together!* "Likes him," I said again. Every muscle in my body screamed as I forced myself to stay put and not go after her.

Dominic didn't miss my sparking rage. He stood up, moving behind the couch, putting a safe distance between us. "I can call Mac," he blurted. "See if she found out anything this morning."

"This morning?" My voice was a growl. My scent flared. His mask splintered and cracked. He paled. His head bowed. I was falling apart. I could feel it deep within my gut. My nostrils flared as I sucked in more and more of her lingering scent. *Mine,* my inner-wolf, growled into my mind. Dammit! She was mine. Every instinct I had was urging me to go after her. *Pull it together!*

"Yeah." Dominic tugged a hand through his blond hair, his head bowing further. "I sent her over there this morning."

"Dammit, Dom!" I jumped up and started to pace. My skin was crawling, my inner-wolf howling, begging to be let out. "Can't you follow anything I say? I told you both to keep away from her. She wanted space."

"Aidan," Tommy choked out in a hoarse voice. He stood up and stepped in front of me, placing a hand on my shoulder, and squeezed. "Keep it together, kid."

I closed my eyes, taking in a deep, centering breath. It didn't help. God, was her scent getting stronger?

"Jade doesn't know what she wants," Dominic

whispered. "And Trevor found tracks outside Mac's house this morning. She can't stay at home. Her dad won't let her move in with her mate, and he won't let Trevor stay there, so being at Jade's with the team always hanging around is the safest place for her."

I glanced at him then, my scent still flaring, and he shuddered. His eyes were full of concern, full of misery.

"Aidan," Chris growled through his teeth. "Tone the scent down. It went well. She'll see her dad in the morning. Play up the Jared bit and then meet us. He won't see it coming. And it will give you exactly what you need. The more time you spend with her, the better chance you'll have at getting her away from Jared. We went over this."

"You don't get it!" I snarled. "That team has never agreed with anything I've said. And, Jade, she's not that easy to convince of anything. Something's not right here. Something else is going on." The rational part of my mind knew he was right. Everything was going as planned, and tomorrow I would have the entire day to try and talk to her, begging her to forgive me, but the other part was crazed, furious that she had left with him — again. Right then, I was certain she had given up on me.

An uneasy silence crowded the room. Tommy dropped his hand from my shoulder and took a step back. He huffed out a breath. "Look, kid, we have to get going," he said. "You heard Jared. He wants us to stay with Landon. Don't want to give that team any reason not to trust us. We'll email you with anything we find out. Get some sleep. It'll look better tomorrow."

JADE

I had to force myself out of the house, one foot in front of the other. I felt wrecked. Shattered. Jared wouldn't talk to me. I got in the truck. We dropped off the team. And still, he hadn't said a word.

Aidan's scent clung to me. On my skin. In my hair. Could Jared smell it? Was that the reason for his maddening silent treatment? He had to know I let Aidan take me into his arms. He had to know that my heart was still racing, that my inner-wolf was doing backflips, begging me to go back. That had to be it. The problem was I didn't really care if he knew. Did that make me a bitch? *Probably.*

He pulled into my driveway. Turned off the truck. He didn't move. I shifted in my seat, opened my mouth, and then shut it. His knuckles were white. His jaw clenched. The muscles in his forearms, straining. He had never been this mad at me before, not even when I wasn't one of them and despised the pack. I swallowed hard, popped the door open, and got out. He would talk when he was ready. Hopefully.

Mom was sitting on the couch when I walked in. She glanced at me as I went by and frowned but didn't say anything. I figured I looked as bad as I felt.

I went straight to my room, sat on the bed, and waited. And waited. And waited.

The glowing red numbers on my alarm clock flipped by, minute by agonizing minute. An hour passed, and still, Jared hadn't come in. I wondered for a moment if he had left, but I knew I would have heard his monster of a truck startup if he had.

I sighed and spent a few minutes debating on whether I should go back out there and try to talk to him. But instead of facing him (yeah, I was being a coward), I dug my phone out of my pocket and fired off a message to Erika asking her where she'd been all afternoon. She should have been accessible. She should have been by my side through that meeting. Erika answered immediately. *At home studying.*

I stared at the message for a long moment. Had Jared even tried to find her, or was she lying to me? I wasn't sure. Jared didn't like Erika, like at all, and she loathed him. I wouldn't have been surprised if she'd simply ignored his calls, and at the same time, it wouldn't have shocked me if he hadn't even tried to reach her.

God, I hated feeling like this. Lost and confused and sad. Really, really sad. The pack had always seemed so close from the outside looking in. A tight-knit group. But the reality was so different. It was like living in a constant power struggle, never knowing who you could trust and who wanted to watch you crash and burn. I was certain Aidan was up to something with his little plan of spending time with Jared and me, and I knew Jared was up to something. He always was. And I was stuck in the middle, wanting someone I shouldn't want, and with someone I didn't want. On top of all that, if Aidan's plan worked the way he wanted, I would be forced to pass judgment on my dad. As a friend of the pack, his betrayal meant I would be issuing a death sentence. The thought of sentencing my father to death was just too much, way too much. No matter how evil he was, he was still my dad. I was still his little girl. Was it completely wrong that I didn't want to be part of the hunt? *Most likely.*

Another twenty minutes passed, and the front door finally opened and closed. I heard Jared's whispered conversation with my mom, too low to really make out what was said. Then his footsteps, clunking up the steps. A knock on a door. "Trevor knows you're staying here?" Jared asked.

"Um, yeah, you want me to call him?" Marcy asked. She sounded nervous.

"Yes." Jared didn't sound happy. I squeezed my eyes shut, pulled in a deep breath, and pushed myself up. Jared didn't turn around when I opened the door. He stiffened, his neck tensed. "Jade, go wash that smell off of you," he said, the words clipped, brisk.

I felt sick. Hot and cold and sick. "Is everything okay?" I asked, looking at Marcy. I took a step and placed a hand on Jared's back. He flinched, and I let my hand fall away. *I'm such an ass-hat.* "She can stay here if she wants, Jared."

"Not if her mate hasn't okayed it, she can't. I'm not housing her without speaking to him. Jade, go." His tone was cold, challenging even.

Marcy smiled. It was forced, a little shaky. She mouthed *It's okay*, and made a shooing gesture at me.

I hesitated for a second, staring at his back, willing him to turn around, but he didn't. Marcy scrolled through her contacts and gave me a pointed look before thumbing the screen and bringing the phone to her ear.

I turned away, took the few steps to the bathroom, and let the door click shut behind me, sinking to the floor. At that moment, I hated, *hated*, being at home. It didn't feel like home, not anymore. It just felt like one big lie.

I hugged my knees to my chest. I hated feeling like this. Since taking over as alpha female, I'd spent the last few days doing what I thought was right. I had stayed away from everyone, the pack, Aidan ... I'd been convincing myself that working with the team was the right thing to do. Pretending to be with Jared was the right thing to do. Stay away. Keep them safe. But as I sat in Aidan's house, listening to his plan, realizing that he needed help, something had dawned on me.

I was no better than him. I had condemned him for lying to me, for manipulating me, but really, I was just as guilty. And watching him glare at Jared made me realize that I was hurting him just as badly as he had hurt me.

God, I suck!

Marcy was already sleeping by the time I finished scrubbing Aidan's scent from my body. I stood outside her door for a few minutes listening to her soft snores, debating on sneaking in there and hiding until the morning. But I didn't.

The lights were off in my room when I eased the door open. Jared's steady breathing came from beside my bed. I listened for a moment, trying to judge if he was really sleeping. I couldn't tell. I tiptoed across the room and eased myself into bed, trying not to disturb him. His breath hitched. He shuffled around, and I let my head hang over the bed, glancing down at him. "Jared, I know you're awake. Will you just yell at me already and get it over with?"

He was lying on his back, the comforter pulled to his waist. Moonlight streamed in from the window, basking him in a silvery glow. He didn't have a shirt on, and his hands were folded behind his head. He sighed. "I don't know what you're talking about."

"Come on," I said, hating how raw my voice sounded and how guilty I felt. "This cold shoulder crap is getting old. I know you're pissed."

"Pissed is so not what I'm feeling right now, little girl. Not even close."

I shimmied off the bed, sinking down beside him on the floor. "Then enlighten me."

He groaned, long and loud. "Go to sleep, Jade. It's going to be a long day tomorrow."

"I can't sleep knowing you're pissed off at me." I inched a bit closer. "What was I supposed to do?

Refuse to go? He sent that Tommy guy. He literally had me dragged from school."

Jared opened his eyes then and rolled over, propping his head up on an elbow. "You think this is because you were at his house?"

I threw my hands up in the air. "Well, what else could your mood be about?"

"This was your idea." He waved a hand between us. "You wanted this to be believable. You wanted us to be believable." His eyes flared bright gold. "His scent was all over you. In your hair. On your neck. What did you do? Trip and fall into him? This may just be a game to you, Jade, but to me, it's not. So stop jerking me around."

I felt his words like a slap in the face. Something splintered inside me. It was as if I were being held underwater. The pressure built and built until my insides felt as if they were filled with hairline fractures. Tears — damn tears — filled my eyes. I would have preferred him yelling or telling me off. But this ... this hurt. I couldn't breathe. I gasped for air, and it burned through my lungs. There was just so much pressure. Be an alpha. Claim a mate. Stop the cougars. Deal with my dad. Maybe even have him killed. Forget or forgive Aidan. Learn pack laws. Fix the pack. Run the pack with a man that made my body sing and my blood boil and one that I couldn't trust. Pretend to be in love with Jared without hurting him. I gasped again. The tears stung, brimming in my eyes and spilling over.

"Don't do that," he said, brushing a thumb hastily across my cheek. "Don't make me feel like the asshole here. You were practically panting over him. Do you really think no one noticed?"

"I'm sorry," I said and hiccupped. "I ... I ..." I huffed and hiccupped again. I shrugged my shoulders. "I don't want to feel this way about Aidan, but I'm his. He's mine. I can feel it in my bones." I pressed my hand to my chest, gripping my shirt in my fist. "I feel it here."

Jared rolled onto his back, and he closed his eyes. Clearly, he was done with the conversation. I watched his chest rise and fall for a few breaths, noting the tension, the unevenness of each lungful.

"I'm going to tell him the truth about us, Jared," I whispered, turning from him and climbing back in bed. I pulled the comforter up to my neck and waited for a response, but when all that followed was another unsteady breath, I continued, "I'm sorry that this situation sucks so much for you. And I'm really sorry that I'm such a crappy fake girlfriend. I won't blame you if you want to call it quits, but I have to tell him the truth."

"I'm not going to give up on you, Jade," he said, his voice thick with emotion that sounded more like anger than anything else. The man didn't have a warm cell in his body. At that moment, I was sure of it. Anger and hatred always won out with him.

"You should," I said, meaning every word. "You really should." *Because you don't have a chance,* I thought, not able to say it out loud.

AIDAN

I was a wolf, and I stood below her window.

I knew I shouldn't have come here, but after seeing Jade today, I needed more. Maybe I was just a sucker for punishment. Yeah, that was probably it. The window was open, just a sliver, and her sweet, sweet scent washed out. She sounded ... sad, angry, frustrated. Her voice was just barely a whisper by the time it reached my ears, just loud enough that I could pick up bits and pieces of the conversation. I shouldn't have been listening. I shouldn't have come. And I knew I needed to leave, but I couldn't.

Maybe it was my guilt that held me in place.

There were many things a wolf could do that wouldn't actually complete mating, and in the last hour, I had done pretty much all of them.

After everyone had left my house and I'd been alone with Jade's tormenting scent, I'd needed a distraction. And I found it in the all too willing arms of Erika. I wasn't proud of it. Truthfully, I felt more than a little sick about what I'd just done, but even if I felt bad about it, I had still done it.

I had left my house five minutes after Dominic went home, and I'd ended up on Erika's doorstep. I told myself it was because I wanted to know why she hadn't been available for Jade. Erika was her beta, and as far as I was concerned, there should never, *never*, be a reason for her not to be reachable when Jade needed her. Dealing with Erika was the one thing I knew I could do. But one thing had led to another, and before I knew it, I was in her room with her tearing off my clothes. She had been more than happy to provide her alpha with the relief that I'd needed, and dammit, I'd been more than willing to let her. Her lips, her hands, caressing my entire body was ... a short-lived relief, effectively shattered by a text message from Jade.

I couldn't believe how easy it had been for Erika to lie to Jade — her alpha. She had glanced at the phone and quickly fired off a message: *At home studying*.

That small interruption had been more than enough to stop everything. I had grabbed my clothes, yanking them on as she tried to convince me to stay.

And now here I was planted on the lawn outside Jade's house, listening as she begged Jared to forgive her.

I'd been telling myself that Jade was probably doing

the same things with Jared as I had been doing with Erika. She might not be mated with him yet, but I knew they were sharing a room, and I was sure her bed.

Jade's voice rose. I could hear the tears. Damn, I could feel the heartbreak as her voice reached my ears. "I don't want to feel this way about Aidan, but I'm his. He's mine. I can feel it in my bones." She paused and then whispered, "I feel it here."

Clearly, I'd been wrong. So very, very wrong.

I'm his. He's mine. The words beat at my mind, repeating over and over. My throat started to close up. My heartbeat started to race. The beginning of a growl built in my chest, and I fought against my inner-wolf to keep quiet. I began to back away. Self-disgust filled me like a nest of snakes writhing in my gut. My inner-wolf tried to hold me in place, demanding me to go and retrieve her, get her away from Jared, but I fought it. I'd been sure she'd been hiding something from me, but I hadn't imagined it would be something like this. Not with the way her inner-wolf reacted to Jared. I backed up a little more. I needed to get out of there. I needed to think. I needed to process this. And after a few steps, I pivoted and ran.

I'm such a jackass.

CHAPTER 8

JADE

I woke up alone. Jared's bed was gone, the blankets, the pillows, all put away. It was weird. He never picked up anything. Never. His wallet wasn't on the dresser, neither were his keys. I rolled over, glancing at the clock: 6:08. My heartbeat doubled, and a nervous knot yanked tight in my belly.

Panic fluttered through me. I yanked the blankets off. He wouldn't just leave. He wouldn't. Not with Dad coming home today, even if I was a crappy fake girlfriend, even if I'd said I was going to tell Aidan the truth. Jared wouldn't ...

I was out of bed in a flash, and just as my feet hit the floor, the door swung open. I skidded to a stop. Jared stood in the doorway, a towel cinched low on his hips. His black hair was wet. Beads of water slid down his sculpted chest. My breath hitched. A hot flush rushed to my cheeks, and I dropped my head, peeking at him through my lashes. My heartbeat skittered within my chest, and my panic eased slightly.

His nostrils flared, and he shuddered — a little — as he scanned me over. "What's wrong, kitten?" he asked, his voice husky. He crossed the few steps to me and cupped my cheeks, forcing me to look at him. He searched my face. Whatever he saw there made him smile.

"I thought you left," I said, hating the tremor in my voice. "I thought you just up and left."

He frowned. "I told you I'm not going to give up on you."

"But your stuff?" I flailed a frantic hand toward the dresser and then to his missing bed. Right at that moment, I realized something. Jared wasn't just the leader of my team. He wasn't just my pretend mate. At some point in the last few days, he had become a friend. A person that I could count on.

He smirked and chuckled, clearly enjoying my panic and knowing him, reading something into it that wasn't there. "Put it away. You're always bitching at me to pick up after myself."

He was looking down at me in a way that was far too personal. His hands fell from my face, dipping to my shoulders. A whole new panic bloomed within my belly. I took a step back, wanting to put some much-needed space in between us. Jared's presence in my life might have started to feel comfortable, but he wasn't home — he never would be. "Nothing's changed, Jared," I said evenly. "I'm going to tell him today."

He opened his mouth, and he looked as if he were about to protest when I heard someone clear their throat and a familiar gruff voice said, "What the hell do you think you're doing?"

I'm not ready for this, a voice in my head shrieked. The temperature in the room dropped to freezing. My stomach twisted, my throat closed up. Jared turned and backed up a few steps, and I swiveled and blinked.

"Daddy?" I said. He looked furious. I took a step back, right into Jared. His face was streaked red, his hands balled. His large frame filled the doorway, and his jaw started twitching. I'd never seen him like this before. Never.

His clothes were rumpled, his jeans filled with dirt stains. Tired lines littered his eyes. Dad's lips thinned. "Get some damn clothes on, boy!" he shouted, his fists clenching tighter.

A rock-hard lump formed in my throat, and the door across the hallway swung open. "Mr. Shaw, what's going on?" Marcy asked. I couldn't see her past the wall that was my dad. Dad didn't turn around, didn't give any indication that he had heard her. His face reddened further, and his gaze was fixed on Jared.

"Jeff," Jared said coolly. He slipped a possessive hand on my hip. "Nice of you to finally come home."

Dad took a step into the room. He was a big man, burly and thick, but he had never looked so much like a bear before, snarly, angry. "Don't test my patience, Jared."

I brushed Jared's hand off me and took a step away, my cheeks burning with a flush. "Daddy, we were just ..."

"In the middle of something," Jared said, cutting me off. He snaked an arm around my waist and pulled me back against him.

"Let go," I said, tugging at his hand. His arm was like a vice grip. Maybe it was the decision I'd made last night, but Jared's hands on me felt more wrong than they ever had before. Even my inner-wolf squirmed and shrunk, wanting away from him.

Act the part! a voice screamed through my head. I stiffened, fighting back the growl that worked its way through my chest, and I softened my smile and batted my eyes. "Daddy, you knew he was living here. I told you. I thought you were happy about it."

His eyes landed on me then, burning like fire. "And you also told me you were mated, but you're not."

Crap! Crap! Crap! This was so not the plan. I sucked in a breath. He wasn't supposed to know. We needed him to believe I was mated. *Crap!* I didn't know what to say. I sucked in another breath and blurted, "What? He is my mate."

He stepped closer. "Don't lie to me, Jade. By now, I'm sure you've been told what I am. I can smell it. You haven't mated. And you're not going to. Not with him." His blazing gaze rose, looking over my head. "Now, you listen to me closely. Take your hands off my daughter and call the alpha. I want him here, now." His tone was nothing short of a challenge.

Jared bristled, and he growled, long and low, tightening his grip on me. His muscles started to shudder, rippling beneath his skin.

"Mac," I shouted. "Mac, get back in your room and call Aidan!"

AIDAN

The wind cut through my fur as I broke into a full run. Her scent was thick in the air, teasing my senses, making my heart race. She yipped, a playful sound, and I set chase. I needed to find her.

From the corner of my eye, I saw her dash out of the trees. She skidded to a stop in front of me. I slowed. Stopped. Sunlight streamed through the branches overhead, winking off her midnight black coat. She licked my nose and rubbed along my side before sitting on her haunches in front of me. Her body trembled. Her fur receded. My heart stopped. Anticipation clawed through me. If I were human, my palms would have been sweating. Her face started to shift. Her smile was shy but bright, like the sun and the moon basking me in light.

And then my phone rang.

I groaned, sitting straight up. The phone rang again. I groped at the nightstand, snagging it up. I thumbed the screen, brought the phone to my ear, and said, "Aidan."

"You need to get to Jade's, like now." Marcy's voice screeched through my groggy brain, and I jerked the phone away, waiting for the ringing in my ears to stop before pressing it back in place.

I groaned again. "Breathe, Mac," I said, scrubbing at my face. "What's going on?" My voice was thick and heavy with sleep. I blinked a few times, clearing my fuzzy eyes.

"I can't breathe. Mr. Shaw is about to take off Jared's head." She sucked in a loud, shaky breath. "The team's not here yet. Jade's starting to freak out. Jared looks like he's about to shift. He's holding onto her, Aidan. He won't let her go."

Shit! I was out of bed and yanking on my jeans before she'd finished her tirade. *This isn't the plan!* I launched out of my room, taking the stairs at a run. "Mac, go to your room, okay? Lock your door." I grabbed my keys off the table and bolted out the door. "Don't come out until I get there, no matter what. Call Dom. Call the team. Get them there. And call your mate."

"Aidan, she needs ..."

"No," I snapped, cutting her off. My chest squeezed tight. *Shit! Shit! Shit!* I got in my car and started it up as I sucked in a steadying breath. "Jade can take care of herself. Stay in your room." I thumbed my phone and tossed it on the front seat, praying I was right.

JADE

Dad's nostrils flared. He stood deathly still, his blazing gaze fixed on Jared. Where the heck was Aidan? It had to have been five minutes since Marcy had retreated, locking her door. I really didn't know how much longer I could keep this up.

Dad's lips thinned. He waved a hand, beckoning me to him, and I shook my head. He didn't try to come closer. I figured he could see how close Jared was to losing control. As it was, he was just barely holding onto his human form. The tension in the room was suffocating, pressing against me from all sides. Right then, I knew I couldn't wait any longer. I needed to calm Jared down. I needed to act like an alpha.

I turned in Jared's arms, reaching up, resting a hand on his cheek. I smirked and said, "No dogs allowed in the house."

He growled. His eyes were completely gold, not a speck of the typical black-brown left. They were fixed on the doorway, on my dad. His claws dug into my back, sharp enough that I gasped as they shredded through my shirt. Any harder, and he'd break the skin, too.

My imprint heated. I needed to get his attention, to calm him. My scent gathered, and I sent out a small short burst. Jared snapped his gaze to mine. He growled again. His muscles rippled. I grinned, rolled up on my toes, and pressed my lips to his. His claws dug deeper, and I bit back a screech as a sharp pain shot through my back. I looked up, my lips still against his, and whispered, "I said no dogs allowed in the house."

Another growl sounded from behind me. Lower. Deeper. I stiffened. So did Jared. A familiar scent filled the air. My nostrils flared. Raw power trembled around me. Jared's knees buckled. Another spasm raked through him, rippling against me. He stiffened and then gave his head a good, thorough shake, and he let his arm fall from me. His breathing evened out, and darn it, mine quickened.

A short burst of adrenaline rushed through me. "Aidan, stop!" The challenge was there, the command clear in my voice. He was going to ruin everything. My inner-wolf clawed through me, trying to rip free. His scent worked through me, stronger, pushing on my nerves, speaking to my inner-wolf in a way only he could. I spun around as another growl ripped through my room, and my gaze met his.

The alpha. I couldn't breathe. *The alpha.* I'd never seen him like this before. *My alpha.* His presence filled the room. His broad shoulders rolled back, his chest puffed out. Corded muscles lined his neck, shoulders, arms. I licked my lips and pulled in a breath. *Home.*

Aidan studied me for a few seconds, and the power, hunger, and strength in that stare left me feeling dizzy. "Jade," he whispered on a breath. He held out a hand, and I reached for it. I saw my hand moving, my inner-wolf forcing me forward, and I couldn't stop it.

Dad barked out a laugh. It slid through me like ice in my veins, and I stopped mid-step. He stepped toward me grabbed my shirt, tugging the neckline down just enough to reveal the burning imprint on my chest. "So my daughter won the games."

AIDAN

Rage pounded through me like a series of waves crashing against my skull. I couldn't think. A growl worked its way out from my chest. There was another man, basically naked, pressed against my mate. Her lips were on his. His claws raked along her back. The rational part of my brain told me this was okay. She was playing a part. She'd confirmed that last night, even if she didn't know, I knew it yet. The guy holding onto her wasn't a real threat, but my inner-wolf growled anyway, *I'll kill him.*

Jeff's voice barely registered in my ears. I heard nothing but the rage. Saw nothing but her. I reached for her whispered her name. She froze. A hand tugged at her shirt. A light shine of sweat covered her forehead as she stared down at her imprint, flickering with a soft white glow.

And then a fist swung at me. It connected. My nose snapped and crunched, and blood rushed down my face.

"Dad!" Jade shouted. Her voice was panicked, scared.

The rage pounded again. Harder. Faster. Her fear fed it. I could taste my own blood seeping into my mouth. My scent thickened. I had to protect my mate. Nothing else mattered. My chest heaved with each breath. Right then, I was more animal than human. I grabbed Jeff, tossing him against the wall, the meaty palm of my hand pressed against his throat.

"Aidan, stop it!" Jade commanded. I felt her voice in my bones, vibrating through me. She growled. Her hand wrapped around my wrist, tugging, as she tried to dislodge my palm from her father's neck. "Think!" she screamed. "You need to think!"

"Take her and get out," I growled, shifting my gaze to the useless enforcer, standing off to the side of the room with his gaze cast to the floor. "You touch her, though, and I'll kill you." It was more than a threat; it was a promise.

"Screw off, Aidan," Jared snarled. He lifted his head slightly, and his face contorted with fury.

I got in his face, tight and fast, dropping my hand from Jeff's neck. "You'll do what I say."

CHAPTER 9

My nose throbbed. Blood still flowed freely down my face. Jared squared his shoulders, dipped his chin, and let out a low growl. The look he gave me was pure challenge.

Every muscle in my body stiffened. I rolled my shoulders back and puffed out my chest only an inch from his. A growl built in my throat, and at that moment, all I saw was red.

"Jared, you need to go," Jade said, her tone a sweet melody of power and authority. She turned to me, jutting her arm between us, and placed a hand firmly on my heaving chest. She shoved, trying to push me back a step, and I let her. "Aidan, you need to calm down."

My nostrils flared, and my throat tightened. I wanted to rip him apart from limb to limb. *No one touches my mate. No one.* Not now. Not after hearing the truth of how she felt last night.

Jade shoved at me again. My nerves were on fire, searing within me. I fixed my gaze on her. Shivers chased down her shoulders and back. She was breathing hard and fast in ragged bursts. The sight of her shivers broke through the murderous haze that was clouding my brain a little, and instead of launching at Jared and ending him, which, yeah, was exactly what I wanted to do, I growled, "Get him out of here." My scent ramped up, and I hated to admit it, but I thoroughly enjoyed watching Jared shudder under its weight.

"Aidan, I'm serious," she growled. Golden veins streaked through her eyes, and she gritted her teeth. "I can't deal with all this testosterone. Everyone needs to calm down."

I watched as another shiver rushed over her skin, and then I forced my eyes closed, and I took a long, long moment to breathe. It was the only thing I could think of doing, to try to calm myself down. Her hand stayed on my chest, shaking. I was exhausted and torn up from the inside out. My self-control was cracking under the pressure of the rage that crashed through my veins, but for her, I would do just about anything. So I breathed and breathed, forcing my inner-wolf to stand down. When he finally receded to a far corner of my mind, I looked down at her, and my heart pulled and squeezed as if a hand had wrapped itself around it and was determined to rip it from my chest.

Her hand dropped from my chest. I almost reached out to grab it. I hated the disconnected feeling. Hated it. But I didn't stop her. Her shivers increased, and she shouted out a slew of obscenities that I'd never heard from her before. And as I listened, resolve tightened in my chest. Whatever game she was playing with Jared was going to stop. Now.

I watched her closely. Couldn't pull my eyes away from her, actually. She looked up at me, really looked at me, and she whimpered a deep, throaty whimper. Her swearing stopped, and her eyes softened as she brought her fingers to her full lips. That small gesture almost did me in — almost — and again, I found myself fighting not to take her in my arms.

And then Jeff laughed, a deep rumbling sound. "You son of a bitch," he said. I glanced at him over my shoulder before I turned to meet him straight on, ready to throw myself in front of Jade if I had to. Sharp clarity washed over me. Jeff — the monster who had been ready to take some of my wolves for his sick, twisted pleasure — stood in front of me laughing.

The blood still trickled down my face, but it was starting to slow. The pain was dull, just a small throb as my nose began to heal. The rage was beginning to fade, and in its place, something cold settled in my bones. *There goes the plan.*

But as I watched him, if I hadn't known any better, right then, I would have thought he actually cared. Although he was still chuckling, his eyes were glassy as they shifted between Jade and me. His expression was a mix of shattered amusement. He pulled in a breath, shook his head, and said, "You made her fight. Tricked her into competing in the games, and then you just let her go. You've been lying to me for days while I've been out there risking everything I have for you and your damn pack." He laughed again, a shocking kind of sound, and his lips curved into a bemused smile.

"You broke my nose," I said and grabbed the hem of my shirt, pulling it up to mop up some of the warm blood that was still dribbling down my chin. I kept my glare focused on him as I tried to make sense of his reaction. But, oh hell, I couldn't. He had to understand that Jade being alpha female, put a gaping hole in his plans to secure female wolves from Tiffany, but if it bothered him at all, he wasn't showing it. But then, he wouldn't know that we knew his plans.

I let my now bloody shirt drop, and Jade whimpered again, her eyes fixed on my face. I smiled at her, just a small twitch of my lips. I couldn't help it. Honestly, it was kind of nice to see that she cared for once. It was just too bad. It took a broken nose for her to show it.

"You deserve more than a broken nose," Jeff said with a chuckle. "You're the sorriest excuse for an alpha this pack has ever had. She's supposed to be your mate, and you let Jared move in here." His grin widened, and he smacked me on the back as if we were old friends. "Why the hell haven't you claimed her yet?"

Okay, so that wasn't what I had expected. Jeff was grinning at me, all the tension he'd had moments ago was gone, and he looked ... happy? I looked him over. His eyes were bright with curiosity, not even a stitch of fear. His scent seemed ... calm and way too human. I didn't know if he could mask his emotions the same way he could hide the cougar smell. My gut told me that he didn't have a clue how much we knew. He wouldn't seem so relaxed if he did, so I went with it. I shrugged, a lazy lift of my shoulders. "Jared was your idea," I said, lifting a brow in question.

Jeff rolled his eyes and grunted. "Because you told me she lost. Mating her with one of the enforcers was the next best option."

JADE

"Enough," I hissed. "I'm not some darn prize. I'm not a piece of property you guys can just give away to any random guy you choose." I spun on my dad, the back of my neck and face burning with a flush. "God, Dad, how can you even talk about this in front of me? I'm supposed to be your little girl, remember?"

Dad looked a little ashamed. He cleared his throat and shifted awkwardly from one foot to the other. I threw my hands up in the air. This was so not cool.

My dad chatting about me having sex was just not cool. I figured it shouldn't surprise me. I knew what kind of animal he really was, but still, he was my dad. Blood rushed to my face. Talk about embarrassment. At some point, the entire team had crowded in the doorway. Dominic was there, smirking, so were Marcy and Trevor. Leave it to my best friends to enjoy this epically embarrassing situation.

Aidan turned to me, staring down at me. The hem and collar of his shirt were soaked with blood. I scanned him over, watching the muscles tick in his arms and neck. His gaze went to Jared, hard and cold, before shifting back to me. The blood on his face was starting to dry, crusting up under his nose, down his chin.

And just like that, my humiliation shattered. I made a sound, a mix of a growl and whimper. I swallowed hard. He'd never looked so powerful before, so much like an alpha even with the blood and broken nose. His muscles were bunched, straining beneath his shirt. His chin dipped. His broad shoulders, squared. Confidence. Authority. It emanated from him.

My lips parted, my jaw dropped. *My alpha. My mate.* The words echoed through my mind. Right then, I couldn't remember why I had been so determined to stay away from him. My inner-wolf stirred as I deeply breathed in his scent.*Mine,* she agreed.

Something had changed with him. Something big. It was as if he were just now, in that very moment, finally stepping into his full authority as alpha male. I'd seen him do this before with the pack, but never with me. Never. He was soft with me. I made him weak. Even when he tried to stand strong, he always relented way before his point was made. But now he didn't look weak, not at all.

The butterflies in my stomach awoke, flapping and

fluttering with excitement. *My alpha.* At that moment, all I saw was him. Everyone else faded, melted until it was as if they were just gone. It was just us.

Jared's hand settled on the small of my back, pulling me back to reality, and I quickly stepped away. If the plan hadn't already been blown apart, that small step had done it. None of them of my dad, Aidan, Jared, or the team missed that step. The step away from the man I claimed to want. I felt cold. Cold and drained and tired, as if every ounce of fight I had in me was just gone. Everything was ruined. Aidan's plan. My plan. All of it ruined.

I needed to get out of the room.

My thoughts began to leap and jump, nothing making sense. I needed a new plan, that was for sure, but my brain wasn't working. My dad looked so calm, caring even. It was wrong. Everything that was happening was just completely wrong. I glanced around a little frantically. There were enough pack members here to make sure he didn't go anywhere. I stepped toward the door. "Move," I said, pushing at the wall of enforcers blocking my way out, but they didn't budge. Clearly, I wasn't the only one feeling the power shift in our alpha male.

I shoved at Beck's chest, none too gently, but he stood firm, blocking my exit. He wouldn't look at me, his gaze fixed over my head, most likely on Aidan. He lifted a questioning brow, and after a long second, he stepped out of my way.

I glanced back at Aidan, waved a hand, beckoning him to follow me, and I headed into the bathroom.

CHAPTER 10

JADE

The bathroom door clicked shut behind me as I grabbed the washcloth from the towel rack. I didn't have to look to know that it was, in fact, Aidan that had followed; his presence filled the room with waves of power. I took the cloth to the sink, turned on the hot water, and shoved it under the flow. My muscles bunched and rolled beneath my skin, my inner-wolf begging to come out.

I kept my eyes fixed on the porcelain top of the vanity, and the bottom edge of the ornate, copper framed mirror, studying the swirls and twists of its floral design. The bathroom was large. My parents had renovated it a couple of years ago, pushing walls back and turning it into a spa-like retreat, with double sinks, a walk-in shower, and a separate soaker tub, but with the door closed and Aidan's heady scent filling the space, it felt tight and small and airless.

Once the cloth was soaked, I turned off the tap and slowly rung it out before finding enough nerve to turn to him. His expression was void of emotion, a blank slate. He leaned against the door, arms folded over his chest, his brown eyes watching my every move.

My hands were shaking, my heart pounding. I closed the short distance between us. I looked back up at him, and darn it, but I whimpered again. *So much blood.*

The sound softened him a little. He reached out and caressed my cheek, but when I pressed into the touch, he let his hand drop, hanging loosely by his side. His eyes searched my face, looking for something, but what I didn't have a clue. I felt the sting of tears welling up. I don't know why. The last thing I wanted to do was cry. Not for the alpha that had destroyed my life and ripped out my heart. His nose had already healed. He was fine. *But there's just so much blood.*

I blinked fast, banishing the tears. "Does it hurt?" I asked and then swallowed hard. I lifted my trembling hand and dabbed at the blood, wiping it away as best I could. "I hope it does. You've ruined everything." Even though I said the words, they held no real meaning. My voice was weak, straining against an onslaught of emotions blooming within my chest.

"No," he grunted. "It's already healed." He grabbed my wrist, holding my shaking hand still. "I did what was needed. You're not staying here any longer, Jade. This little game you're playing ends now. I'm taking you home, where you belong."

I clucked my tongue and dropped my gaze. More butterflies surfaced in my belly, and I breathed, "This is where I belong."

"Look me in the eyes and tell me that," he said. When I didn't lift my head, he chuckled a deep rumble that turned my knees to mush. "You can't, can you?"

"I can't trust you," I whispered, my voice wobbly. My heart started pounding painfully fast. "I don't even know who you are."

He tipped my chin up with his free hand, forcing me to meet his eyes; his eyes were pleading. "Your wolf knows me, Jade. She trusts me. You feel it. I know you do. We can work on the rest. I can make this right."

I shook my head, pulling in a deep breath. He was right. He was so bang on, and it scared me to death. At that moment, I wanted nothing more than him. I wanted to feel delicate, wrapped in his arms. And I never ever wanted to feel the dark, frantic need that Jared brought out in me again. But the tendrils of longing and desire that weaved throughout my chest scared the heck out of me. How could I feel this way about a guy who had done nothing but lie and manipulate me?

I heard the shuffling steps outside the door and then the thump of feet on the staircase. I listened until the last step had been taken and strained to hear if anyone else had hung around upstairs. The silence that greeted me seemed too loud, and uneasiness wormed its way through my belly. My nerve started to falter, and I squeezed my eyes closed, and then I murmured the words that I was sure could only lead to my heart being ripped out again. "I don't know if you can make it right." I sucked in a full breath and let it hiss out slowly. "But I guess that doesn't really matter. I need to ..."

He growled low in his chest. My eyes snapped open as his grip tightened on my wrist. I searched his face, trying to read what was there, but all I saw was rage. "Don't say it, Jade," he spat. "Don't even think of saying you need to stay with him."

AIDAN

Jade was still trying to play the game, and it confused the hell out of me. Maybe she had changed her mind from last night. Maybe she wasn't going to tell me the truth anymore. I didn't really deserve it, especially after what I'd done with Erika, but damn, I wanted to hear her say it.

She knew I'd seen her shudder away from Jared's touch. She felt the connection, the chemistry, between us. I could see it in her eyes. I knew she didn't believe she should stay here, stay with him, but she still tried to convince me that she wasn't mine. It was wrecking her — wrecking me. Her expression was shattered, her body trembled.

"Will you just shut up," she hissed, keeping her voice low so no one would overhear, and her defeated gaze dropped to my chest. She shook off my hand, which was still clamped around her wrist, and when I let go, she hugged her arms around her waist, pressing the damp washcloth into her side. The water seeped into her light blue nightshirt, the thin cotton soaking it up and darkening where it touched, but she didn't seem to notice. "I'm trying to confess here," she huffed, "and you are so not making it easy."

"Confess?" I asked. I shook my head. Damn, clearly, I had read her wrong. The way she had closed her eyes, squeezing them shut, as if she couldn't handle looking at me, and that sad, sad smile that curved her beautiful lips. I sucked in a breath, steadying my racing heart, and I tapped her chin again, tilting her face back up to meet mine. "You want to confess?"

"Never pictured this happening in a bathroom," she muttered. She puffed out a breath and tugged her bottom lip between her teeth. She held my gaze for a moment before pushing my hand away and letting her eyes drop again. "Jared and I aren't really together," she whispered.

I held my breath, waiting for more. I craved to hear her say that she was mine, that I was hers. I needed to hear it, needed to watch her say it, but she didn't say it. Her shoulders slumped, her breath hitched, as if talking to me was physically painful for her.

My inner-wolf howled within me, and the alpha in me shot to the forefront of my mind. Pieces I hadn't even considered last night started to fall into place. I'd been so busy feeling like an ass that I hadn't seen the whole picture. But at that moment, I saw it all in crisp, clear threads playing out just behind my eyes. Not only had my mate been lying to me, but the head enforcer, probably the whole damn team, had also been. My inner-wolf took over, and through my teeth, I said exactly what my inner-wolf wanted to do, "I'm going to kill him."

"Oh no, you're not." Jade shuddered back a step and jammed a pointed finger into my chest, the cloth still clutched in her hand, leaving a wet print on my shirt. "You're going to stay away from Jared."

A growl rumbled in my chest, and I closed the small space she'd placed between us, pressing against her and glaring down at her. My biceps flexed, and my eyes washed over with a golden haze.

"I'm serious, Aidan," she whispered. She took another step back and then turned away from me. The back of her shirt was shredded and angry. Red welts littered her skin, the remnants of Jared's claws raking over her. Her shoulders rose and fell quickly, and she said in a soft, airless tone, "You will leave him alone. None of this was his idea. I care about him, and I'm asking you to leave him alone."

I growled again. I couldn't seem to do anything else. Right then, I was more animal than human. Coarse hair layered my forearms and then receded. Shots of adrenaline pounded through my veins. Another growl erupted, and another shot of adrenaline followed.

Jade spun on me, narrowed her eyes, and planted her hands on her hips. "Will you stop this! God, when did you turn into such a freakin' caveman?" She sighed long and loud and shook her head a few times. "Jared was following my orders. I put him up to it all. I didn't want you to know. He lied to you for me. Maybe I wanted to hurt you as much as you hurt me, I don't know. I tried to tell myself I was doing it for the pack, for you, even. But I guess that doesn't matter anymore. I asked him to keep it real and keep it quiet. And he did exactly what I wanted."

"You're just digging his grave, Jade," I said in a low growl. "Word of advice, keep your confessions to yourself. Don't give me another reason to get rid of him."

Her eyes narrowed further until they were only little slits. She swallowed a few quick swallows and then asked, "Who are you?"

"I'm still the same person you fell for. The same person you fought for a few days ago. The same person you killed for. I haven't changed. I'm your mate." She made a shocking noise from the back of her throat and brought her fingers to her lips. Her eyes widened. "What? Did you really think I didn't know how you felt?" I'm not sure what made me say it. The truth? Until yesterday, I'd actually believed she hated me.

"Of course, I didn't think you knew," she muttered, turning the cutest shade of rosy pink. She took a step back toward me and reached out, running a finger along my cheek. She cocked her head to the side, and her nostrils flared, then she smirked. "You need to chill out before you end up shifting in my bathroom."

I chuckled, but it sounded strangled and forced. I needed to know something, and I was pretty sure the answer would completely suck. "I can't believe I'm going to ask this, but why him? Why would you pick someone that you knew wanted to mate with you?"

She lifted her shoulders in a small, delicate shrug.

"Because at the time, he was a better choice than you. At least with him, I knew where I stood."

Yep, completely sucked.

Her answer burned, and the small ounce of peace I'd started to feel under her touch splintered. I growled again. I couldn't stop it. My inner-wolf was going crazy. I was going crazy. I reached out, cupping her cheeks in the palms of my hands. "I'm taking you home. Your Dad knows who you are, Jade. The best thing we can do right now is walk out of this house together." I paused for a second, searching her face, waiting for her protest, but she said nothing, so I pushed on. "You're going to tell him you freaked out after taking Tiff's life. You'll tell him you were scared about mating, that you weren't ready for that kind of commitment, and that the pressure of it all was too much. And then you're going to pack your bags, and you're going to finally come home."

For about half a second, she smiled, a soft, sweet smile, but it didn't last, and before I knew it, she was frowning. I ran a hand over her forehead, desperately wanting to smooth out the lines and bring the smile back. As I tried to brush them away, she said, "This is my home."

"Not anymore." I dropped my hands from her face and took a step back toward the door, ready to walk away. I couldn't listen to her try to tell me any different. I didn't trust myself to keep in control. Not right now. "I'm not arguing about this. Right now, I need to fix what just happened. I need to cover this up, and the best way to do that is to take you home with me."

I waited for a second, hoping to see something — anything — to tell me that she agreed, that she felt the same as I did, but she gave me nothing. I sighed and started to turn away from her, but as I did, she placed a hand on my chest, stopping me. "Lean back," she said. "You still have blood all over your face."

CHAPTER 11

JADE

I finished cleaning the blood from Aidan's face. My pulse was pounding, my ribs aching, as if my heart was trying to break through with each frantic beat. I had to admit that telling him the truth had a freeing effect, even if I hadn't been able to say everything I had wanted to. It was as if there had been a barbed wire cage around my heart, squeezing and cutting, but as I told him that I wasn't actually with Jared, the barbs had loosened, although they hadn't completely vanished.

I wanted to say something. He had to know how ridiculous he was being. He had to know that there was absolutely no way I would just pack my bags and follow him home just because he said so, even if that was exactly what I wanted to do. He'd had his chance, and what had he done with it? He had set it on fire and watched it burn. And I really didn't think I was ready to give him a chance to do it again.

The problem was I couldn't make my voice work. Maybe it was because deep down, I didn't really want to fight it, or it could have been that my inner-wolf was clamping down on my protests, reminding me that I had essentially done the exact same things that I'd been blaming him for. Whatever it was, it was definitely annoying.

His shoulders were set, a determined glint in his eyes. There was no reasoning with him, at least not now. His scent raked through me, calming my nerves and, at the same time, doubling my heartbeat. All I could do was focus on breathing, slow, steady breaths.

I rinsed out the cloth and draped it over the edge of the sink. I sighed. I could feel his eyes on me, scanning down my backside, most likely inspecting my tattered shirt. I'd felt the gashes close up some time ago, and the dry crustiness of blood was starting to itch. I grabbed another cloth from under the sink, wet it down, and tossed it to him.

Aidan caught it easily and moved in behind me as if he knew exactly what I needed. His fingertips, warm and smooth, teased my skin as he lifted the hem of my shirt, and I really had to focus on not leaning into him as he gently stroked the cloth along my tender skin. But darn it, I wanted to.

I knew he was waiting for me to tell him no. During the last few minutes, while I couldn't find my voice, he had been coaching me. Telling me exactly what I had to do. He was sure my dad didn't know everything. He claimed that the *Jared cover* being blown was just a hiccup. And he had made it very clear that I would be in a crap-load of trouble if I didn't make the story I needed to tell Dad believable.

On the other hand, I had been trying to think of a way out of this. I knew I could make the story believable. It was all the truth. I had freaked out. But really, who wouldn't have? I had killed someone. I had fought to the death for a pack that, for the last two years, I had loathed with every fiber of my body. And, yeah, Aidan was right. When I really thought about it, in the end, I'd been fighting for him. It had been his voice, his encouragement that had helped me win. His cries to me had been full of heartbreak, desperation, fear, and it was all of that that had given me the strength in the very last second to finish Tiffany off; I was sure of it.

But I knew in my gut that moving in with Aidan wasn't such a smart idea, even if it was only until we dealt with my dad. I didn't trust him, I didn't trust myself to be alone with him, and I was sure that staying here, near my dad, would be more useful. Really, that had been the reason behind everyone agreeing that I should pretend to be with an enforcer, so we could keep an eye on things.

When Aidan finished up on my back, he tossed the cloth into the sink, and I slowly, almost reluctantly, turned around. And again, I found myself wanting to tell him how stupid he was being. He was acting like a freakin' caveman, puffing out his chest, giving me a look that clearly said, *You're mine, accept it and deal with it.* The same look he'd given me when I had won the games and had melted into his arms. But again, I couldn't because, darn it, no matter how I looked at it, I was his.

Like the earth needed rain, I needed my mate.

He leaned back against the wall and gave me a thorough once over before he asked, "Is there anything else you want to tell me?"

"I'm not sure I can do this," I said, feeling a slight tremor in my bottom lip. "He's still my dad. I feel like ... like I'm betraying him."

He frowned. "Your dad betrayed your pack."

"You're not helping, jackass," I snapped, cutting him a dirty look. "It's not that simple, and you know it." But then, maybe it was that simple. I knew I was desperately trying to hold on to an image of my dad that couldn't have ever really existed. It was just that a part of me, the scared little girl within me, really, really wanted her father not to be the devil.

"Come here, sweetheart." Aidan's voice was soft, soothing. He held a hand out to me. I took a tentative step and then another, and as soon as I moved close enough, his arm coiled around my waist, pulling me flush against him. The gesture felt so incredibly right, so perfectly natural that I found myself liquefying, melting into him, and leaning my head against his chest. As he brushed some stray hair from my forehead, the barbed wire around my heart loosened a bit more.

He pressed a kiss onto my brow line, and all it took was just a light brush of his lips, and my heartbeat tripled. "You're the strongest person I know. You can do this." He squeezed me tighter and rubbed a small circle on my back. "Nothing needs to be decided today. We can go on the defensive. We'll watch and learn what we can about his pack and his involvement. Figure out what they want with our town. That's it."

"Okay." I nodded against his chest. "Okay, I'm ready." He didn't say anything else as I wriggled out of his arms, straightened my shoulders, and raised my chin. And he didn't try to stop me as I nudged him out of the way and went out the door, but then he'd already said everything he'd needed to, giving me the strength I needed.

I found everyone in the living room. Dad sat in his recliner, completely at ease. Dominic was grinning at me. Trevor, too, with Marcy pressed against his side. Jared was scowling, but thankfully he had ditched the towel and gotten dressed. The team, all five of them, were squashed together on the couch. Tommy and Chris stood behind them like statues. They looked incredibly out of place amongst our young pack members, but for a split second, I was really glad they were there, their strong, controlled presence balancing out the youthful recklessness of my team.

The glad feeling didn't last nearly long enough. There was so much tension I could barely breathe. Aidan was behind me. I could feel the heat of his glare hitting my back in waves. I could only imagine the furious, determined glint that had to be in his eyes because, honestly, I was a bit too freaked out to turn around and actually see it. *You can do this*, I coached myself. Too bad my little pep talk wasn't working for me.

As we approached, heads bowed and shoulders drooped. I gritted my teeth. Again, I felt like something big had changed. And I really didn't know if I liked it. Since when did my team show any kind of respect to the alpha? They hadn't been with Ray, and they had challenged Aidan's every move since he took over. I knew the show of respect wasn't for me. For me, they would have grinned and said something ridiculously annoying. Whether they meant to or not, their silent show of reverence only managed to make my nerves waver.

I stopped beside the couch, wishing I could squeeze in with the guys and hide. I was about to try it, too; I even took a step closer.

Aidan must have figured out what I wanted to do. His hand clamped down on my shoulder, stopping me. The profound silence that followed the gesture and the dark look from Jared twisted my stomach into pinching knots.

My dad spoke up first, and I couldn't stop myself from cringing at his question. "Is what Dominic told me true, Jade? Did you turn your back on your mate?" The disappointment I heard in his tone pulled the knots in my belly tighter and made me want to throw up. My cheeks cramped, and my mouth flooded with water. I didn't know how he could sit there looking all heartbroken like he actually cared. Not with everything he'd done, was doing, and was going to do again and again until we stopped him. I swallowed a few times, trying to bury the sick feeling.

At least his question explained Dominic's grin, and I cut my former best friend a dirty look. He winked, clearly enjoying my discomfort.

"I did," I whispered, dropping my head. Aidan squeezed my shoulder, probably trying to reassure me, but it didn't help. I pulled in a breath. "I was scared. I'm still scared."

"Do you understand that he could have you killed for this?" Again, the disappointment. Again, the heartbreak. Bile rose in my throat again, and I swallowed it down.

"At the time, no, I didn't," I said, shaking my head from side to side. "I thought I actually had to go through the mating process to break that law."

Dad sighed and said, "As soon as you won the games, your mate was chosen, pumpkin. The alpha male and female always mate. It's what makes the alpha pair such a strong force. The combination of your scents mixed with your imprints, it would give you both complete authority over your wolves, being able to draw on each other's scents or use them both together ..." He sighed again, long and loud. "A mated alpha pair is the strength behind any pack."

I blinked. I hadn't really thought much about the whole scent merging thing. Really, I had kind of figured that the purpose was solely to ward off other wolves, like a *mate nearby* warning function. But hearing it all put so bluntly, well, it made me feel a little sick. I knew love wasn't supposed to have anything to do with it. Erika had told me as much when I'd stepped down from the games. The alpha pair was never supposed to be about love. Call me crazy, but I still thought love should be a factor. It was the reason why I won in the end. I figured there was something to be said for that. Love had given me strength when I needed it. I had killed for Aidan, and I would do it again. But in the pack's eyes, it was about strength and dominance and leadership. And with our scents merged, working together ... *Oh God, I think I really am in love with Aidan.*

I blinked again and shook myself a little. I sucked in a breath and another. I needed to stay focused. I quickly shrugged off Aidan's hand from my shoulder, stepping over to my dad. I crumbled to my knees in front of him.

"I'm scared, Daddy. I'm not ready for this. Any of it. I'm only eighteen." My voice held a high squeal of terror, and I held onto that feeling as I launched into the story. I told him how I had stepped down and walked away before the games ended. I explained that when Tiffany had won by default, she'd told Erika that she'd made a deal with Bruce and that Tiffany had promised Erika would be the first to go to the cougars, all the while dodging around the video that condemned him. It was Aidan's idea. He had wanted to see Dad's reaction, see if we would get anything out of him, but to my dad's credit, he looked shocked, disgusted even, and I went with it. I cried about killing someone, and he tried to soothe me, telling me that as a wolf and as an alpha, it was expected and probably wouldn't be the last time I would have to kill to defend my pack.

When I finally finished, tears were streaking down my cheeks. Dad brushed them away with his thumb before his gaze shifted to Aidan. He was in full diplomat mode now. A side of him I'd seen from time to time when Ray had come pounding on our door, usually in the middle of the night, waking the entire house. "Are you going to officially bring her in front of the enforcers for this?"

Aidan didn't answer for a long moment. He took his time, looking the team over. To my surprise, Beck actually looked a bit misty. His eyes were fixed on me, and Tommy and Chris had their hands planted on his shoulders as if they were holding him in place. When Aidan finally looked back at my father, his expression was like stone. "There won't be any need. My mate will be coming home with me today." A crooked smirk curved his lips, and he looked over his shoulder at Jared. "She'll also be stepping down from her role as an enforcer."

What? Okay, I hadn't agreed to that. There was no way I would step down abandon my team. I jumped up from the floor and closed the space between us. My emotions ran wild, and a new wave of tears brimmed in my eyes. I grabbed Aidan's bloodstained shirt, bunching it in my hands, and cried, "Aidan, stop this. Please. I'm not ready for this. I don't want this. Please."

"That's enough, Jade." He took my hand, prying my fingers off his shirt. "I've let you have your fun for the last few days. It's ending now. Your Dad's right, you know. If you fight me on this, you'll force my hand. I'll put you on trial if I have to, and the enforcer you've been screwing around with will stand right there beside you."

"I think I hate you," I whispered. I pulled my hands from his, letting them drop to my sides. He held my stare for a long moment, and I knew exactly what he was waiting for, what he'd told me I had to do. And darn it, but I did it. I bowed my head, showing my submission to the only person I was actually allowed to submit to — my mate.

I heard a few quick intakes of breath from behind

me. The significance of that bow spoke volumes to the team. And when I shifted, presenting my vulnerable neck to Aidan, the intakes turned into loud gasps that resonated around me.

Aidan took a moment to press his nose against my throat, taking in a deep breath, showing everyone that he was accepting my submission. As he did, his lips fluttered little kisses, sending hot shivers cascading down my back. I figured he was trying to reassure me; with the angle, we were standing at, no one would notice the kisses, but when he pulled back, his eyes still held that hard glint. "I'm fine with the hatred," he said coolly. "Alpha pairs aren't about love, sweetheart. They never have been."

I straightened, looking up at him. I knew he didn't mean it, but it hurt. Bad. Really, really, bad. A hissed cry slipped out of my lips.

Suddenly Dominic was in between us. "Dammit, Aidan," he growled. "You have no right to speak to her like this!" His fists were balled, knuckles turning bluish-white.

I placed a hand on his bunched forearm. "Dom, don't do something you'll regret," I whispered. I met his eyes for a brief moment, pleading with him to shut up. He cocked his head to the side, understanding burned in his eyes. His jaw clenched, his eyes blazed brighter, but he stepped back, clamping his lips shut.

I turned to my father, pulled in a deep breath, and held my head high. "I want to stay here. I've shown the alpha the respect he wanted, now please, talk some sense into him."

But Dad only shook his head, and a disgusted sneer spread across his lips. His gaze morphed into an ice-cold glare. "You don't want to go, then step down and let the games start again. It's the only way out of this, Jade. Step down. Let someone else run the pack with him and leave town. Either way, you won't be staying here."

I gasped. I didn't mean to, but really, that wasn't the reaction either Aidan, or I had expected. His words were like a physical punch in the gut, knocking the wind out of me, crippling me. Where was the man I had called Daddy, the big teddy bear that was always there for me? Where was the man that, a few moments ago, while locked in Aidan's arms, I had wanted to protect? Tears streaked down my cheeks in earnest now as I searched his face for any resemblance to the man I had loved all my life, but all I saw was the monster I didn't want to believe he was. I backed up a step. Something dawned on me then, my last thread holding me here, to this house, to this man. "Where's Mom?" I asked, looking around. I knew there was no way she would have been able to sleep through all the commotion. "I want to talk to Mom."

My dad frowned and looked at me as if I were crazy. "She's at work, Jade, but even if she were here, you wouldn't get a different answer. Your mother knows pack law. She knows how this works."

But she hasn't worked in days. Why would she go back the morning her husband came home?

I glanced over my shoulder, looking at Jared. I must have looked pretty freaked out because he offered up a smile and said, "She left around 5:30 this morning."

A hand slipped into mine, and then another, squeezing silent support. I glanced from one side to the other, not missing the grim expressions marring my best friends' faces. "Come on, honey," Dominic said. "We'll help you pack."

CHAPTER 12

Jade's tears had looked real.

I dismissed the team, Tommy and Chris included, as Jade disappeared upstairs with Dominic and Marcy. Trevor followed them. I was sure he didn't want to leave Marcy alone, not with the enemy so close. Jeff rambled on, trying to make sure I wouldn't hurt his *baby girl*, and I tried not to think about how real her tears had felt.

A strong swell of sensations stirred within me. It started with fury and ended somewhere near disgust. This man, the one that claimed to love his daughter, was using her as a puppet in his sick, little game; I was sure of it.

At first, I had expected him to fight, beg for her to stay under his roof. I had never expected him to kick her out, basically disown her, and then in his next breath, beg for her life. None of it really made sense. He would have more control over her if she stayed, but I started to understand as he spoke. He had known Jade would follow me. He could see that we were *attached*, hell, I was sure everyone could see that, and he was simply playing into our weaknesses. And that was when I learned something very valuable about this man. He didn't care who got hurt, but instead, he took pleasure in watching the pain. He was certain that he would win the end game, and he planned on enjoying every second of the battle in between.

By the time Jade finally came downstairs with her bags, I was sure of two things. One: I needed to know what the hell the end game was. Two: his certainty that he would be victorious was by far his greatest weakness.

Jade didn't say goodbye to her dad, didn't even look at him. She took her bags out to my car, piling them in the trunk, and then climbed in the front seat, waiting.

Jeff made me promise to take care of his baby girl. He even went as far as to tell me not to wait any longer to make our mate status official. It was one hell of a struggle to accept the hug he offered, and really, all I could do was nod my agreement on the not waiting thing because I knew if I opened my mouth, I would regret whatever came out.

Outside, Trevor asked me to call Marcy's school and her father, pulling her out for the day on pack business. He made it clear that he didn't want her out of his sight, and honestly, I couldn't blame him, so I did it. Marcy's dad hadn't been happy about it, but in the end, he hadn't argued, which was probably a good thing because I wasn't in the mood to deal with it.

Once that was settled, I sent them back to the pack headquarters with Dominic, asking them to call all available pack members together. I figured it was probably better to let them see Jade and me together before the word spread about her show of submission. Dominic hadn't said much, only that he hoped to hell I knew what I was doing, but the truth was so did I.

Jade didn't look at me when I finally got in the car. Her gaze was fixed on the forest, but her eyes looked blank as if she wasn't really seeing anything. I started the car. I didn't know what to say. I'd never seen so much turmoil in one person before. As I sat beside her, I didn't know whether to pull her into my arms and let her cry or leave her alone and let her pretend that she was okay. She needed time to process, that was for sure, but I could see that she was holding this all on her shoulders, even if it was my fault everything had gone to shit in the first place. She was struggling to keep her tear-filled eyes dry and not let her shoulders sink in defeat.

The urge to pull her to me, to give her some comfort, was physical, winding through my body, my soul, like a living organism, but I couldn't do it. Jeff was watching out the window, and after our little show, well, hugging her wasn't really an option. So I put the car in gear and backed out of the driveway.

"If you're ever that cold to me again, you'll be sorry." Her voice was hoarse and raw.

My entire body stiffened, and a sharp ache settled in my chest. I sighed, shifted the car into gear, and eased my foot off the clutch. "It wasn't real, sweetheart." I gave her a quick sideways glance, but she was still gazing out the window.

"It felt pretty real to me," she whispered.

I didn't say anything as I gave the car more gas, let up, pressed on the clutch, and shifted again. The truth? The coldness felt pretty damn real to me, too.

JADE

My brows were drawn in severe slashes over my eyes. I tried wiggling them. Anything to ease the tension from my face, neck, and shoulders, but each time I began to relax, I would take another breath and catch a scent that shouldn't have been coming from Aidan.

I had missed it earlier. I wasn't really sure how. Maybe it was the stress, or maybe it had been his scent overpowering the light spring fragrance that now seemed to cling to him. But right now, enclosed in this car, I couldn't smell anything else, and it was really starting to make me feel sick.

I figured I couldn't blame him for carrying her scent on his clothes. As far as he had been concerned, I had moved on. I'd been with Jared. And the fact was, we were never actually together — really together. Sure, we'd had a strong attraction to each other, but the second that we'd been able to act on it, be more than just two people who liked each other, I had walked away. So yeah, I couldn't blame him, but that didn't change the fact that it hurt. Bad.

The five-minute drive back to Aidan's house felt like five hours. For the last few days, I had craved time alone with him. But now that we were actually alone, my nerves replaced the cravings, jumping around like a field of grasshoppers in my belly. I wondered if my nerves were because of the scent that stuck to him or if it was because I knew exactly what I wanted for the first time since I'd joined the pack, and with that darn smell, I didn't know if I could still have it. I figured I could thank my dad for that. His bluntness made something click inside me, gave me clarity, and forced my irrational brain to accept what I had known all along. Aidan was mine. The pack was mine. And there was no way I would let someone else have either. Not without a fight.

Most likely, though, the nerves were just something else for my stubborn brain to think about. I guessed they were better than dwelling on my father kicking me out, which pretty much sucked.

When Aidan pulled into the driveway, I still hadn't looked at him. I would have killed to know what was going through that gorgeous head of his, but yeah, I was a chicken, way too scared to ask. So I got out grabbed my two bags, a backpack, and a duffle bag out of the trunk. They weren't heavy, only about half full. I hadn't really wanted to stick around long enough to really pack. I made a mental note to ask Marcy and Dominic if they would go back and pack up the rest of my things because there was no way I was going back there with my father home.

Aidan waited by the car door. He looked exhausted, maybe a little defeated, and the ache in my chest grew and pulsed. He met my eyes, smiled a little, and held out his hand to me. I was at his side in a breath, lacing my fingers through his. The scent may have been there, clinging to him like glue, but he was making it clear what he really wanted. So he slipped up a little. No big deal, right? My inner-wolf was so calm, elated, content, just being near him. Clearly, she wasn't freaking out about it, so I probably shouldn't be either, definitely, maybe. He squeezed a little, his silent reassurance, and together, we headed in.

I let my bags drop to the floor just inside the door. I sighed and then sighed again. The scent was still only on him. I hadn't realized how freaked out I'd been to walk in and smell it in his house, too, but it wasn't any stronger than it had been in the car. At least he hadn't brought her back to his house. Another sigh hissed from me in a long stream of air.

Aidan chuckled a bit nervously. "Don't know whether to take all your sighs as a good thing or not." He squeezed my hand again. "Want to talk about it?"

Yes! That's exactly what I wanted to do. Talk. I'd known him for just under a month, and we had never really talked. I wanted to know him — really know him. And I wanted him to know me, especially since it looked like I would be staying with him at least for a bit. But instead of answering, I only shook my head. Sometimes opening up and letting someone in was the hardest thing to do.

I tugged on his hand, pulling him from the doorway and over to the couch. I plopped down none too gracefully, dragging him with me. I sat there for a moment, sinking into the leather, staring at nothing. I could feel him watching me, waiting, but for the first time ever, I had absolutely nothing to say to him. No snippy remarks, nothing.

Another long-winded sigh pushed out of my lips.

I shook off his hand. I needed to get comfortable. I needed to get closer to him, and I wanted to feel his arms around me. I scanned the length of the couch and smiled a little before shifting toward him. Then I placed a palm on his right hip and another on his right knee, and I pushed.

Aidan chuckled, and he was looking at me as if I had lost my mind, but really, I was pretty sure I actually might have. Maybe I was just tired of being pissed off at him. Who knows, but right then, I felt beyond relaxed. I grinned up at him, what I hoped was verging on a flirty grin, and pushed again. "Move. I need more room."

"Yeah, sure," he said, chuckling again and shaking his head. He went to get up, most likely to move over to his chair and give me space, but as he started to stand, my hands slid to the top of his thigh, pushing him back down.

"No," I said, glaring up at him. "Just shove over."

He chuckled again, still shaking his head, but he shoved over. I nudged him again, and he kept sliding until I had him pressed tightly against the arm of the couch. Satisfied, I flipped around, my back to him, and swung my legs up. I'd thought about sitting like this with him more times than I could remember. I flopped back, my head landing square on his lap, and then I grabbed hold of his arm and brought it around me, pulling it tight, just below my breasts.

He stiffened suddenly, his thigh turning into a rock under my head. His scent changed, thickened, leaving a sour taste in my mouth. *Guilt,* a voice within my mind chimed in, and my inner-wolf growled within me.

I closed my eyes, trying not to let it get to me. I tilted my head into him, my nose pressing against a clean patch of his shirt over his stomach, and I inhaled a long breath, letting it out in a strangled growl. I almost told him to go change. I wanted to get rid of that smell so bad it made my teeth itch. And the dried blood along the hem wasn't helping either. For a split second, my entire body went rigid against him — or was that his body going ridged against me? I didn't know for sure. Whichever it was, it didn't last, and he, or maybe it was me, relaxed again.

He ran a finger along my cheek, letting it drift down my neck. The sour scent thickened, masking everything else for a moment. "Sweetheart, I can't stay here." His voice sounded strained. "I have work to do. The pack is unsettled, and I really need to meet with the team about your dad." I snuggled deeper into his lap. I had no intentions of letting him up, not anytime soon, at least. Not until we settled a few things. I was about to tell him as much when he huffed and said, "And there's something I really need to tell you before whatever is happening between us goes any further."

Crap! Was he actually going to tell me? My breath hitched. I didn't think I wanted to hear it. "I'm pretty sure I already know what you have to tell me," I said, my voice tight and my body stiffening again. I took a breath, let it out, and took another. "Work can wait, so can the pack. This, right here, is more important."

He laughed, but there was no humor in the sound. "You wouldn't say that if you actually knew what I need to say."

I pulled his arm a bit tighter around me and swallowed a few times. I was pretty sure I knew exactly what he was going to say. My nerves jumped again. I opened my mouth, closed it, swallowed, pried my eyes open, and decided to just get it over with. "I can smell Erika on your shirt and jeans, Aidan. Guess you didn't think that one out when you threw on the same clothes from yesterday, did you?"

"Guess not." He frowned, searching my face. "And you're okay with that?"

"No, not really," I said, deflating like a popped balloon. I'd really hoped there had been another reason for the scent. "But I'll get over it, just like you're going to get over Jared sleeping in my room for the last few days."

For a long moment, Aidan just stared down at me before he finally said, "Huh." He ran his free hand through his hair, blinked, fixed his blank stare back on me, but said nothing more.

"Really?" I asked sharply, elbowing him lightly in the ribs. He winced. "All you're going to say is 'huh.'"

His jaw twitched, so did his forearm that was lying across my chest. "Um, yeah, right now, huh is pretty much all I've got." The blankness began to recede from his brown eyes, and in its place, something that looked a heck of a lot like panic settled in. "Wait, why aren't you pissed at me? You're always pissed at me. This can't be a good thing."

I laughed, a cold, empty sound. "I can assure you, alpha, that on the inside, I'm a blazing ball of fire. Of course, I'm pissed, but ..." I paused, and my inner-wolf brushed against my chest, urging me on. She knew what I wanted — what I needed — and she wasn't about to let me chicken out. I sighed. "Well, I figure you lied to me, I lied to you. I was with Jared, and you moved on. It'd be pretty horrible of me to hate you for the same things I was doing." Something dawned on me then, something I probably should have clued into yesterday. Erika never studied. "It's really too bad, though," I continued. "Guess I need to find a new beta."

A swarm of emotion passed across his face so quickly that I really couldn't pinpoint exactly what I saw there. His scent told me he was guilty, angry, hurt. He growled, a deep rumbling sound, and his eyes filled with specks of gold. "Screwing around with the alpha isn't grounds for stripping her of her title, sweetheart." The roughness from the growl tinged his voice, dropping it lower, but I wasn't going to let it stop me.

"No, but blatantly lying to me when I needed her is," I said with a matter-of-fact air. He looked a bit confused, and I furrowed my brow. "Tell me you weren't with her when she sent the text message last night." His lips parted, and his scent spiked with more of that throat closing, tongue-tingling sourness, and I huffed. "Yeah, that's what I thought." I closed my eyes again, pressing my cheek against the hard contours of his stomach, and muttered, "I guess I should be glad you weren't stupid enough to go all the way."

Aidan petted my hair, just a light touch. "It went pretty far last night, Jade." His voice was low, just barely a whisper. "You should know that before you make any decisions here."

Okay, I really didn't need to hear that, but I had to admit it, I was impressed. I was so used to Aidan holding everything back, hiding things that would hurt me or piss me off. It was kind of nice hearing the truth directly from him. It gave me hope that maybe, just maybe, things could change. Warmth spread through my chest, swelling and pulsing. "I can't condemn you for doing the same thing you thought I was doing."

"Are you really saying you want to just start over?" He looked so serious and incredibly confused as if he were just waiting for me to lose my cool and storm out, but I was done with that. If my dad had shown me anything today, it was that I needed to suck it up, get over everything, and, in one way or another, move on. The thing was, I didn't think I could handle moving on to a life that didn't have Aidan in it. It was a truth I'd been trying to ignore, one that I hadn't wanted to accept. And it was a truth I wasn't going to brush off any longer.

Right then, though, I needed to fix all the seriousness that was marring his expression, so I smiled wickedly. "Yep, that's what I'm saying, but I do want to know something. How far exactly can you go without the whole scent merging thing happening?"

His jaw dropped a little, and he coughed a choked sound, and yep, he actually blushed a bright fire truck red. His eyes widened, and he gave me a look that begged me not to force him to give me all the details.

I smirked. It was totally evil, but I loved his awkwardness. "Seriously, I need to know in case I get the urge. Landon was looking pretty yummy today, oh, and Beck. Yep, Beck has potential." I laughed and winked.

His eyes flared with a dangerous warning, and his arm tightened around me. "That's not funny, Jade," he growled.

"I think it's only fair," I said, pushing at his chest half-heartedly and giggling. "If we're really going to start over, then we should even everything out. I only ever kissed Jared when people watched to make our fake relationship believable, and I can assure you, there was no pleasure in it. You had some fun. I should, too."

He folded over me in a blink, and his lips came crushing down on mine. It was a possessive kiss, rough and demanding and oh-so-amazing. I squealed in shock, my lips parting a little under his. His tongue was suddenly in my mouth, claiming every deep crevasse and fold, marking my mouth as his. He dug a hand into my hair, settling it at the nape of my neck, pulling me closer, holding me still, and before I knew it, my body was liquid against his.

Aidan broke away way too soon, only moving an inch from my swollen, tingly lips. I was panting. My heart was racing. "Let me make one thing clear," he growled. "As of this moment, you're mine. I'm not letting you out of my sight again, and I'm not stupid enough to let you go twice." I jutted my bottom lip out in a fake pout, and he nipped at it before he said, "By the way, I was also outside your window last night. I heard everything."

My eyes widened, and it was my turn to blush. I felt the heat blaze up my neck and settle in my cheeks. *Oh, God.*Last night I'd told Jared that I belonged to Aidan. Was he really saying he heard that? "Everything?" I asked. My voice was choked, and he chuckled and nodded.

I squeezed my eyes shut for a quick second, wishing I could just vanish. I didn't know if I would regret this, but I didn't care right then. The truth? I'd spent the last few days lying my face off, and it felt so amazingly good to have it all out in the open. And I was kind of regretting never talking to him before now. So much pain could have been avoided if I had. I was sure of it.

I felt him shift, and my eyes popped open. He

lowered his head, coming in for another kiss, but I lifted my hand, placing a finger on his lips. I took a deep breath and said, "I'm Jade Valerie Shaw. My favorite color is plum, not purple. I'm eighteen, and before I joined the pack, I spent my free time drawing. I love using charcoal and my favorite time of the year is fall. There's just something so perfect about being able to wear jeans and a hoodie. It's not too cold, not too hot."

Aidan's eyes lit up with amusement, and he laughed, a full belly roll of a laugh. "What are you doing?"

"I think it's time we got to know each other," I said, grinning.

He laughed again, giving me a wide smile. He lifted a brow and asked, "You ever going to stop surprising me?"

"Probably not." My smile stretched almost painfully wide, and more warmth pooled in my chest. Right then, I was pretty sure I could love this man, really love him.

"Good," he said with a bob of his head. He took my hand, the grip was awkward with my head still in his lap, but he made due, shaking it once before lacing his fingers through mine and letting his arm fall back to my chest. "Nice to meet you, Jade Valerie Shaw. I'm Aidan David Collins."

CHAPTER 13

AIDAN

When we pulled up to the pack headquarters, the parking lot was already full. Jade was quiet beside me. She was a bit nervous, but she was still smiling.

It was her smile that made my stomach sink and my nerves light on fire. The pack, especially my males, were a little ... upset with Jade. I'd been trying to explain it to her, but I didn't think she was taking me seriously. Maybe she was at her maximum stress limit for the day. Maybe she just didn't want to believe that they were all that pissed off. I didn't know for sure, but I was starting to think I should have just left her at home because that smile wasn't going to help matters. It was a sweet smile, a happy one. It reached her eyes and lit up her face, and I loved it. I really did. It was just that I was sure it would give the wrong impression as if she were trying to lighten the seriousness of what they believed she had done.

The thing was, most of the males felt as if she had abandoned them while she'd been hiding away with the team for the last few days. And then there was the issue that she had turned away from me. That alone had gotten a lot of backs up. I didn't really know what the response would be when she walked in. I hoped that seeing us together would ease some of the tension, and if she would just stop grinning, it might actually work, but I just didn't have the heart to tell her to stop.

I pulled into a spot at the back of the lot and turned off my car. This was the last place I wanted to be. I wanted to be alone with Jade, but my phone had been buzzing nonstop against my left hip for the last twenty minutes; Dominic had been trying to let me know everyone was waiting.

Pack members milled about outside the glass double doors, the team of enforcers among them. I watched their cagey pacing for a moment, the way their muscles shuddered as they moved along the concrete exterior of the building as if they were wired, ready to shift without a second's notice. They were alert, working as a team to scan the tree line for any sign of a threat. Even from this distance, their tension was evident. Tommy and Chris were with them, but Jared wasn't. I didn't know whether to be happy he wasn't among them or pissed off that he hadn't bothered to show up.

I puffed out a breath and pulled the keys from the ignition. "Erika's going to be in there," I said.

Jade stiffened in her seat, but her smile didn't fade, not even a little. "I know. I'll be discreet, Aidan. I don't want your night broadcasted any more than you do."

"Okay, good." I nodded a few times quickly, more to reassure myself that this was actually good, but really, who was I trying to kid? Her calmness about the whole thing was kind of eating at me. I understood her theory, that she couldn't blame me for doing things that I had believed she was doing, but still, it was just … odd and not what I had expected from her. And it made me uneasy. I wanted to kill Jared for even looking at her, let alone touching her. My inner-wolf wanted blood, but Jade, Jade was the picture of calmness.

I puffed out another breath. "You ready for this?" I asked as I popped my door open.

Jade nodded, a stiff bob of her head, as she got out. She met me in front of the car, holding her hand out to me, and I took it. Her smile widened further as she weaved her fingers through mine. Damn, I loved that smile and the content glint in her eyes. I really didn't know how I had gotten so lucky or why she had decided to forgive me, but I wasn't about to question it. I didn't want to give her a reason to rethink her decision to start over. I was pretty sure if she thought about it, she would realize that I had done so much more wrong than she had, even if she claimed we were even, and then she would walk away again. There was no way I would let that happen, so, yeah, I wasn't going to ask. I was going to just suck it up and not worry that she didn't seem to be all that bothered about the whole Erika thing. I didn't need to know the full why of her decision. All that mattered was that she was with me. Yes, that was all that mattered, definitely, maybe. I breathed in a deep, calming breath of the crisp air, and together, we started for the doors.

As we crossed the parking lot, our pack began filing inside. I tugged on Jade's hand, slowing our pace. I wanted everyone inside before we walked in. I wanted them to see our clasped hands, our nearness, but most of all, I wanted them to see that I'd accepted her submission and that I wasn't going to hold her actions over the last few days against her.

When we reached the door, she squeezed my hand. "Will you relax," she whispered. "It's going to be fine. I can handle this."

I looked down at her and forced a smile. "I know you can," I said. Jade didn't buy it, not for a second.

She rolled her eyes, reached for the door, yanked it open, and pulled me inside.

"Look at this. The alpha female is finally deciding to grace us with her presence," Phil, one of the older pack members, spat as the doors shut behind us. His eyes sparked with speckles of gold. He wasn't a big man, slim and lanky, but the hatred that burned in his eyes as he scanned Jade over made him look threatening, and my inner-wolf stirred restlessly. I tugged on Jade's hand, pulling her behind me, and a growl built within my chest.

The silence that followed was deafening. I could barely hear the whispered breaths of all the people around me as the buzz of anger built in my ears. The pack, minus Jared, were all gathered in the sterile waiting room. The stark white floors and walls and the scent of bleach and various cleaners assaulted my senses as I made my way into the center of the room, tugging Jade along with me. Some sat on the hard orange plastic chairs, some paced, and others just stood there, glaring at Jade. Whispered criticisms invaded my ears, too many for me to even try to comprehend. The stress coming from my pack was palpable, rippling through the air like an electric current.

Phil sneered at Jade, and I let out a low warning growl. "That's enough," I said. The words were snarled, and by the way his eyes dropped to the floor, and he slid back a step, I figured he knew I wasn't asking.

"Aidan, I don't need you to defend me," Jade said calmly. She pushed out from behind me, tugged her hand free of mine, and moved to stand a few paces away from me. She took her time to look at every one. The urge to grab her and pull her closer, to keep her safe, was unbearable, but as she moved, the division within the pack had never been clearer, and that was what held me still. She needed to see it. She needed to understand what had happened within the pack over the last few days.

Our werewolves began shifting to positions that clearly reflected who they considered their alpha to be. The females crowded in behind Jade, the males moving closer to me. She didn't need me to keep her safe; she had her pack at her back.

"You've been alpha female for three days, and you're already destroying this pack," one of the men said under his breath. It came from behind me, a mumbled whisper, so low that I really wasn't sure who had said it.

I let out another growl, pivoting in place to glare at my wolves. "She's one of your alphas, and you'd better start addressing her as you would me."

"No, she's not," Phil countered. He waved a hand toward the females. "She's the females' alpha. She's nothing to me. Not without you as her mate."

I blinked, stunned at the defiance, I saw stoning his face. Yes, he was right. Without us mated, without our scents combined, the pack was divided, but damn, she still deserved their respect. I opened my mouth, ready to tell them all exactly what I thought, but Dominic jumped in before I could.

"We called you all here to tell you that our alpha female made a public display of her submission to Aidan this morning." He stepped up, standing in between Jade and me. "I was there, so was the team, and Aidan accepted it." He paused, letting everyone process the information for a moment before he continued, "The alpha pair will now be living under the same roof and are to be considered mated from this moment on."

Jade made a strangled sound from somewhere at the

back of her throat. I glanced over my shoulder just in time to see the vibrant red flush rushing to her cheeks. "Dom!" she called, her voice strangled. "We are so not discussing that."

For a split second, everyone was silent, but it didn't last. It started with a chuckle and then a giggle, and in no time, the entire pack was roaring with laughter. I met Jade's eyes, smirking, and she blushed brighter.

CHAPTER 14

JADE

My face was on fire, and darn it, Aidan was smirking. The tension that had filled the room moments ago was almost completely gone, although the visible split between the pack was still very evident. The laughter continued, I even heard a few snorts, and my face burned hotter. I planted my hands on my hips, scowling.

Aidan closed the space between us. He was chuckling, too, and his eyes danced with amusement. I figured the laughing was better than the tension, but this was just not funny, well, at least not to me. He leaned into me and planted a sloppy kiss on my cheek. "Have I ever told you how cute you look when you're all embarrassed?" he asked.

I shoved at his chest, rolled my eyes, and pursed my lips. I was about to tell him that I didn't find any of this funny. Really, how many more times would my sex life (or lack thereof) be brought up and discussed today? I guessed it shouldn't bother me. Mating was a huge part of pack life. I thought it had something to do with a werewolf's protective and oh-so-possessive nature. Claiming and possessing that one person you couldn't live without. At least that's how I felt when I thought about mating with Aidan. The idea of possessing him in a way that no one else ever could sent hot chills careening through my body.

My embarrassment clearly dissolved a lot of tension, so I figured that was a good thing — kind of. But really, there were so many more important things to talk about. Like my dad being home or how the search was going for the cougars' location. We needed to find them before they moved again, but no, discussing the status of my mating was so much more important. *Ugh!*

And then I spotted Erika. She was in red leather pants and a jacket with a black tank underneath that was cut so low the black lace of her bra was showing. Her midnight-black hair hung straight over her shoulders, and her lips, coated in a devil red, were parted. Her lust-filled eyes were fixed on Aidan. Any embarrassment I had felt vanished, replaced by an ugly surge of jealousy.

I placed myself in front of Aidan and growled. Yep, I growled. Somewhere in the back of my mind, I knew, just knew, I would regret the reaction. I was so not this person. I wasn't psycho jealous, and I was secure enough with myself that I didn't need to worry, but right then, none of that mattered. Aidan was mine, and that tramp was basically drooling over *my* man. I didn't care that technically she was still my beta or that Aidan and I weren't even officially together. God, we'd just barely passed the forgiveness point. But as far as my inner-wolf was concerned, no one — absolutely no one — could look at him like that.

My growl didn't faze her. She actually sidestepped and tilted as if she were trying to look around me. Her eyes dropped to his chest and then back to his lips.

"Erika, you did hear Dom, right?" Even I felt the chill rolling off my tongue. My tone was so cold. "The alpha male has a mate. I suggest you fix that gaze of yours elsewhere."

Erika shook herself like a wet dog shaking water out of her fur. She slowly pulled her gaze from Aidan, fixing it on me. She opened her mouth as if she were about to say something but snapped it shut just as quickly.

My reaction earned me another round of laughter from the werewolves who didn't know me all that well. But the ones that did, my team and Dominic, they moved in, flanking me. "Is there something we need to know about?" Beck asked, letting his booming voice carry throughout the room.

The laughter died abruptly. No one missed the pointed question or the lethal glint in Beck's eyes. The lobby was so quiet that the only sound I heard was my racing heartbeat pounding in my ears.

My blood was pumping, hot and fast. My skin, shuddering. All I could see was her with her hands all over my mate. *There goes being discreet,* I thought. I opened my mouth, ready to tell the team about her little rendezvous with Aidan and the text message she had sent me, but I snapped it shut when Aidan said, "Meeting's over." He weaved his arm around my waist, holding me still. He glanced down at me and grinned, a sexy as hell half-grin, and winked. If I had to guess, he actually looked happy about my reaction.

Aidan held my eyes for a long moment. His were dancing with humor and what looked a heck of a lot like relief before he finally looked back up at the stunned crowd. "Thank you for coming on such short notice," he said, his tone light and, yep, happy. "We didn't want to wait to share the news with you all that Jade has finally come to her senses and moved in with me." There were a few chuckles, and Aidan paused, grinning like a fool as he waited for them to die down before continuing. "As you know, Jade's father came home this morning. Jade and I will be working closely with the team, and we'll call you all together again when we're ready to act. Remember, our phones are always on, and our door, always open. If you need us for anything, come find us."

No one questioned Aidan's dismissal, which shocked me a little. Marcy had told me that the pack had warmed up to him, that they listened to him, but even so, it seemed weird to me how quick they moved toward the door, no questions asked.

I barely noticed the curious glances in Erika's direction as people started shifting toward the door. I was too busy trying to tone down the swarm of jealousy-induced emotions that kept thrashing around within me, and on top of that, I couldn't figure out why Aidan was happy about it. I received a few hugs, some whispered congratulations on my move, and it sucked that pretty much all I could manage was grunted responses.

I don't really know how long I stood pressed into Aidan's side before he stepped away from me. I vaguely noticed him talking to Beck and then whispering something to Dominic. My focus was fixed on Erika. Her complexion was paling fast, going a little whiter with each person that left the building.

When the last person left, and all that was left were the team and Dominic, Erika whispered, "I thought you were with Jared." She put her feet in motion, coming closer, and when she was only a foot away from me, she dropped to her knees. "I swear. I would have never let him in the door if I knew you were going to take him back."

She dropped her eyes to the ground, tilted her head, and presented her neck to me. I wanted to take a step away from her. I wanted to ignore her offer and tell her to get the hell away from me, but the team stopped me before I could. Beck and Landon were suddenly beside me again, their hands pressing into the small of my back, holding me in place.

I heard the growl the second they touched me. It was a predatory and extremely possessive sound, and I shuddered. I shouldn't love it, but coming from Aidan, I did, so very, very much, and just as quickly as their hands had settled on my back, they were gone. Aidan growled again, and his scent swamped my brain, bogging me down, although I wasn't complaining. Man, I loved that smell, the power mixed with the greens of the forest — best smell ever. My heart skittered in my chest, and my inner-wolf decided to wake up, moving around within me as if she thought that my belly was the perfect stage to do the salsa.

The team moved, so did Dominic, clearing a safe distance from me, and my stupid mate secured me around the waist with a stiff arm. Erika didn't move from her position, her neck still craned out before me, but she did whimper.

"Will someone explain what's going on?" Craig asked. He crouched down beside Erika, his freaked out light blue eyes met mine, pleading, and his usually soft features were sharp and hard.

Erika squeezed her eyes closed and pulled in a noisy breath. Her shoulders drooped a little more, and she blurted, "Jade's upset because the alpha came to see me last night."

Craig looked at her and blinked. His jaw started to drop, and he gave his head a shake, and as he did, he growled, a deadly sound. He stood up slowly, his jaw ticked. "Is that why you were late?" His cheeks flamed, his eyes flared. "Why you showed up at my place freshly showered, hair still dripping, with all that awful perfume?"

Erika straightened, rising up to face him, and she shrugged. "I wanted to keep my options open."

Right then, I wanted to slap her, if not for me, for Craig. I hadn't known that they were actually seeing each other. Erika hadn't said a word, and Craig was more of the quiet type. If I had known, I wouldn't have said anything, not with him here.

Craig's fists flexed, released, flexed. He was vibrating, his skin starting to ripple. He glared at her, grinding his teeth so hard that I swore I could hear the enamel chipping.

I pried off Aidan's stiff arm from around my waist and went to him, placing a hand on his forearm. "Why don't you go take a walk," I said.

"No, I need to hear this," he growled, shaking off my hand, never taking his fuming gaze from Erika. "She promised herself to me last night." His voice cracked, and another shudder rushed along his skin. "She's supposed to be mine."

Aidan cleared his throat, drawing everyone's attention. "Craig, it was my fault," he said, looking everywhere but at me. "I'm the one who sought her out. I'm the one who let it get out of hand."

I spun on Aidan, my eyebrows shot up. "You've got to be freakin' kidding me! You're defending her?"

Aidan's mouth twisted into a wary frown and his hands rose in what I thought was supposed to be surrender. "No, not defending," he said. "You have every right to ignore her, strip her of her title, and throw her out of the pack. I'm just thinking we should consider showing her the same kindness you showed me."

Erika huffed and planted her hands on her hips. "You can't throw me out of the pack just because I gave the alpha the relief you wouldn't give him."

Craig's eyes fell back on her, slicing like blades, and

his stance stiffened. He lifted one side of his mouth in a sneer, and as he did, I got a glimpse of the tips of his lengthening canines.

"You're right," I said. "But that's really not the problem. When I was looking for you last night, you told me you were at home studying."

Erika smirked. "Well, yeah," she said, waving a hand in Aidan's direction. "I was studying, and I was thoroughly enjoying it, too."

My jaw dropped. Honestly, I didn't know where Erika was getting the balls from. It wasn't that long ago that she had cowered in my bedroom, trying to hide from Jared. Maybe she was just getting used to the enforcers, or maybe she knew there was really no way out of the shit pile she had found herself in. More likely, she was just reverting back to the epic bitch she had been for the last two years. My mom had always told me that people could only hide who they really were for a week or two before the truth came out. Whatever it was, though, it was making me see red.

I took a step toward her, my fist clenching. I saw it all play out in my head, the satisfaction of smacking that smirk off her face. And I was going to do it, too, for Craig, if nothing else. I took another step, my jaw clenched.

And then Tommy stepped in front of me. "Jade," he said. He ran a hand along his shiny head and then met my eyes. "This is the girl that brought you the video, right?"

"Yes," I said through my teeth. "This is the girl. But right now, I don't really care about the damn video."

He grimaced, and he dropped his eyes from mine. "I've been wondering how she got it without the enemy picking up her scent. Before you sentence her, maybe we should consider that."

I gritted my teeth and almost snapped at him. I was

just too mad to think. Aidan must have noticed because suddenly, his scent wrapped around me, and I pulled in a long breath of fresh greens. I shifted, glancing at him over my shoulder, and he gave me a look that clearly told me I had to hear her out before I made any decisions. I hated that he was right.

CHAPTER 15

AIDAN

"Hold up a second, Aidan," Tommy whispered, placing a firm hand on my forearm as Dominic began leading the group down to the meeting room.

Jade must have heard his whisper. She stopped abruptly and gave us a funny look. Her eyes drifted to Tommy's hand clamped on my arm, and then she looked back up at me, arching a brow.

I sighed and then forced a smile. "I'll be right there," I said. "Don't start without me, okay?"

She frowned a little, but then Chris moved in beside her and placed a hand at the small of her back, nudging her forward. She quickly stepped away from his hand and cut me another questioning look. I smiled what I hoped was an *everything's okay* smile. It must have been convincing because she nodded and then followed the others down the hallway, with Chris right behind her.

I turned to Tommy, squinting against the bright sunlight that streamed through the glass doors. He wasn't frowning, but he also wasn't smiling; his expression was stuck somewhere in the middle. "Can this wait?" I asked.

"No." He rubbed a hand over his hairless head as he

waited for the others to clear out. Once they were far enough down the hallway that they wouldn't overhear, he said, "Jared took off."

I huffed a loud gusty sound. "What do you mean Jared took off?" I asked. I didn't need anything else to deal with. Not today. Out of every possible scenario I'd considered after what happened this morning, Jared leaving hadn't been one of them. I had figured he would give me the cold shoulder, or he might even try to challenge me, but leaving, well, he didn't strike me as the giving up type, and leaving was definitely giving up. He'd be giving up his home, his pack, his friends ...

"Just what it sounds like," Tommy said. "He took off. But I got to say, I don't think it was because he wanted to go. Pretty sure the guys told him to get lost for a bit and cool down. I came in at the tail end of it."

It's temporary, I thought, surprised that I actually felt glad about that. I knew it would kill Jade if he left because of her — because of us. I folded my arms over my chest and frowned. "You think the guys pushed him out?"

Tommy nodded. "Yep. They're pissed at him, and I'm sure that if he showed up right now, they would go at it. Specifically Landon. With the way he talked last night, it sounded like he was ready to kill Jared. Don't have a clue why, though."

Charming. Just what I needed. The team at each other's throats.

Through my teeth, I said, "So you haven't really found out anything." I knew it wasn't a fair statement. Tommy and Chris had only just gotten to town yesterday, and in all fairness, I hadn't really expected them to find out anything from the team anyway.

Tommy glowered at me, and when he spoke, his voice was a gravel pit, rough and jagged. "Not fair, Aidan. We've only had one night with them, but I do know that Jared hasn't been sticking around at your mate's house just because he wants her. There's more to it than that, but thanks to Beck, Landon clamped up when I pressed."

I laughed, a cold, frustrated sound, and scrubbed at my face. "Well, I can't very well act on your speculations now, can I?"

Tommy was uncharacteristically quiet for a minute. He studied me closely; his eyes were alight with a curious seriousness. "You are nothing like your father, you know that?"

I didn't respond immediately. My father most likely would have taken the information as grounds to throw the whole team in lockdown and tortured them with his alpha scent until he got what he wanted to know out of them. And although the idea was an appealing one, since the last thing I needed was the team fighting right now, I wasn't going to do it. Jade would never forgive me for it, and well, I didn't want to run a pack by inflicting fear and pain on my wolves. It just wasn't me.

I finally looked back at him and asked, "Did you really volunteer to come here?"

Tommy hadn't expected the question. He furrowed his brow. "Sure, why wouldn't I?"

"Oh, I don't know," I said with a lazy lift of my shoulders. "Maybe because you've hated me since I was born."

He gave me an odd look, one that I couldn't even begin to understand, and in a low, calm voice, he said, "Never hated you, kid. If we were all soft on you like Lance was, you'd never be where you are now. Probably would have died in your fight for alpha."

I really didn't know what to say to that. He might have had a point, but I wasn't ready to admit it, so I just shrugged and started down the hallway. "Come on," I said. "Jade's waiting."

JADE

Time, even the last twenty minutes, had given me some perspective as well as a much-needed reality check. To put it simply, the pack was a freakin' mess, clearly divided. There had been no mingling between the males and females, no friendly gestures. If anything, there was a hostile tension wrapping around the room, well, until they started laughing at me.

I hadn't believed Aidan when he had tried to explain how upset everyone was with me. Really, I figured he was exaggerating, but after seeing them all together, one thing was clear: I couldn't hide behind the team any longer.

I had never gone further than Aidan's office in the headquarters before, and I was a bit shocked at how large the building actually was. Tommy had suggested we move our little meeting from the lobby to a more appropriate setting, so Dominic had led our group down the main hallway to a meeting room at the back of the building. There was a network of hallways that branched off the main one, and every few feet, there was another closed door. I had no clue what all the rooms were for or why we needed such a big building, but after this was all over, I was definitely going to check them out.

I was in a meeting room with the team: Beck, Landon, Mark, and Craig. Tommy and Chris were there, as were Aidan and Dominic. Jared still hadn't shown up, but I was starting to think he probably wouldn't. The room smelled of wolves, angry, nervous wolves. And there was a hint of lingering staleness as if the space had been sealed up tight for some time. That was the first thing I had noticed when I had stepped in.

And it was quiet. So very quiet. Everyone was looking at me, waiting expectantly, but I didn't know what to say. I hadn't been in the pack for all that long, not to mention I had no clue what I was doing as an alpha. The sound of my footsteps was loud, echoing around the room as I paced back and forth. Heat pooled in my cheeks, so hot that I was certain my face was a bright scarlet.

Once Aidan and Tommy had come in, we had listened as Erika recounted the events leading up to her capturing everything on video, and I hated it. Still, her story had an undeniable ring of truth. She had driven Tiffany to the meeting with my dad. Her best guess was they didn't notice her scent so close because they had known she was there, although they had thought she was waiting in the car. She'd been certain that Tiffany would win the games, and she had done what she could to get in Tiffany's good graces before that happened.

But after waiting for a little over thirty minutes, Erika had wandered into the woods, following Tiffany's trail. She said they were just beyond the tree line, and the moment she had picked up what they were discussing, she had crouched down, hiding behind a bush, and started recording. When they had broken up their little meeting, Erika had bee-lined it for the car. She drove Tiffany home, listened to Tiffany brag about her little get-together, and as soon as Tiffany was out of her car, Erika had found me. According to Erika, Tiffany had been so certain she would win the alpha female games that she hadn't felt the need to hide her plans, especially since Erika had sworn her alliance.

Once she finished her story, I had dismissed her,

sending her back to Aidan's office to wait. I needed time to think everything out, figure out what to do with her. I wasn't sure if she would stick around, but then I guessed she really had nowhere else to go, and she knew we would hunt her down if she left.

The light coming into the room was dim; the windows, covered by light filtering roller shades, the same sterile white as the shiny ceramic tiles, were pulled down and the lights off. A long, rustic wood table that looked like a slab was taken from the center of an enormous oak tree filled the room, with the enforcers surrounding it, sitting in matching wooden chairs.

Aidan smiled. It was a bit shy, a lot sweet, and it made the butterflies in my belly dance and shiver. The air around me warmed as if I stepped into a patch of sunlight. He sat at the head of the table in jeans and a light gray zip-up hoodie, the sleeves pushed up to the elbows. His light brown hair was sticking out a little, but then he'd been running his hands through it constantly as he listened to the recount. He hadn't shaved, his jawline looking rough with stubble, and as I scanned him over, if I had to guess, I'd say he hadn't been sleeping much lately.

"Sweetheart, she's telling the truth. You can smell it." The smile that Aidan gave me shifted to something that looked like a challenge as if he were daring me to disagree, and I resisted the urge to groan and roll my eyes. I knew she was telling the truth, but darn it, I wanted it all to be a lie. He noticed and got up, crossing the room to me. He leaned in close, his voice dropping to barely a whisper as he pressed his lips to my ear. "I love the whole jealousy thing. It's hot as hell, but you need to be sure your decision wasn't because of my bad choice last night. You need to be fair to her."

When he pulled back from me and retook his seat,

my heart was pounding, and I seriously hoped I didn't look as guilty as I felt. I looked at Aidan, silently cursing him for pointing out what had already been eating at me. I swallowed down a frustrated sigh.

"Okay," I said. "Okay." I nodded a few times, more to reassure myself than anyone else. "I think we can all agree that Erika can't be my beta. And I can't very well throw her out of town. She may suck most of the time, but she's loyal to the pack, and right now, we need all the loyalty we can get."

Craig didn't look happy, but he grunted, "You're right," along with the rest of them, and I started my useless pacing again. I just didn't know what to do with her. I knew the way the pack worked to a certain extent. If I stripped her title, they would eat her alive. She would be marked as a weak link, which never went well. *God, I don't want to make this decision.*

"Where the heck is Jared?" I blurted, stalling. "He should be here for this."

The second the words left my mouth, I heard Aidan's growl. I stopped in my tracks and cut him a dirty look. "Will you stop that? Seriously, what's with all the growling?" His response was a sexy smirk and another soft growl.

"Jade, he can't help it," Tommy said, chuckling. "Give him a break. It's his inner-wolf voicing his claim on you. It'll ease up after you two are officially mated."

Tommy grinned when I shifted to face him. It was a playful grin, one that told me I was, in fact, as red as my cheeks felt. I laughed a little and smiled sweetly. "The next person who brings up my sex life is going to be sorry. I swear it."

Beck laughed, Landon rolled his eyes, and Mark snickered. I groaned. "Okay, if she stays here, she needs a mate. The threat of a pissed-off mate should keep the pack off her back, and I think we owe her that much for what she's done for us."

I glanced at Craig, and he quickly shook his head. "I won't mate with her, and I won't house her either." He let out a painful-sounding sigh. "I just can't do it. I won't be her fallback plan. I can't deal with the fact she was with him or anyone just before she crawled into my bed." He glanced at Aidan then, and I was a bit stunned that there was no hostility or blame in his gaze. "At least I understand why she said she wanted to wait." He stood up slowly, glancing at Beck. "Will you watch out for her? The pack owes her protection. The team owes it to her for bringing Jade to us. Once she's stripped of the title, she'll be looked at as weak, and with how unsettled the pack is, that won't end well. I just can't do it."

Beck nodded, and Craig shifted his focus to me. "You good with this?"

I nodded. I couldn't really do much more than that. My throat was burning and my eyes stinging. I wanted to hug him. I wanted to tell him I was sorry, but the words were jammed in my throat. But the nod seemed to be enough.

"Good," Craig said. He nodded, too. "Good." He looked at Aidan and said, "We need Jade on the team. I know you want her to step down, but it'll be a mistake. We need her. She's the only thing that's keeping Jared sane right now."

"Is he okay?" I asked before Aidan could say the blunt *no* that I could see written all over his face.

A ripple of tension passed through the team, and Landon said, "Nope, he's far from okay. But you need to stay away from him. And I don't agree with Craig. You need to step down, keep clear of him until everything is ..." he smirked and chuckled, "settled between you and Aidan."

I clucked my tongue and began fidgeting, playing with the strings on my hoodie. Aidan was frowning, but at least he wasn't growling. My stomach dropped, and I huffed. "He's still my friend, guys. I'm not going to just ditch him."

"He's not your friend, Jade," Landon said. "I hate to point it out, but he didn't give a shit about you until Aidan showed his interest. Might want to ask yourself why."

Ouch. That was pretty much the only thing that went through my mind as I stared at Landon, my jaw-dropping.

"Landon," Beck said. "Not your place, man. Let it go."

"What's not his place?" I asked. My voice was a little rocky, and I swallowed hard. I glanced at Beck, but he only shrugged. He gave me a look that clearly said *Let it go* and glanced in Aidan's direction.

Mark leaned forward, his elbows on the table, and he rested his chin in his hands. "Did anyone else pick up on Jeff's eye twitch when Jade told him about Tiffany's deal with Bruce?"

CHAPTER 16

AIDAN

Looking back on it, I thought I should have known that there was more trouble with the team than just their normal jerkiness. But with my pack, pretty much everything equaled some kind of trouble, and it was beginning to become extremely hard to see the real problems when they surfaced. They were all so testy and high-strung right now that even looking at someone the wrong way caused an issue. So when Jared failed to show at the pack's headquarters, I really hadn't thought much of it. I figured he was pissed off, and not showing was his version of throwing a tantrum.

Except this wasn't just a tantrum. Whatever the problem was, it went further than Jared being pissed off at me. I hadn't wanted to believe what Tommy uncovered, but after listening to Landon tell Jade to stay away from Jared, I was sure this really did have something to do with the entire team.

Awesome. Another problem to solve. Just what I need.

I pulled up to a stoplight and glanced at Dominic in the passenger seat. He looked as if he were somewhere else, completely lost in his own thoughts. His face was utterly blank, not guarded as usual, and it made him look a lot younger than eighteen.

It only took about five minutes for everyone to agree that I needed to chat with Jade's dad and get a briefing on the cougar situation. As far as Jeff was concerned, I'd sent him back to the cougars to gather information for me, and if I never bothered to ask him what he found out, sooner or later, he would clue in that something was up.

It didn't take long to set it up. Jeff had been more than happy to meet, and within fifteen minutes, I was back in my car. And although I tried to convince Jade to come with me, she'd ended up hanging back at the headquarters with the guys claiming she wanted to work on strategies.

The light changed, and I eased off the clutch, feathering the gas. After another moment of silence, I said, "So, Jared's gone. Tommy said that he thinks the guys forced him to leave for a bit."

Dominic blinked and pulled in a loud breath. "Yeah, figured as much," he said. He fiddled with the window button, letting the glass fall an inch and then rise again. "Maybe it's a good thing. Gives you both time to simmer down."

"I don't need time to simmer down," I said, making a right on Clearmont Drive. "I promised Jade I wouldn't touch him, and I won't. God, I can't believe I'm saying this, but we need him. We need all of them right now."

Dominic grunted and cut me a sideways look that clearly said he disagreed. Whether his disagreement was about me needing to cool down or us needing Jared, I really wasn't sure.

The park came into view, and I pulled into the lot, parking at the far end. It was vacant, not a single car other than mine, and I wondered if maybe, just maybe, Jeff wouldn't show. As I pulled the keys from the ignition, Dominic said, "Aidan, be good to her, okay? I know you were just following my advice the last time around, but don't hurt her again."

So that was what his quietness was about. I should have guessed. The only time Dominic got that remote look on his face was when he was thinking about Jade. I sighed as I opened my door. "She wants to start over. Clean slate and all that."

He smiled a little and nodded as we got out of the car. "Yeah, I figured she'd do something like that." He scanned the parking lot quickly and asked, "You think he'll show?"

"Hopefully not," I said. "It'll give me a reason to go after him."

Unfortunately, Jade's dad was exactly where he said he would be. Jeff was sitting on a worn wooden bench nestled under a large oak tree, sporting a lime green windbreaker and khakis. When he spotted us coming across the field at a leisurely pace, Jeff got to his feet, leaving the bench behind as he came toward us. He was smiling a casual *nice to see you* kind of smile as if he hadn't just broken my nose this morning.

He stopped a few feet away from us, jamming his hands in the pockets of his jacket. "Didn't expect to hear from you so soon," he said. "Did Jade settle in at your place, okay?"

I had to give him credit; he was great at the *concerned father* act, so good, in fact, that I could almost believe it. Almost.

I returned his caring smile and ignored his question. "Where are they, Jeff?"

Jeff raised his hands, obviously noticing my no-nonsense tone. "Okay, fine, right down to business then." He let his hands drop, and a frown curled his lips. "I'm not too sure. They were relocating when I left. Supposed to get a call in a day or two when they settle in."

"Did you know the cougars have been coming into town?" Dominic asked in his typically calm, cocky demeanor. He smoothed a few non-existent wrinkles from his sweater.

"Nope," Jeff said. He smiled, a cool and confident kind of smile, but his eye started to twitch. "Maybe they're looking for Tiffany. She made a deal, right? They're probably trying to find her to collect on it."

I studied him for a moment as a gust of wind blew through the park. His eye was still twitching, and I wondered if it was because he was lying or if it was nerves. Either way, it made me smile. I might not have been able to pick up the scent from him, but the eye twitch, that was something to go on. *Thank you, Mark.*

"I got to say, Jeff, I figured you'd have something to tell me by now," I said, folding my arms over my chest, my biceps curling up thick. I might have promised Jade I wouldn't hurt him, but I said nothing about trying to intimidate him. I narrowed my eyes. "What were you doing with them?"

Jeff's smile lost confidence. "Like I told you," he said. "I was stalling the recruitment for more women. And I was trying to get a full count for you."

"What's the count then?" Dominic questioned.

"I'll know in a couple days," Jeff blurted a little too quickly to be believable. His throat worked fast in a bunch of swallows, and his smile returned. "Some of the guys were out, and no one knows how many were gone. They're not an organized bunch. I blame it on having no females."

I took a step closer, and he took a step back. "You know, I'm starting to feel like you're jerking me around."

His eye started to twitch again as if it had a pulse. "I'm not your enemy, Aidan."

"Oh yeah?" I chuckled. "You're one of them. Kind of makes you the enemy."

Jeff froze like a snapshot, blinked, and then shook his head, and he laughed a humorless laugh. "Careful there, alpha. My daughter might be upset with me, but she's still my daughter."

I shrugged. "She'll forgive me," I said, except I really wasn't sure if she would.

JADE

Landon was trying to draw.

Okay, so it wasn't really a drawing. It was supposed to be an attack plan. There were stick figure wolves, what I thought were supposed to be trees, and I had no clue why there was a half-moon in the background.

Aidan had been gone for forty-two minutes, and I thought it was totally lame that I actually knew the minute count. But, yeah, I did. I didn't like that he was meeting my dad. I knew he was more than capable of handling himself, and Dominic had gone with him, but still, it didn't seem like enough. And it also seemed like a waste of time. It wasn't like Dad would tell him anything, but Aidan said we had to play it cool and keep my dad thinking we didn't suspect him of anything.

I hated that he was right.

I glanced back at the drawing, tilting my head. Maybe if I looked at it from a different angle, the thing would make sense. Nope. I tried the other way. It didn't work. I seriously had no clue what I was looking at.

I got up from my chair and went to the jumbo pad that Landon hovered over. "What is that supposed to be?" I asked, pointing at the half-moon that couldn't really be a half-moon.

Landon stopped drawing and made a tragic face as if I had insulted him by asking. "It's the mountain. I was trying to give it a backdrop. To make it look realistic."

"You drew the wolves as stick figures," Beck pointed out, chuckling. "I think you lost the whole realistic feel with that."

"What's the point of this?" I asked as I turned from the drawing and returned to my chair, pulling my legs up and crossing them.

Landon shrugged. "Just trying to be prepared," he said. "And we could use a playbook, don't you think?"

Craig groaned and leaned forward, planting his elbows on the table and resting his chin in his hands. "If you are going to be drawing our playbook, we're in serious trouble."

"Come on, it's not that bad," Landon said, cutting everyone an exaggerated *I'm wounded* kind of look.

"Yeah, man, it is," Mark said as he looked over the drawing. He patted Landon on the back roughly in mock consolation. "But keep practicing. You might get better at this whole drawing thing."

I rolled my eyes at the guys as they continued badgering Landon about his lack of art skills and glanced at my phone, wishing again that it would beep or ring or do something. I'd sent Jared at least five messages since Aidan left, and each one had gone unanswered. I understood why. Really, I did. But still …

"Jade." Beck's tone was a harsh bark, letting me know he knew exactly what was on my mind as I started to reach for the phone. He moved silently to the table and leaned against it to face me. "If you even think about texting him again, I'll confiscate that damn phone."

I let my hand fall back into my lap. Not for the first time today, I grew angry with the guys, and when I spoke, it showed in my tone. "I just want to know where he is."

"Not your concern anymore," Mark said softly and firmly as if he were trying to be absolute on the subject, but at the same time, he wanted to be compassionate.

I felt a little hurt, but not so much for myself. I felt it for Jared. Beck looked troubled, but I didn't think he had the right to be. I rubbed my face, my gaze drifting again to the phone.

"What is that?" Aidan said, drawing my attention to the doorway. He was staring at Landon's drawing with a seriously confused expression painted on his face.

"It's supposed to be our playbook of attack strategies," I said, uncrossing my legs and twisting around. "Did Dad tell you anything?"

He shook his head and said, "Nothing useful, but I think the eye twitch happens when he's nervous."

CHAPTER 17

My head hurt, a throbbing pain right behind my eyes. With each throb, a needle prick pinched at the bridge of my nose. My butt was beyond numb, and I couldn't feel my toes anymore. Aidan's hands kneaded at my shoulders and rubbed up my neck. His touch felt like heaven — simply amazing.

It was closing in on three in the morning, and still, the team was in strategy mode. Each one of them had picked up on different things during our interaction with my dad at my house yesterday morning. Mark noticed the left eye twitch. Beck picked up on a light apple butter scent when my dad had passed him in the hallway. Craig heard a hint of excitement lining Dad's tone when he had kicked me out. Dominic noticed how Dad watched Aidan as if he were waiting for an opening to rip out his throat. And Tommy and Chris, well, they seemed to notice a lot about Jared. Like the way, he watched me as if he wanted me dead. I didn't really blame Jared for that. If I were him, I figured I would probably want me dead, too.

We had taken a quick break at noon, long enough for Beck to sneak out and stash Erika at his house until he could figure out what to do with her. Craig had gone with him, and when they had gotten back, he looked completely wrecked, and as the hours passed by, he didn't look any better.

The table was scattered with empty pizza boxes and burger wrappers. Someone had pinned up a town map on the wall, and beside it was a jumbo pad of white paper hanging from an easel. Since Aidan had gotten back from the useless meeting with my dad, they had been mapping out each area they had searched for the cougars. Aidan pinpointed each spot he'd sent Trevor to as well. They marked each location with a red X and then placed a blue X on every place they had found tracks.

I'd thought we had made progress, but as I scanned the map from my seat, all I could see was how much territory we still had to search. Dog Mountain was secluded, surrounded by thousands of acres of bush, and there was also the entire mountain to cover. There were three times as many blue marks as there were red.

Aidan's fingers moved up my neck again, working the muscles along my spine, and I released a long groan when they hit the tender knot. I wasn't really sure how we had gone from barely speaking to this in less than twenty-four hours, but I didn't really care. Since seeing him yesterday, a longing, deep and close to unbearable, had settled within me, and having him close eased it a little. He leaned forward, resting his chin on my shoulder. "How you holding up, sweetheart?"

Sweetheart. It sounded so perfect and, at the same time, so weird. His fingers kept working at the kink in my neck, and his breath tickled along my cheek.

"I think my brain died about five hours ago," I said with a groan.

Aidan chuckled. He pressed his lips to my ear and whispered, "I'm taking you home."

Home. Another way too perfect-sounding word. His hands dropped from my neck, and his chin lifted from my shoulder, and then he was in front of me, taking my hands in his and pulling me up from the chair. He fired off a bunch of quick commands, telling everyone to get some sleep and meet back here at eight tomorrow morning, and then he led me out of the building and to his car.

I must have dozed off in the car, and Aidan must have carried me inside. The last thing I remembered was buckling up my seatbelt. Now I was tucked in a big bed, surrounded by Aidan's scent. My jeans were gone, so were my hoodie and socks. All I had on was my underwear, bra, and tank.

A number of sensations struck me all at once: the emptiness of the bed, the coldness of the room, Aidan's scent clinging to the sheets. But above all that, I felt a bitter stab of loneliness. I shivered, and a sharp roll of needles chased down my spine.

The room was black as pitch. Not even a stitch of light came through the drawn curtains. It took a few blinks for my eyes to adjust, but once they did, I tugged on the comforter, wrapping it around my shoulders, and then wiggled off the bed. The last thing I wanted right now was to be alone.

The upstairs of Aidan's house was as empty as it felt. There was a bathroom just off to the left of the room I'd been sleeping in, the door open and lights off. I kept moving, tiptoeing down the hallway. A bit of moonlight streamed in through a small window, casting shadows that I swore were trying to jump up and trip me. I picked up my pace, passing another bedroom that was again empty, not even a stitch of furniture, and I kept going, sneaking down the stairs as quietly as I could.

I found Aidan snoring on the couch. The curtains

were drawn. The only light coming into the living room was through the tiny frosted peek-a-boo window on the door. He was on his back, one leg on the floor and one arm draped over his eyes. There was a blanket pulled up to his waist.

I stood at the base of the couch and tugged the comforter more snuggly around me, cocooning myself in its warmth, as I watched his chest rise and fall with each steady breath. My chest expanded, my heart warmed. He looked ... happy in sleep, a soft smile on his lips, his muscles relaxed and loose.

I sighed. My chest expanded a little more. I didn't know exactly what I was feeling, but it felt a heck of a lot like love. I sighed again and smiled as I turned away from him. I figured I should probably go back to bed even if I could have stood there all night and watched him sleep. I took a small step, a floorboard creaked, and Aidan's soft snores stopped. He didn't move, but his abs and pecs flexed. He pulled in a loud breath, and his muscles relaxed again.

I waited for him to say something, but he didn't, as if he were waiting to see what I would do. I hesitated for a second, watching him pull in breath after breath, and then I sat down, squeezing myself into the small space on the couch between his bent knee and stretched-out leg, pulling my feet up underneath me.

I felt him tense again and then relax. He kept an arm draped over his eyes but lifted the other and wound it around my waist, pulling me closer. He kept tugging until I shimmied around, and then he tugged some more until I was settled on top of him, my comforter still snug around me. I buried my head at the hollow of his neck. I could feel him swallow, his Adam's apple bobbing against my forehead. He tightened his arm around me. "Thank you," he said.

I leaned up, tucked my comforter under my arms,

and planted my forearms on his chest. "For what?" I asked.

He smiled but still kept his arm over his eyes. "For forgiving me."

I grabbed his arm, lifting it so I could look at him. My heart skittered within my chest as he settled his beautiful brown eyes on me. "I'm really glad you stuck around long enough for me to come to my senses," I said.

Aidan cupped my cheek. "I would have waited forever," he said.

I sighed, and once more, my heart expanded. I really didn't know how this would work out, but I was determined to try. He let his arm fall back over his eyes, and I put my head back down on his chest, listening to the steady thump of his heart. He lifted his leg from the floor, and I wiggled around, tugging at the comforter until it loosened enough that I had one of my legs on either side of his thigh. I thought about telling him that we should move, head to the bed where there was more room, but I was too comfortable wrapped up in his arms, lying on top of him, and frankly, I didn't want more room.

We lay there in a perfect kind of silence for a few moments when a thought surfaced that effectively rocketed my blood pressure up about ten notches and set my skin on fire. I planted my forearms back on his chest, lifting myself up again to look at him. "Did you undress me?" The question came out as a whisper.

"What?" he asked. He slid his draped arm from his eyes to his forehead and squinted down at me.

"Did you undress me?" I asked again, louder this time. The butterflies in my belly became soaring birds, and my skin heated just about everywhere.

Aidan shifted, scrubbed at his face, and groaned. "Don't get all modest on me, Jade. I'm too tired. It's not like I left you naked. You're still covered. And I'm pretty sure I saw more of you that day when you were in that little towel than I did tonight."

"Chill out, alpha," I said teasingly, settling my head back down on his chest. "I was just asking. I don't remember coming in."

He chuckled. "I tried to wake you up, but you were completely out," he said and finished it off with a long yawn. "We've got to be up in a few hours." He lifted his head from the armrest that he had been using as a pillow and pressed a light kiss on my forehead. "Are you staying down here?"

"Would it bother you if I did?" I asked, snuggling deeper into his arms.

He squeezed me tighter and whispered, "It would bother me if you said no. I love having you this close."

I smiled. I was sure we would both be seriously cramped in the morning, but I didn't care. I closed my eyes, breathing in a deep drag of his scent, and the world softened and then dissolved as sleep took me.

CHAPTER 18

AIDAN

Two days after Jade moved into my house, her dad asked for another meeting.

I probably shouldn't have been relieved that Jade refused to come with me to see her dad, but I was. I needed a break. I never thought living with Jade would be easy, but I never imagined it would be this hard.

The biggest problem: Jade wouldn't let Jared go. He had been MIA for the last two days. The team said he needed some distance, and frankly, I was glad for it, even if we could have used his help with the hunt. I didn't want to see him, and I didn't want Jade to see him, either. I had promised her that I would leave him alone, and I planned to keep my word, but it was seriously getting harder and harder to do.

All Jade could talk about was Jared. She claimed she was just worried about him, but I knew it was more than that. Even after telling her everything Tommy found out, she still held onto him. She cared about him — a lot. I knew we had agreed to move on, forget about the past, and start over, but I just couldn't do it. Maybe I didn't trust her; I knew she still didn't trust me. And I was sure that our trust issues were the reason we still hadn't moved forward, why we still hadn't made our mate status official, and it made the whole living together thing seriously tense.

I'd lost track of how many times over the last few days I'd found her outside trying to call him. It wasn't that I cared that she was checking in on him. It was more that she felt the need to sneak outside and hide it from me. How was I supposed to move on when she was sneaking around? I even asked her as much this morning. Her response: an intense kiss, a cute smile, and then she told me I worry too much.

So now Jade was at home getting ready to meet up with the team, and I sat in the coffee shop, sipping a steaming cup of java. I needed time to clear my head before seeing her dad again, and I needed some peace and quiet to review the latest email report from Tommy and Chris.

The faux red leather booths were lumpy and uncomfortable, and the coffee was burnt, but I sipped it anyway. The coffee shop was relatively quiet, with only a few tables occupied. The waitress rushed by with steaming cups of coffee and a tray of pastries.

I scrolled through my phone, brought up the email from Chris, and scanned through it again. The report wasn't much. Chris said the team had something they figured they should probably share with me. Chris was leaving it up to me on whether I wanted to hear whatever it was from the team or if I wanted to meet with them first. The email was clear that they thought I should let the team tell me. I didn't know what to think, and honestly, with all the crap going on at home, I didn't think I could take many more confessions.

I hit the reply and was about to start tapping in my response when a woman said, "Aidan, could you spare a minute?" I glanced up to find a short blond moving over to my booth, looking nervous and out of place. I'd seen her before, but I couldn't place her. She looked to be in her mid-thirties, and she wasn't part of my pack. She wore the typical fall Dog Mountain outfit: jeans and a heavy sweater. She smiled, showing a brilliant flash of white teeth, and stopped beside me.

I glanced back at my phone; I still had about ten minutes until I was supposed to be at Jeff's. I gestured to the empty seat across from me and said, "Sure, what's up?"

She slid into the booth and extended her hand to me. "Rachel," she said as I clasped her hand. "I don't think I actually introduced myself when I ran into you a few weeks ago." She had a firm, steady grip as she pumped twice before letting go. "How are you liking Dog Mountain?"

I chuckled. I couldn't help it. The look she was giving me was all business. "I know that look," I said. "You're not here to chat. What's on your mind?"

She laughed and tucked a lock of her shoulder-length hair behind her ear. "Oh, you're good."

"Well, I do live with Jade," I said and chuckled again. "She's the queen of that look. I get it at least five times a day."

Her expression sobered a little more, and she leaned forward, placing her hands on the table. "Those guys at the bar," she said, jutting her chin and keeping her voice low. "They've been in here a lot over the last few days. Asking a lot of questions about Jared and the enforcers."

I glanced over my shoulder, spotting Tommy and Chris, and groaned. I hadn't even noticed them come in. Tommy nodded to me, and Chris chuckled. "Morning, boss," they chimed in unison.

I rolled my eyes and groaned again. "Please tell me you guys just walked in," I said, hoping that was the case because I seriously should have noticed their scent as soon as the doors opened and they came in.

Tommy laughed, a loud rumbling sound. "Been here for about ten minutes," he said. He got up and made his way over; Chris followed along. "You had that *I want to strangle Jade* look again, so we figured you needed the space."

I shook my head, turning my attention back to Rachel. "Next time they pester you, tell them to screw off," I said.

"Oh." She brought a hand to her mouth, and her eyes widened. "I didn't know you had new members. Shit!" She blushed, a deep crimson, and glanced at Tommy, her cheeks reddening further, and then she looked back at me. "I'm sorry for giving them a hard time, then."

I smirked. "Don't be sorry, knowing them, they deserved it."

"Hey," Tommy said, punching my shoulder playfully. "Don't give the lady the wrong idea about us, kid."

"See what I mean?" I said to Rachel, rolling my eyes. "They deserved it."

Rachel laughed, a nervous kind of laugh. "You're nothing like Ray, are you?" she asked, arching a brow and tucking more of her thick hair behind her ear.

I wasn't really sure what she meant by that, but I really hated how nervous she was sitting across from me, so I smiled the crooked smile that always worked to mellow out Jade and shook my head. "Nope. Nothing like him."

♥

Jeff was sitting on the porch steps when I got out of the

car. He didn't look up as I approached. He was in jeans and a light gray fleece sweater, and he wore a black baseball cap that shadowed his face.

The sun was obscenely bright without a cloud in the sky, but the wind was brisk and heavy. The chain links that held the porch swing creaked and cracked as it swayed in the breeze. The van was gone, the driveway empty, but then I guess I hadn't really expected Pam to be home. According to Jade, she had been working like a dog since Jeff got back, furious at him for kicking her daughter out.

"My daughter didn't bother to come?" he asked, a hint of hopefulness in his voice, as he glanced back at the car as if he might have missed her at first. He kept his chin dipped and his face hidden under the brim of his cap.

I took a deep breath, trying to keep calm. I figured he knew I didn't like him; I was sure he could smell my distaste, but I didn't really care. "She doesn't have anything to say to you right now," I said evenly. "You did kick her out of her house."

He shrugged as if kicking out his only child was no big deal. "You were going to make her leave anyway."

A gust of wind hit my back as I stopped in front of him and my nostrils flared. The copper scent of blood was thick on the wind, and it carried the now familiar smell of cougars. It was an odd scent, almost like a house cat, but not. It was stronger, harsher, and had a hint of dried birch bark mixed with lemon.

"I don't have time for this shit, Jeff. She'll talk to you when she's ready, or she won't," I said, forging calm remoteness. I took another breath, trying to determine which direction the smell was coming from, but the wind was making it seriously hard to pin down. "What was so important that you needed to see me in person for?"

He lifted a hand, tipping up his cap with a fingertip, giving me a clear view of his blackened and swollen eye along with a busted up lip.

"What the hell happened to you?" I asked, scanning him over. There was a tear in his sweater, right at the neckline, and what looked like the remnants of a bruise on his cheek. His lip was healing, although it seemed slow for a shifter, or maybe he just really got his ass kicked. Either way, I didn't really care. The man deserved what he got.

"Jared came to see me this morning," he said. "He's on the outs with his brothers again. It never goes well when those boys are fighting. People get hurt."

I narrowed my eyes, folded my arms over my chest, and glared down at him. "Jared doesn't have any brothers, and I doubt he could do this."

Jeff smirked, causing his lip to split open again. "You sure about that?"

Was he joking? Damn, I couldn't tell. His scent gave nothing away. I was pretty sure Jared wouldn't show up here just to beat the crap out of him. If he was going to try and beat someone down, it would most likely be me. And I was certain he didn't have any brothers. From what Dominic had told me, Jared was the product of a one-night stand. He was the only enforcer that grew up in Dog Mountain. He'd never met his dad, and his mom died three years ago from an overdose.

Another gust of wind brought the scent of blood swamping around me. I breathed it in and turned, looking toward the tree line. The wind shifted, blowing from the other direction, and again, it brought the coppery smell back with it.

"He got a phone call while he was here, and he took off pretty quick," Jeff said and chuckled, a cruel sound that put ice in my veins. I shifted my gaze back to him, and he smiled wide. "I'll give you one guess who called him."

I gritted my teeth. I didn't need a guess. I knew exactly who had called him. "Jade."

Jeff didn't confirm it, but I guessed I didn't really need him to. I'd known something was up with her when she practically shoved me out the door this morning. But I had really been hoping it had nothing to do with Jared.

Jeff stood up and walked to the door. He was still smiling, enjoying the pain he was inflicting on me; I was sure of it. "Before you go running off to track down that mate of yours, I called you here to tell you I finally got a full count of the cougars, and I also picked up a little something for you that will lead you right to them." He shoved the door wide open and stepped back.

For a long moment, I didn't have a clue what I was looking at. The stench of cougar and blood was suddenly so thick that I almost gagged. I moved up the steps, holding my breath as I did. Sitting on a chair, tied tightly enough to cut through the skin, was a man about my age. His eyes were closed, his head lolled to the left. Blood dripped to the floor around his feet.

"Richard," Jeff said. The man lifted his head and slowly opened his eyes. "Meet Aidan, the alpha of the Dog Mountain pack."

CHAPTER 19

"It's official. I'm going to flunk out of high school," I said, slapping my textbook shut. My whole plan of studying for an hour before meeting up with the team was not going to happen. I couldn't focus my mind on anything other than what my father could possibly want. He had been lying low, avoiding us completely, and Aidan had sat back and watched, just like he'd promised me. But this morning, Dad had called, waking Aidan and me up, demanding a meeting.

Marcy giggled a trill sound that burst through the speakerphone of my cell. "You're not going to flunk out, Jade," she said. "Half your teachers are part of the pack. They wouldn't dare fail you." Clunking footsteps and a rustle of fabric flitted through the phone suddenly, and she squealed a little breathlessly. "Trevor, stop it. Alpha on the line."

Trevor grunted something that I thought might have been an apology, and I rolled my eyes, flopping back on the couch. "Don't you guys have Erika duty today?" I asked, picking up the list of late assignments and scanning it over. It was ridiculous how much homework could pile up over a week. As far as I was concerned, there should be some kind of law about homework. How the school system expected people to sit in class all day and then spend hours each night cramming in more knowledge was beyond me. Not that I had been sitting in class much lately, but that was beside the point. It was a sunny Saturday morning, and I was stuck on the couch surrounded by a mountain of work. Where was the home/school balance?

"Don't remind me," Marcy said, her voice sounding further away and a bit fuzzy as she switched me to speakerphone. "She's driving me insane. Tell me again why we're putting up with that ... that ..." she groaned. "See, she has me so pissed off I can't even think of a good name for her. I get the whole going after the single alpha thing, but I don't know how she could do this to Craig."

"I'm supposed to be diplomatic now," I said, dropping the list to the couch. "And protecting a wolf that helped the pack is diplomatic."

Marcy snorted. "You, diplomatic? Yeah, right."

"Hey, I totally resent that," I said, except she probably had a point. I really wasn't the diplomatic type, but still, I was trying to be somewhat reasonable. "I can be diplomatic. You've got to admit it, I've got skills. If I didn't, you wouldn't be lounging in Trevor's bed right now, would you?" And pulling that one off had taken mad skills. I'd sat with her dad for hours trying to explain the whole mate status thing and what that actually meant. In the pack world, she was literally married now. I'd done a crapload of bargaining and more negotiating than I'd ever done before, but in the end, we'd finally come to an agreement, and Marcy had moved in with her mate. Seriously, the whole thing had been a perfect example of exactly how diplomatic I could be when I needed to.

"How's everything going with Aidan?" Trevor asked casually.

I took a deep breath. "I don't know. He's been crazy bossy, and I swear he hasn't left me alone for even a second in the last two days. It's like he thinks if he turns his back, I'll just vanish." I'd known that trying to start over would be work — a lot of work — but he was being impossible. Whenever he was around, the problem was that birds flapped in my belly, and my heartbeat pretty much tripled. He made my body sing and my inner-wolf dance. And I loved him. I really did. There was no denying it, not anymore. I just didn't have the strength or energy to do it anymore. But sometimes, space was a good thing, and Aidan hadn't been giving me much space (or any space) over the last two days.

And yet here I was alone. Actually alone. Sure, I had basically shoved him out the door this morning, but still, after two days of his hovering, it felt weird not having him standing over my shoulder, and whether I liked it or not, his absence made my inner-wolf uneasy.

"He's your mate, Jade, and an alpha," Trevor said. "Of course, he's bossy. His inner-wolf wants to keep you safe. It's probably all he can think about. Give the guy a break."

"He's not my mate," I countered, the weight of my words close to unbearable, and I suddenly found it hard to catch my breath. "I don't know if this whole starting over idea was such a hot idea."

That wasn't entirely true. I didn't regret starting over. In truth, even with Aidan's constant closeness, and his increasing possessiveness, I was glad I was here — with him. But if I took that step, I wasn't sure who I would be anymore. I wasn't even really sure who I was now. I had adapted to my new life. I had survived. I thrived as a werewolf. And well, it had become comfortable. The truth? I was terrified that if I took that step with Aidan, I'd lose myself, that I'd become just another piece of him. There had to be a balance — somewhere.

Never fall so hard that you can't live without him. You need to stay your own person. Mom's advice to Marcy when she'd broken up with Trevor for the first time never strayed far from my mind these days. I thought they were supposed to be words of wisdom, except I didn't know how to stop myself from falling, and I was falling fast. It didn't help one freakin' bit that our inner-wolves knew there would be no one else. They were done with waiting, and darn it, but the thought made me glow from the inside out.

"Has the last few days really been horrible?" Marcy asked.

"No," I said a little grudgingly, staring at the phone on the coffee table. "They've been perfect. He cooks, cleans. He's considerate, and he even lets me have the television remote. It's sickening. He's not supposed to be this sweet. But I need to just be *Jade* for a while. I need to find my way through this make a place for myself in the pack. I might have won the games for alpha female, but it's almost as if the males can't see me as my own person, like I'm just another arm of him, not important but there anyway."

If I had been hoping they would disagree with me, I was left disappointed. The silence stretched on for a long moment before I asked, "Have you guys seen Jared? The guys won't tell me anything, and with Aidan hovering, I haven't really been able to check on him."

"It's for the best, Jade," Trevor said. "You need to forget about him. If you would move on and embrace your mate, you'd see a shift in everyone's attitude." His tone was firm but not cold. Trevor was one of the few male pack members who hadn't shunned me over the whole Jared thing, although I was pretty sure it was only because he was mated to my best friend. He had to play nice, and so did I.

"How is this fair?" I asked. "Aidan actually messed around with Erika, and no one batted an eye at it. All I did was pretend to have a boyfriend, a few public kisses, that's it." A frustrated growl rumbled around my chest.

"Aidan hasn't hated the pack for two years," Trevor said, his tone measured and tense. I figured Marcy was probably giving him a look to stop him from telling me off. "We all know how you felt about us. It's not like you hid it. You didn't bother to try once you became one of us. You showed complete disregard for our ways, decided you didn't need to follow our laws, and you publicly humiliated our alpha — your mate — and walked away with an enforcer."

He was right. Yes, I had done all that, but in all fairness, I hadn't known that I was doing it. No one had bothered to tell me the rules.

The sound of a car pulling into the driveway drew my attention, and I glanced out the window. I watched for a moment as a white Honda pulled to a stop, and then a pack member got out. "Got to go, guys. Luken's here," I said as I watched him walk up the driveway. He knocked on the door, thumping three bangs that rattled the hinges. "Get to Beck's. He needs a break." They both mumbled a reluctant agreement before ending the call.

I crossed over to the door, pulling it open. I didn't even get a chance to say hi before Luken asked, "Where's the alpha?" His arms were folded over his massive chest, and he focused a dark glare on me. The werewolf was close to enforcer status, just one row down in the pack's pecking order. He was built like an enforcer, too, tall with more muscle than any one person needed. He was in jeans, a black baseball cap, and an off-white fall jacket.

"You're looking at her," I said, aware that I had hesitated way too long before answering him.

He stood perfectly still for a moment as his nostrils flared, and then he leaned forward, taking a deep sniff of my scent. His lips curved in disgust. "You're not my alpha. Where is he?"

I laughed, a startling sound, and brought a hand to my chest in mock hurt. "Ouch. You know if you guys keep this up, I might actually start to believe you don't want me here."

He lifted one shoulder in a small shrug. "We don't," he said. An easy smile curved his mouth. "Where's Jared been?" He sounded cautious as if he were testing how far he could push me without crossing the invisible line that would lead to me telling Aidan or unleashing my alpha scent on him. Even so, tension slid down my spine, awakening my inner-wolf and ratcheting up my anxiety. I was sure that the pack males knew I was clutching onto my independence with a fiercely tight hold. Luken wasn't the first in the last two days to talk to me like this or ask me about Jared, and I was sure he wouldn't be the last.

"What do you need, Luken?" I asked, planting my hands on my hips and giving him my best *no-nonsense* look. The wind ruffled his jacket, filling the space between us with a light rustling of fabric. "I've got stuff to do."

I held onto my inner-wolf tightly, keeping her growing annoyance balled and contained. She was getting tired of the constant challenge of our authority, but really, so was I. In my mind, it shouldn't matter that I wasn't a mated alpha. I had taken out every challenger. I deserved their respect even if I had walked away from my mate.

"You wouldn't understand." He paused for a moment and then said, "Just tell him to call me." And with one last disgusted look my way, he turned from me and stalked down the driveway to his waiting car.

I stood there for a moment, feeling like a piece of crap, at least until the car door slammed. It was amazing how much damage I had done to the pack without even trying, and I was actually starting to feel guilty about it. I blinked, watching him pull out of the driveway before retreating back to the couch.

So that sucked, I thought. I didn't want to believe it, but maybe Trevor was right. Maybe I needed to move on. But I knew I wasn't wrong either. Wanting to be my own person, not be defined by who I was with, wasn't wrong.

I glanced at my phone, reached for it, and pulled back. I knew there really was only one thing to do. I had to fix things, and I knew exactly where I needed to start. I reached for my phone again, snagged it up, and made the call before I could change my mind.

CHAPTER 20

I sucked in the fresh air. My lungs couldn't get enough of it. Clean and crisp and cool. The jog over to the clearing had been refreshing and relaxing. I stood hunched over, my hands on my knees, pulling the air into my lungs and expelling it in slow, deep puffs.

The sun was out in full force this morning, coating the clearing where I had spent many hours in training with Jared and Beck in a warm glow. Leaves rattled across the dried-out grass as they were carried in a cool breeze.

I knew he was behind me, watching from the tree line, but I needed a moment to just breathe. His scent was thick in the air, a mix of caution and a hot spike of tempered anger. I figured he was waiting for someone else to show up. I didn't really blame him for that, but it hurt a little that he assumed I'd try to set him up.

Another couple of minutes passed before I heard the crunch of leaves underfoot behind me. I pulled in a few more deep breaths and slowly straightened, turning toward him.

"Hey, little girl," he said, looking me over with cool eyes as he walked toward me. I didn't really know what

I had expected when I saw him, but what I saw definitely wasn't it. Jared looked ... good. Really good, actually. He had gotten a haircut, his black hair short, spiked, and gelled. His face was clean-shaven, smooth, and fresh-looking, and there wasn't a stitch of darkness under his eyes. The tension he had carried around with him while he had stayed with me was gone. I didn't recognize the leather jacket he was sporting, and underneath he had on a light green tee that I was sure I had never seen him wear before. He usually kept to blacks. It hugged his sculpted chest, outlining his thick pecs.

He stopped a few feet away from me, and his eyes swept over me in a thorough inspection. His nostrils flared a few times, and then he smirked. I knew what he was looking for, a change in my scent, and I seriously hated that smug look that was etching itself onto his face. "Does he know you're here?" he asked, amusement thick in his voice.

"Does it matter?" I countered blandly, lifting a brow. A gnawing sense that I was walking in a gray area surfaced, and it scared the crap out of me. My muscles tensed, my stomach started to twist, and I tried to breathe through it, hoping he wouldn't notice.

Jared chuckled, a husky sound. One that usually sent my inner-wolf into a round of manic backflips, but oddly enough, she was calm and steady. It was strange and, well, amazing. But then I guessed living with Aidan had calmed her. But still, I had kind of expected the franticness, the racing heart, but it didn't come, and my coiled muscles began to unwind.

"Nope," he said. His smirk widened. "Just didn't figure he'd loosen up on that short leash he's been keeping you on long enough for you to sneak away."

Ouch. Okay, the truth of his statement kind of sucked. I tried not to frown, but it happened anyway.

Yeah, Aidan had been keeping me close, but frankly, I was just as bad as he had been. I hated having him out of my sight.

But was I really so transparent that Jared could see that I had snuck out, or did he just know me that well? I could feel the scrunch in my forehead and a knot deep in my belly twisted and yanked. The gray area flapped in front of me again. *I probably should have told Aidan,* I thought. I should have given him a choice to come with me, too. But honestly, I hadn't wanted to get that look again. The one who told me he didn't trust me enough to go alone; the same one I would have given him if he had told me he wanted to see Erika.

"I didn't sneak away, and he doesn't have me on a leash," I snapped, except it didn't sound believable. I took a step toward him, and he backed up a step, putting up a hand as if he were asking me not to come any closer.

My frown deepened, tugging at my lips. I huffed. He looked at me as if I were the dangerous one out of the two of us, which was pretty much a laughable notion. I never thought I would see the day that I would make the head of the enforcers nervous. And, man, had I tried to make him nervous in our training. But Jared didn't get nervous, not usually. He fought. Sometimes he lost, mostly he won. His job as an enforcer was black and white for him. *Fear and nerves are for the weak,* he'd told me. *Win or lose, don't show fear.*

I plopped down onto the grass, stretching my legs out in front of me, and leaned back, propping myself up on my elbows, trying to make myself look unthreatening. "Where have you been?"

"Around," he said with a lazy lift of his shoulders. He scanned the length of my body again, letting his scent thicken in the air. When I gave him no reaction, he lowered himself to the ground, sprawling out on his back still a few feet away from me.

"Really?" I asked. "That's all you're going to give me?"

Jared sighed long and loud as he stared up at the cloudless sky. "What did you expect, Jade?" he asked in a hushed tone. "You made your choice. I didn't want to stick around and watch."

I groaned and cut him an exasperated look. Too bad he still wasn't looking at me. "There was never a choice, Jared. I never hid that from you. You knew from the start I was his. Don't you dare try to make this about *us* because you know damn well that there never was an *us*."

He lay on his back as still as rocks except for the steady, even rise of his chest as he breathed. He was quiet for a crazy long moment before he finally said, "I needed a break. The team is a nightmare with Aidan's newbies hanging around."

I laughed. "Nightmare?" I said and laughed again. "You want to talk about nightmares? Hell, I'm living in a damn nightmare."

Jared chuckled. He shifted onto his side, propping his head upon his hand. His dark brown eyes searched my face with an intensity that made me shiver, not a pleasurable one. His eyes were cold and calculating and hard, and they traveled along my skin as if he were watching the shiver spread down my body. His lips quirked into a cocky, one-sided grin. "Awe, kitten, is that soon-to-be mate of yours not treating you as good as you thought he would?"

I bristled like a porcupine, and my inner-wolf became seriously agitated within me at his insinuation. "He treats me just fine," I said through my teeth. "It's keeping him from hunting you down that's the freakin' nightmare. On top of that, most of the males hate me. And you hiding away like I've ripped out your heart is only fueling their anger. It makes us look guilty."

That wiped the smirk off his face. His brown-black eyes hardened and cooled again. "Maybe we are guilty."

I rolled up to my feet and paced the few steps over to him. "I'm not buying this *poor me* act," I said, smirking. "And by the way, you suck at it."

That earned me a throaty chuckle. "Come on, I know you felt a little bad."

"The team needs you, Jared," I said, ignoring him. "Aidan needs you. He might not want to admit it, but he does." I extended a hand to him. For a minute, I didn't think he was going to take it. He schooled his expression into a blank mask of indifference, and as he did, I whispered, "Please."

As soon as the whisper left my lips, he took my hand and pulled himself up. He stood in front of me for a moment before he tugged on my hand and wrapped me in a tight hug, resting his chin on the top of my head.

I stood stiff in his arms, waiting for my inner-wolf to perk up at his nearness, but she didn't, not in the way she usually did, so I wrapped my arms around his waist and squeezed back.

CHAPTER 21

"What am I supposed to do with this?" I asked, waving a hand toward the man, tied and bleeding out onto the floor. I felt cold and tired. I probably should have been mad, but I just couldn't drudge up the emotion. Jade was with Jared. Cold and tired and disappointed was pretty much all I had right then. Ice slid over my skin. I wanted to dig out my phone and call her. How long had I been gone? An hour? She didn't have a car, but he could have picked her up. My brain raced and swirled with all the things she could have done with him in the last hour. My stomach rolled. I swallowed hard. "He can barely hold his head up."

Jeff chuckled and shook his head. "He'll heal," he said. "The count's eighteen." He chuckled again. "Seventeen now." He moved into the house, rounded Richard, and placed a hand on his shoulder, his grip hard. "I was supposed to kill this one, but I figured he could be of use to you. Like I told you, they were moving locations when I left, and he's been to their new hot spot." He dug his fingers into Richard's shoulder hard enough that the man groaned and winced, and then he let go, shrugged his shoulders, and said, "But if you don't want him, I can dispose of him."

I couldn't focus. I knew I needed to. I knew that Jeff was playing me, and I needed to pay attention, read between the lines, but all I could think about was Jade. Was it so wrong that I wanted to keep her close, protect her, hold her, to have her in every possible way? She seemed to think so. *Stop being such an overbearing dog,* she'd said to me this morning, laughing. She had kissed me, kissed my cheeks, my lips, my neck, a flutter of delicate presses along my skin. *I'm yours, Aidan. You have nothing to worry about.*

But she wasn't mine. Not really. Not fully. Most of all, I wanted her to want me the way I wanted her. To be with me. I thought that was the part that was eating at me the most. When she was with me, she wasn't really with me. Her mind was with him. I was lost to her. Completely lost. At some point, those ideas of love had gripped me, turning into so much more than just ideas. And knowing that she was out somewhere with Jared, that she clearly didn't feel the same as I did, was wrecking me.

I guessed that was probably why Jeff had told me where she had run off to. I figured he wanted me distracted. "What's his death sentence for?" I asked, trying to push her out of my mind, even for a second.

"He fell in love, took off with one of the women just before the accident." Jeff's tone held a note of remorse, remorse that I knew he didn't feel. "He was stupid enough to go back, and when he was caught, they called me to get rid of the problem."

The rage I had been missing surfaced and thrashed against my skull. *Accident.* The way he said it was as if it were actually an accident such as a car crash or a house fire. But it was nothing like that. His pack had brutally used two women, used them until they died. It wasn't an accident. He didn't care that they were dead. I was even willing to bet he had known they would die.

"I can help you," Richard rasped. He struggled to lift his head enough to meet my eyes. His were a cool blue, hard and full of conviction. "I want to help you."

"We'll take him," I said, fished my phone out of my pocket, and thumbed the screen. 9:30. Jade had been alone, or with *him*, for an hour and a half. I should have killed him. I could have, too. In the eyes of pack law, Jared had done enough to be put down, but Jade ... she wouldn't even let me throw him out of the pack, claiming none of his crimes was his fault. They were hers.

Another rush of ice pushed through me. I stared at the clock. A minute ticked by. I knew I needed to call the team in the back of my mind. Get them here. Deal with the cougar. If nothing else, I wanted time to question him before he met his death, but I stood there frozen, staring at the clock. Another minute passed, and then another.

"I know what you're thinking," Jeff said blandly. I glanced up as he stepped away from Richard. There was a pitiless, callous glint in his eyes as he approached me. "You're wondering how long she's been gone, counting the seconds, minutes, maybe even hours since you left her this morning. She probably told you she would take a shower and meet up with the team. She's been trying so hard to help, and you wanted to believe her. You want to trust her, but you can't, not really. Not when you know he can speak to her inner-wolf and that she cares about him enough that she has to hide it from you." He paused, smiled, and chuckled. "I bet you're trying to figure out how long she's been with him this morning. Did she actually take that shower? How long could that have taken?" He stopped in front of me, his smile widening. "You should have taken my advice. You shouldn't have waited to claim her as your own. If you had done it, you'd see Richard as something of value to you and not just another problem for you to solve."

Listening to him speak about his daughter as if she were a piece of meat was like walking through the pits of a garbage dump. Stomach-turning and vile. But even if listening to him made bile rise in my throat, he'd summed up everything that was racing through my head. I forced out a laugh that I hoped sounded somewhat believable and lied, "Actually, I was thinking you have a lot of cleaning to do before your wife gets home from work."

He chuckled and said, "I'm sure that's exactly what you were thinking."

For half a second, I entertained the idea of shifting and ripping out the man's throat. Oddly enough, it was my inner-wolf who pushed the thought away. I'd promised our mate that I wouldn't hurt her father, and it seemed as if my inner-wolf was determined to make me keep that promise. He wasn't willing to make a move that could jeopardize my chance at claiming her.

I thumbed my phone again, bringing up Beck's number, and tapped it as I headed down the steps of the porch, putting some distance between myself and the bastard Jade called a father. It rang twice before he answered. "How'd the meeting go?" he asked.

"Gather the guys and come to Jeff's," I said, walking down the driveway, away from Jeff. I let my voice drop low and added, "And send someone to track down Jade."

"What do you mean 'track down Jade?'" he asked, his voice taking on a hard edge.

"She's with Jared," I said and swallowed the rotten taste that had filled my mouth that was full of my useless anger.

"You let her go see him." It wasn't a question. I didn't miss the blunt accusation in his voice. Beck had taken on a *big brother* kind role with Jade. The whole team had, actually. She had them wrapped around her finger, and they loved it, loved her, and right now, Jared wasn't in their good graces.

"She told me she was going to study and then meet you guys," I growled. The rotten, rusty taste filled my mouth again, and I tried to swallow it down.

"Shit," he said, summing the whole situation up perfectly. He growled out a few more obscenities before he said, "Let me go for her."

I clenched the phone tighter, feeling every muscle in my body flex right along with my fingers. His reaction wasn't helping my mood, even if it was exactly what I had expected. "I don't care who goes for her. Just send the guys to me and have someone bring her back to the headquarters. Jeff is giving us one of the cougars." I didn't wait for his response before ending the call. I shoved my phone back into my pocket and focused every bit of energy I had on reining in my emotions.

JADE

Jared's arms felt solid wrapped tightly around me. He was taller than me, not a lot, but enough that he had to bend a little to whisper in my ear. "You sure about this?"

I nodded. "Yes. I wouldn't be here if I weren't. Aidan's never going to get over it if you keep running, and like I said, he needs you now more than ever."

He moved back slightly to meet my eyes and brushed a strand of hair from my cheek with a big warm hand. "He might not agree," he pointed out.

I shuddered. No, Aidan probably wouldn't agree. I

had no doubt that he would want to throttle me when I brought Jared back, but it was a risk I had to take. The longer he stayed away, the guiltier we looked. The pack needed to see the three of us working together. They needed to see my reaction. They needed to know that I wouldn't turn back to Jared when things got tough, that I was with them, and most of all, that I was with Aidan.

And I knew Jared wanted to be different. I saw that. Over the last few days, he'd worked so hard to show me that he did care about the pack. He may be a cocky pain in my ass, he may push all of my buttons, but he was loyal. He was pack. He was family.

I grinned. "You leave Aidan to me. He'll come around." Okay, I wasn't entirely sure that he would come around, but I was hoping he would.

Jared chuckled and shook his head, clearly thinking I was mental. Right then, I wasn't sure that I disagreed.

"You have a death wish, don't you?" Beck, his voice rough, pierced through me like a row of sharpened teeth.

"It was just a hug," I squeaked, jumping out of Jared's arms. "What are you doing here?"

Beck was tense but trying not to show it. I could see it in his set face and the way his shoulders bunched, emphasizing the muscles under his jacket. "Aidan sent me to find you." He didn't crack his usual *you're a pain in the ass* smile, but then, neither did I. "Haven't you put him through enough of this bullshit?"

Nice. It was going to be one of *those* days.

"You've got to be kidding me," I said in a stronger voice, although there was a bit of a whine to it. I couldn't help the small smirk, and Beck rolled his eyes. "I'm not doing anything wrong here. It's just a hug."

"Just a hug," he repeated as if I'd said the words in some foreign language, and he couldn't quite grasp the meaning. There wasn't a doubt in my mind that he was disappointed with me, and, man, did it make me feel like an ass. I probably should have stopped at, *"I'm not doing anything wrong here,"* because the look he shot me made me want to find a rock to crawl under, full of animosity and frustration. He paced toward me. He looked as if he wanted to grab and shake some sense into me. "If you really believed that, you would have told Aidan where you were going. You were warned to stay away from him."

I opened my mouth and then closed it when nothing came out. He stopped only inches from me, folding his arms over his chest, still giving me a god-awful expectant kind of look as if he were waiting for a detailed explanation. It was the kind of look Dominic or Marcy would give me, but really, I had nothing that would make this look better, so I kept my mouth clamped shut.

"Beck, lay off," Jared said, pressing in closer to me again. "She was trying to convince me to come back. That's all. Give her a break."

"If you speak again, I'm going to punch you," Beck said softly, but it was clear that he meant it. He glared at Jared. There was a warning in his eyes that I couldn't even begin to understand, but I figured Jared did. He moved in a blink, propping himself against a tree about ten feet away.

Beck's nostrils flared as he fixed his eyes back on me. "His scent is on you," he said, gritting his teeth and digging out his phone. He tapped on the screen, brought it to his ear, and after a second, he said, "I've got her." He paused, scanned me over, and moved a little closer. He grabbed my shoulder, spinning me around, and then he lifted my hair, inspecting my neck and shoulders. "I'm checking, Aidan, just hold on," he barked. He did a thorough once over of my clothes and then said, "There's not even a hair out of place on your mate." He paused, cut a furious look at Jared, and said, "Yeah, I'll bring them both in."

I could hear the heated tone of Aidan's voice as he gave his orders but couldn't quite make out the words. *Oh, God.*Nausea rolled in my belly. I held out my hand and said, "Give me the phone. I want to talk to him." Beck started to pass the phone but hesitated, listening for a moment to whatever Aidan was saying. He scowled at me, shaking his head, and then thumbed the screen and jammed the phone into his pocket. "Beck, what the hell?"

"He heard you and said 'no.'" There was a dry, cutting edge to his tone that I really didn't like.

"Is he mad?" I whispered, my throat closing up. My chin started to dip on its own, and my shoulders sagged. It wasn't that I hadn't secretly seen this coming, well, okay, not exactly this, but I'd had a hunch that Aidan wouldn't be all that pleased with me dragging Jared back into the mix. But I knew that what I was doing was right. If anything, we needed to keep the pack together — keep them safe — and even if Aidan didn't like Jared, as the head of our team of enforcers, he was a big part of the pack.

Beck frowned. "Disappointed, definitely hurt. You've got to stop this shit, Jade. You threw the guy away because he lied to you. Do you really think this is any different?"

"Jared and I are just friends," I said. "It was never anything else. You know that."

Jared's temper flared. The heat in his scent pulled my eyes to him. His face shifted slightly, his eyes flashing gold, and then it faded, but the heat in the air lingered. Beck flashed him another cold glare just as Jared opened his mouth, and he closed it, biting back whatever he was about to say.

"It doesn't matter what I know," Beck said, softening a little. "Finding you in the bush alone with him doesn't look good. What if it had been someone else? What if he'd called Craig or Landon instead of me? You need to start thinking, Jade. You can't just run off like this. You wouldn't do it with the team, and you can't do it with him. He's your partner; you need to treat him like one." He huffed, and then a wicked smirk curved his lips, and he chuckled. "You are going to be in so much shit when he smells Jared on you."

"Not funny, Beck," I said with a sigh and then ran my fingers through my tangled, windblown hair.

"Yeah, it kind of is." His gaze was still dark with disappointment, but at least he was smiling now. "I love seeing that look on your face when he growls at you. It's priceless."

I smirked and stretched out my arms. "Want a hug?"

He shook his head and took a large step back. "Oh, hell no, you screwed up, you pay the price. I'm not getting in the middle of this shit."

CHAPTER 22

Aidan didn't look happy. He was leaning against the concrete side of the building. His arms folded over his chest, glowering, when Jared, Beck, and I emerged from the woods.

My heart did a little flip-flop against my ribs, and I stopped abruptly. Even glowering, he was a sight; tall and broad, with so much muscle. He was in jeans and a long-sleeved white T-shirt. His shaggy, light brown hair was flipping at the sides and disheveled on top, and all I could think about was running my hands through it. His intense brown eyes met mine, and I watched, frozen in place, as they flashed gold. He pointed at me, wagging a finger, beckoning me. My inner-wolf perked up, pushing at my skin, desperate to break free and run to her mate.

But I didn't move. It was as if my feet were pinned in place, no longer connected to my body. A rush of wind kissed my cheeks, bringing with it an assault of scents: leafy greens, hot power, the tang of anger and anxiety, and mixed with it all was a coating of spice. It was the spice that freaked me out the most. I knew exactly what it meant. He was jealous, which was, well, annoying, but it was also a little hot, and I shuddered hard.

Aidan's lips parted, and he growled. His eyes flared brighter. He beckoned me again, his finger stiff as he flicked it. I took a shaky, unsure step. The emotions in his scent were seriously nerve-racking, and they were also overly exciting my inner-wolf, sending hot chills over my skin and warmth pooling in my belly. It wouldn't take much for his inner-wolf to push to the forefront, for him to go all *alpha* on me, and I fought back the feeling that maybe, just maybe, I had made a mistake. I shuddered again, and his nostrils flared.

I took another step, and Beck snagged my wrist, pulling me to a quick stop. "Jade, play nice," he warned.

I shook off his hand. Now was so not the time to touch me, like at all. Not when my inner-wolf was all squirmy, wanting her mate. I put my feet in motion and picked up my pace to a jog. "Hey," I said, meekly, as I approached. "How did your meeting go?"

Aidan didn't answer. His jaw was tense, the muscles along his neck, roped and straining. I picked up my pace further, closing the distance between us as quickly as I could, and as soon as I was close enough, I threw my arms around his neck, pressing myself flush against him. He shifted his gaze, glancing down at me, and I rolled onto tip-toes. I meant to kiss him, ease some of the jealous rage I saw flaring in his eyes, but he wasn't having it. Before I knew it, his nose was pressed to my neck, dipping to my chest, and then back up to my hair, pulling in long, deep hauls.

I felt the growl bouncing around in his chest just before I heard it. His hands wrapped around my wrists, pulling them from his neck, and he glared down at me. His jaw worked as he clenched his teeth, and he growled, "Gym shower. Now."

"Wow, really?" I asked, leaning back. I smiled the

sweetest smile I could, hoping it would soften him. It didn't. He let go of my wrist, folding his arms back over his chest. I huffed and glanced over my shoulder, watching Jared and Beck make their way to us. Beck was already chuckling, a deep rumbling from his chest. "Two guys telling me I smell in the last few days. You know, if you all keep it up, I'm going to develop a serious complex."

"Jade," Aidan said in warning, clearly not seeing the humor in my statement.

"It was just a hug, Aidan," I muttered, feeling about fifty different kinds of guilty. My inner-wolf squirmed and sunk in my stomach as if she were feeling just as bad.

He studied me with a strange intensity, almost as if he were seeing something new in me, and if I had to guess, whatever he was seeing wasn't something that he liked much. "Go wash that smell off of you," he said roughly as if his throat had been shredded and was raw.

I laughed nervously, placing a hand on the swell of his rounded pec. "There's no way I'm leaving you with him, not with you all growly." I poked him in the chest. "And don't look at me like I've done something wrong because I haven't, and you know it. You need him."

If Aidan heard me, he clearly wasn't processing my words. "Jade, please go shower," he said and nudged me toward the door.

I took his hand. It felt warm, good, solid and strong, and perfect. "Come with me?"

I figured it was the right question to ask because his sudden grin was one hundred percent male. He bent, scooping me up in his arms in a motion so quick that I squealed. My arms flew around his neck, holding on, as he yanked open the door and stepped inside.

AIDAN

"How many times do I have to tell you that I'm yours before you believe me?" Jade asked. Her head was cradled in the hollow space between my neck and shoulder as I carried her through the network of hallways to the gym.

Jared's bitter scent clung to her, but it was the underline sharpness of his arousal that stirred the beast within me into a wild, rage-induced frenzy. Another male had been turned on while touching *my* mate. Another male touched *my* mate. Another male ... A growl ripped from my throat.

"If it were really true, we wouldn't be waiting." I knew I shouldn't have as soon as I said it, but I couldn't hold it back. My inner-wolf was pressing under my skin, itching to break free. He wanted his mate, craved to mark her with his scent, claim her as his. But, oh hell, so did I.

"That's such a guy thing to say," she said, cuddling closer. It was as if she were oblivious to the turmoil thrashing around within me. My muscle flexed; my grip on her tightened. "I don't need your scent in me to make us real, Aidan." Her lips, soft and moist and warm, brushed along my neck, but it did nothing to calm my inner-wolf. Her brush-off only agitated him — me — further. "You shouldn't need it either."

I shouldered the door to the gym and stalked to the back changing rooms. My nostrils were flaring, my heart was thundering with adrenaline. My inner-wolf urged me to lock her up, shift, and kill the bastard who had dared to touch her. He wanted to hunt. He wanted blood. And then he wanted to bathe his mate with his scent. It was as if I'd lost all rational thought. I needed to hunt. Kill. Claim. Protect. My mind was functioning on the most primal level, lost within the need of my inner-wolf.

Two pack members ran on treadmills in the far corner of the room. "Out. Now," I growled, my voice sounding far more animal than human. The whirl of the treadmills halted immediately, and they vacated the gym in a rush, keeping their eyes glued to the floor as they went.

I pushed through the doors to the changing room and flipped the deadbolt on the door, locking us in. I set her down, and she twirled around. Her head came to the bottom of my chin as she faced me. She glanced up, her big brown eyes full of concern, and when she met my furious gaze, she took a fast step back.

"You're right. I probably shouldn't," I said, following her as she continued to back up with every step I took. Her eyes were wide, and I watched closely, waiting for alarm or fear to show. If she showed fear, I would have stepped back in a second, but her scent was screaming excitement, so I continued my advance. "But when you throw yourself at another male, come back to me smelling of him, of his arousal, it makes it hard to believe you."

Her lips quirked into a sexy as hell smirk. She backed into the long row of showers, unzipping her hoodie and shrugging it off. My pulse quickened.

"How am I supposed to lead this pack when I can't even keep tabs on my mate?" I growled. "You blatantly lied to me, Jade. You were supposed to be here with the team, but you snuck out to meet *him* instead."

She kicked off her shoes, hopping around from one foot to the other as she yanked off her socks. Her eyes, flecked with gold, were trained on my lips as she licked hers. I continued my slow advance, and she stopped, letting her eyes rake over me.

I was pretty sure she wasn't listening, her scent thickening in the air, calling me to her, but I had to get it out. She had to hear it all. "Do you really think no one notices this crap? That the pack doesn't see it? You're single-handedly ripping apart our pack, and you're doing it with a damn smile." I took one more step and reached out, cupping her cheeks in my hands. "I love you, Jade. Probably more than I should, and I'm beginning to think that's the problem with us. We're the alpha pair. Caring complicates our job."

Jade flushed a rosy pink. "I didn't throw myself at him," she said, her voice husky. "And I don't think he was aroused. We're just friends, Aidan."

I let my hands fall from her face. My jaw locked with tension. "I can smell it, Jade. He wants you." My voice was stiff, low, furious, and my inner-wolf howled for blood.

My inner-wolf challenged me for dominance. I pressed against Jade, letting him take control, and I leaned in, taking her mouth with mine. She whimpered. Liquid fire ran through my blood. There was nothing careful about how I held her. I was done with being careful. She was mine. And by the sugar-sweet change in her scent, I could tell she didn't mind what I was doing.

I stepped into her, pushing her back until she was pressed against the tiled wall, caging her between my arms, and she melted against me. Heat crawled across my skin as her lips parted and her hot tongue pushed and tangled with mine.

The kiss helped to calm my inner-beast, but having our mate near, tasting her, wasn't enough. I broke the kiss and growled against her plump, swollen lips, "You're mine, do you understand me?"

"Yes," she whimpered, her inner-wolf flaring up in her golden eyes. Her fingertips ran along my back, her nails lengthening into claws as they descended along my spine.

"Say it," I growled against her mouth, my voice thick with need even to my own ears. "I want to hear you say it."

Jade took in a shuddering breath. I could scent the alpha within her, pushing for control, and it shocked the hell out of me when she tilted her head back and cocked it to the side, presenting her delicate throat to me. My inner-wolf howled with joy at her quick submission. "I'm yours," she murmured, her voice knotted and rough.

I growled, a soft rumble in my throat, and her alpha scent thickened in the air. Almonds and mixed fruits came at me in waves. My heart was pounding hard.

Her lips curved into a bemused smile. She cocked her head a little further, exposing more of her neck. "Looks like you're stuck with me, alpha," she said, lifting her shoulders in a delicate shrug. She sounded totally confident in that, but then she clucked her tongue, shifting her gaze to her feet. "Something happened that I should tell you about."

"What's that?" I asked, dreading the answer.

She looked up and touched my face with her fingertips, delicately running them along my cheekbone. "My inner-wolf ..." she started, stumbling over her words. Her face paled, and she pulled in a ragged breath. "Well ... she didn't respond to him." She shook her head, her hair falling forward, covering her eyes, and she dipped her chin, fixing her gaze on my chest. "Like at all." Her voice was whisper quiet as if what she was telling me was wrong to say out loud, and I waited for the bad part because I was certain there had to be a bad part to this, but so far, I wasn't seeing it. "She was quiet, calm, even when he hugged me. It was as if she didn't even notice he was there."

"You say that like it's a bad thing."

"No, not a bad thing." She took my hand in hers. "I didn't really get it at first. Actually, I kind of thought something was wrong with me. But I understand now."

She didn't seem willing to say more, but I was still simmering over her meeting up with Jared, and I needed to know. "You're killing me here, sweetheart," I said, trying to keep my voice gentle. I brushed her hair from her eyes, tucking it behind her ears. "What do you understand?"

She sighed, a painful and more than a little frustrated sigh. "That I'd never give you up. Not ever again. As soon as I saw you, even all growly and pissed off, my inner-wolf wanted to come out. She wanted to run to you, rub against you, feel you. But it's not just her. I wanted to do it, too. Me. All of me." She ran her fingers over my lips, and I shivered. "I adore you, Aidan David Collins, and it scares the hell out of me."

She straightened then, leaned up, brushed her lips against mine, and smiled up at me. The featherlight brush was nowhere near enough, and I tried to capture her mouth again, but she giggled, pushing at my chest. She tucked a long strand of dark hair behind her ear as she tried, and failed, to force her smile away. "I wasn't really inviting you *into* the shower with me."

"Sure sounded like it to me," I said, giving her the crooked, half-grin that I knew made her knees weak.

Jade giggled and ducked away from me. I reached out to pull her back, but she sidestepped and headed toward the line of showers.

I stood there, looking after her for a stunned moment, and she glanced over her shoulder, grinning. That grin was all it took for me to follow. I closed the distance between us in a few long strides, letting a low growl rumble from my throat. She squealed, a delighted kind of sound, and I pulled her into my arms.

I dipped my head, pressing my lips to hers. She gasped as I pulled her bottom lip between my teeth. Her gasp quickly turned into a soft moan. She wound her hands around my neck, stepping back into one of the open stalls, pulling me with her.

Her silky hands gripped at my shirt, tugging and pulling, lifting it up. Her fingertips traced along my stomach and up my chest, and she pulled back from me, just enough to tug off my shirt, before leaning in and placing a trail of burning kisses along my shoulder.

I buried my lips against her neck, kissing and nipping my way up to her ear. Her skin was warm, smooth, sweet. I let my hands roam down her back and slip under the edge of her tank top, pulling her as close as I could get her.

"Aidan!" Dominic shouted as a round of thumping bangs against the locked door reverberated through the change room. "Open the damn door!"

"Not now, Dom," I shouted back before focusing back on Jade's sweet and smooth neck.

"You live with her, man," he bellowed. "You can do whatever you're doing later. Get out here!"

I opened my mouth to tell him to screw off when Jade said, "He's right. You should probably go." She squirmed in my arms, pulling back and breaking away, as she blushed, a deep red.

"He can wait," I said, smirking down at her and leaning in for another kiss.

"Aidan," she said against my mouth. "I don't think I'm ready for this. You should go."

I leaned back a little, searching her face. Her lips were red, plump, and swollen. Her skin, flushed, and her scent was full of need, but her eyes held a hint of uncertainty that twisted my gut. I nodded, stealing a quick kiss, and smiled down at her. "I'll go get you a change of clothes," I said, and before I could change my mind, I turned from her and went straight for my locker.

CHAPTER 23

JADE

Aidan grabbed me his spare gym clothes, jogging pants, and a T-shirt, told me not to even think about putting back on the clothes that smelled of Jared, and then left me alone to shower.

My entire body was thrumming. My inner-wolf was a bundle of tender nerves, pressing against my heated skin. I didn't know whether to be glad or furious that Dominic interrupted us. I was trying to be sensible about the whole thing. Yes, I wanted Aidan, but I was only eighteen and him, nineteen. Wolves mate for life. It wasn't like we could change our minds later. It just didn't happen. And really, once our scents mixed, it couldn't happen. I would be his, and he would be mine. So yes, I was trying to be sensible, but my inner-wolf didn't want to be sensible. And her instant need to claim him was driving me crazy.

Keeping Aidan's jogging pants up on my hips took three bunching knots along the waistband. His T-shirt was baggy on me, too, but I didn't care. After securing the clothes the best I could, I gave my wet hair another tight ring-out and twisted it into a messy knot, and then I went to find Aidan.

The headquarters was relatively busy for a Saturday morning, or I guess it was early afternoon now. As I walked through the brilliant white hallways of the hulking maze-like building, I passed quite a few pack members. A few cut me dirty looks, and a few offered causal greetings, but most of them just ignored me, which kind of sucked. But I was working on that, and it would change, definitely, hopefully.

"He hasn't woken up yet. There's a stench to him, but that could just be him. The boys have clammed up, too, since Jared got back."

I heard the lazy, gravelly voice drifting past the slightly ajar door of Aidan's office as I walked through the lobby. I paused for a moment and took a deep breath. Aidan's scent flooded my nostrils, and I went to the door, nudging it open. "Who hasn't woken up yet?" I asked.

Aidan looked up, smiled, and then exchanged a look with Tommy, Chris, and Dominic, sitting on the couch. He gestured for me to come in, and I shook my head, cracking a smile, because, well, I wasn't really asking for an invitation. As I padded across the room and rounded his desk, he pushed back his chair, and I hopped up on the edge, facing him. "Well?" I said, folding my arms over my chest. "Who hasn't woken up yet?"

He scanned me up and down a couple times before his eyes settled on my chest. He let out a frustrated groan and tugged a hoodie off the back of his chair. "Put this on," he said hastily, tossing his sweater at me.

I glanced down at myself, not sure what his issue was. I noticed it fairly quickly, though, and I rolled my eyes at him. I pulled on the sweater and said, "You told me not to put my clothes back on, Aidan. I was wearing a tank with a built-in bra."

"I want you to go home, sweetheart," he said.

"Good for you, but I'm not going," I said, glancing over the scattered papers that littered his desk. Status reports on the team, bank statements, and income statements for the different establishments the pack owned in town were strewn everywhere. "I've got work to do. I was thinking about going out with the team, too, help them search the next section of land." I folded my arms over my chest, looking back at him. "Now tell me, who hasn't woken up?"

Dominic chuckled, and I was pretty sure the gravel-sounding snicker came from Tommy. I swiveled, cutting them each a dirty look, and the laughter died abruptly, although all three of them were grinning.

Aidan's warm hand clasped my hip as he moved in closer. His emotion shone brightly in his eyes, a deep stormy sea of anger and adoration and dread. He puffed out his chest, his lips drawn tight. His scent increased, and, well, I laughed. I shouldn't have, but I couldn't help it. I knew what he was doing, trying to distract me, and it wasn't going to work.

He leaned forward and kissed me on the lips, sweet and warm, with none of the intensity from before. It was gentle, tender. Full of all the emotion that I knew was growing inside him, the same emotion that was building within me. "You're not going anywhere with Jared," he said. "If you wanted to go out with the team, you should have thought about that before you brought him back." He said it as if it were simple and something I should have already thought of.

"Be serious, Aidan." I nudged him back a little and tried to laugh it off.

He let his scent trickle into the air and gave me a grin that was at least half-wolf. "Oh, I am, sweetheart. I'm very ..."

I put my hand over his mouth, stopping him from saying something stupid, and I stared him right in the face with a no-nonsense glare. "Tell me what's going on, Aidan."

I took my hand away slowly, keeping my glare fixed in place. He laughed a little as if he were in shock. "Go home, Jade." There was an unmistakable command in his tone, one that clearly told me he was the dominant one. He was to be listened to.

"Aidan, cut it out," Dominic said dryly. There was a little smile on his lips and amusement in his eyes. "Of course, she isn't going home. You wouldn't be able to watch her if she did." Clearly, whoever was sleeping was important to them if they felt the need to hide it from me. I wasn't sure if that was a good thing or not.

"Don't think he's interested in watching her anymore," Chris said. His face twisted into a frown, and he cut a sharp look in my direction.

Aidan's body went tense, but he didn't break eye contact with me. I cocked my head to the side, narrowing my eyes, trying to ignore the others as he was. I could feel the push of his alpha-wolf, trying to bend me to his will. It was strange. I had no idea what was happening or why there was a shift in him. But there was a shift, one that sent my inner-wolf into a panicked, angry frenzy in my belly. Was he trying to protect me from finding out the truth or manipulate me?

Silence fell. I wasn't really sure what Chris meant, but his words rattled me nonetheless. After what had just happened in the showers, I hadn't thought Aidan would let me out of his sight, at least not anytime soon. But as the silence stretched and I tried to make sense out of what was happening, Jared's first piece of training surfaced. *The moment you show weakness, you'll lose my inner-wolf, Jade,* he'd said. *"No matter what, you need to stay dominant. No matter how much you want to submit, don't. There is a place for submission, but only to your mate and only when it is necessary to appease his inner-wolf. You do it to show your respect. You do it to show you agree, to show others you are backing him. But submit when you shouldn't, and my inner-wolf will decide you are weak. He'll forget you. Never let him forget because if he does, so will I."*

Aidan held strong, his eyes wide, unforgiving, commanding. Was his inner-wolf forgetting me? Had I already lost that piece of him? I had shown my submission to him twice. Once to show I wouldn't argue with his decision to take me home, and once to show him I was his during a heated moment, but I wasn't really his mate — yet.

I gasped and almost lunged into his arms. Almost. For a hot second, all I wanted was his comfort. I wanted to hear him say that I hadn't made another epic mistake as alpha female or as his potential mate.

It was his growl that held me in place, a low and commanding sound that left me short of breath.

And I thought that this probably wasn't the best time to be passive or look for comfort, and I growled back, yep, I actually growled at him.

Quick vibrations littered my skin. "Aidan." My voice was a low snarl. My nails dug deep into my palms as I clenched my fists. My claws were itching to come out. Hair brushed under my skin, waiting to erupt. The need to dominate rushed at me. It was ... weird and a little freaky. It was one thing to show him my submission when we made out. My inner-wolf was happy to let him take the lead there. But here, in front of Tommy and Chris and Dominic, I was his equal, and he would either treat me like one or he would submit. It was black and white in my inner wolf's mind — simple.

His scent thickened, so did mine. My breath quickened, my body started to tremble. Blood rushed from my face in a cold flush of fever as I struggled to keep my chin level, my gaze on him. It was as if I were fighting an exhausting internal battle with my inner-wolf. She clawed for control while I wanted to bow, present my neck, and feel his warm lips flutter across me in acceptance. Or was that my inner-wolf, and it was me that wanted control? I wasn't one hundred percent sure right then.

His nostrils flared for a moment, and then he sat back in his chair and gave me an amused smile as if he'd simply decided to humor me. "Your father gave us a cougar. According to him, the guy had a death sentence for helping one of their prisoners escape, and your dad was supposed to dispose of him. The wounds your father inflicted on him have healed, but he hasn't woken up."

"He gave you a cougar," I said slowly, processing this news. "Don't you think that maybe, just maybe, you should have told me that already?"

Aidan smiled his sexy, crooked smile that never failed to make my heart flutter. "I had other things on my mind, sweetheart," he said and winked. "More important things."

"Going all growly on me because I hugged a friend was more important?" I pursed my lips, trying for annoyed, but I was pretty sure I failed. "Might want to rethink your priorities there, honey."

It seemed strangely unreal that my father would give us one of his own. I leaned against the countertop in the makeshift kitchen of the pack building, sipping on hot chocolate loaded with frothy whipped cream, wondering why he would when I thought it did seem somehow appropriate. Dad had to have guessed that Aidan hadn't believed him about not knowing how many cougars there were or where they were hiding. What better way to show he was on our side than by giving us someone who knew the ins and outs of the werecougars, even if he wasn't able to tell us anything yet.

I squinted against the bright rays of the setting sun that streamed through the window. The parking lot was half full, and a knot of people gathered by the cars. They mostly looked unhappy and on edge, but then I couldn't really blame them. Aidan had decided to tell everyone about the cougar we had acquired, and no one really knew how to take it. For the most part, the pack wanted the sleeping man dead, and no one was all that pleased with me that I wanted to keep him alive.

The thing was, I figured that if my dad had, in fact, been about to kill him, then he might be willing to help us if he woke up. And even if he wasn't willing, there was a reason he'd been given to us. I wanted to know what that reason was.

And I was also almost positive that I needed to get my mom away from my dad, which was absurdly ridiculous. We had no solid reason to suspect she knew anything about what was going on, but we didn't have a solid reason to doubt it either. Pulling her out would tip off my dad, but then, maybe that was a good thing. This defensive strategy wasn't really getting us anywhere, and I was beginning to wonder if going on the offensive was what we should have done all along.

Aidan hadn't strayed far from me since our little dispute in his office. I still felt the weird shift in him, and it hurt, but only a little. At least he still felt the need to stay close by. It was definitely better than ignoring me.

I snuck a peek at him. He sat at a scratched-up round

table, nursing his coffee as he studied the map of the forest surrounding Dog Mountain. We'd made a lot of progress over the last couple of days, but there was still a lot of land to search before we could move on to the surrounding towns.

Aidan glanced up at me, and his eyebrows rose. "What?"

"I think we need to stop watching and act," I said, shocked that I actually voiced my thoughts. So was Aidan, judging by the wide-eyed look he gave me. I sighed. "I've been justifying waiting to myself because we didn't have enough information. Dad wants to use me, but we don't know what for. He also said I was your weakness. I'm going to take a wild guess here, but I figure he's going to use me to get to you, although I don't have a freakin' clue why. The longer we wait because I don't want to hurt my dad, the more people who could suffer — will suffer. And my mom ..." I swallowed, dropping the thought.

"We don't need to rush," he said, but it wasn't believable. I knew he was just saying it to make me feel better, to give me a sense of security that really wasn't there.

"Did you call Luken?"

Aidan nodded. "He wants to join the team. He wants to help find them."

"And he thought I wouldn't understand." It wasn't a question. It seemed crazy that he thought I wouldn't understand that. "What did you tell him?"

"I told him that he needed to talk it over with Jared," he bit out, annoyed.

I huffed. "I know you don't want Jared here, but we need him. The pack needs to see I'm with you, and the three of us working together will help. I should have talked to you first, but let's face it, you've been a bit overbearing lately. You would have told me no.

We would have argued. I'm just trying to fix the mess I made." I waved a hand in his direction. "Clearly, it's a bigger mess than I thought."

"About earlier," he said, raking a hand through his hair and shifting his gaze.

"I get it," I said when he didn't continue. "We aren't really mates. I shouldn't have rolled over to you. But you try and pull that crap again, and you'll be the one rolling over."

He let out a soft growl and met my eyes again. His were crinkled with humor. "Sure, you keep telling yourself that, sweetheart."

I rolled my eyes. "I've got to get going." I downed the last mouthfuls of my drink and rinsed out my mug in the sink. I walked over to him and gave him a peck on the cheek before heading for the door. "They're probably waiting."

"Hey, hold up," he said, snagging my wrist and pulling me to a stop.

"Aidan, don't start," I said, turning into him. My voice was growlier than I intended, and I quickly cleared my throat, attempting to hide my frustration. "I'm going. I need to do something. I can't just sit here. And besides that, my skin is crawling. I need to shift." And it was. My skin was rippling and prickly and itchy. My inner-wolf needed out.

He chuckled, and I couldn't help but smile. Man, I loved his laugh. "I'm not going to stop you," he said. "I just wish I could go with you." He stood up and pulled me into his arms. I wrapped mine around his waist, looking up at him.

"Yeah, well, we don't always get what we want," I told him dryly. "One of us needs to stick around and be available, and you're the better option for that. They like you, me not so much. And I really think it will help my image with you agreeing that I should work with them. You know, let the pack see you're okay with it, with him."

He dipped his head and pressed his lips to mine in a quick kiss that left me breathless and, to my dismay, panting for more. "I don't know what I'm going to do with you." He chuckled. "One minute you're growling at me, and the next you're melting into me."

"I believe you growled first," I said, batting my eyes in an attempt to look innocent. "It's about time I growled back."

CHAPTER 24

AIDAN

I walked Jade to the doors, hating every damn step, and although I'd said all the right things to make her happy, I felt ... on edge and a little empty. I knew she was right, but it didn't mean I had to like it. It just seemed stupid to let her go out to hunt down the cougars. It went against every protective instinct I had.

Oh, hell. There were so many other things to worry about right now, but the only thing on my mind was the weird-ass way my inner-wolf was reacting to her.

For a moment, I indulged myself and imagined what it would have been like to claim her in the showers. What her peachy skin would have felt like against mine. What her hands and lips, grazing all over my body, would have felt like. Seeing that fiery passion in her eyes. I could almost smell the change in her scent and in mine.

The fantasizing was a good diversion, but it didn't help.

It's going to be fine, I thought. I just had to breathe. She wasn't going to be alone. She'd have the team. She'd have Jared. Okay, so that didn't help either. But they wouldn't let anything happen to her, right?

And the cougars were smart. They changed locations frequently. They hid their tracks. Based on the last week of hunting them, the odds of her actually running into one of them were low.

Knowing that should have helped, too. It really should have. But it didn't.

There was still a good crowd in the parking lot when we got outside. At first glance, I didn't think any of them noticed Jade. It hadn't been obvious that they were watching her join the team, and for a moment, I thought that maybe her shifting in private was a bad move. Too discreet to draw attention. But as I followed her out the doors, I realized they were watching. I caught the sidelong glances checking out the matte-black wolf trotting away from me and the arched eyebrows in my direction, and I forced a smile to show I was supporting her.

When she reached the edge of the forest where the wolves were gathered, Jade twisted to look behind her, and her bright golden eyes settled on me. She let out a sound that was somewhere between a growl and an excited yip.

"Be careful, sweetheart," I called, lifting my hand in a little wave. *Just breathe. She's going to be fine. We are going to be fine.* Damn, it would be better not to feel anything right now.

As the team and Jade took off into the forest, I spotted Tommy and Chris leaning against the building with Dominic. And oh, they weren't happy. Even if Tommy's shiny head wasn't redder than a blistering sunburn, the hot spike in the air would have given it away. Clearly, they didn't appreciate Jared telling them to hang back from the hunt.

"Hey," Dominic said as I approached. He was frowning and giving me one of those looks that told me he knew I was on the verge of cracking. I had to give it to him; he knew how to read me. "She can handle herself. She'll be fine."

I nodded but didn't say anything. He was right. I knew it. He knew it, too. But knowing it didn't mean that I liked her going any better. But I made a conscious effort to dial back my anxiety.

My relaxed persona must have been somewhat convincing because as I settled in with them, Dominic chuckled and then said, "You know. She once told me that there's nothing sexier than a man who's in love with his woman and not afraid to show it."

Tommy and Chris chuckled, and both of them rolled their eyes.

Dominic flashed them a bright, pearly white grin, full of exaggerated smugness. "Laugh all you want," he said. "I may not date women, but I know what I'm talking about when it comes to impressing them." And then he grimaced. "Mac and Jade like to talk — a lot."

I had to laugh. If Dominic knew anything about Jade or Marcy, it was only how to piss them off. Except it really did sound like something Jade would say. The question was: how was I supposed to show how much I loved her without coming across as being possessive or overbearing? That's what I wanted to ask, but what I said was, "She's not really *my*woman."

"Keep thinking like that, and she never really will be," he said and clapped me on the shoulder.

Something inside me flinched hard. "Yeah, well, we're still trying to work out our issues."

"Whatever, I'm not judging, man. Just sharing my wealth of knowledge on the mystery of what women want." He smirked, cutting me an angled side glance, and then said, "Come on, these two want a meeting."

"Sure," I said with a nod and pushed off the wall.

"I'm going to check in on the cougar. I'll meet you guys in my office in a few."

The headquarters had once been home to the pack. They had slept here, ate here. There was security in staying together. And the building had everything they had needed: beds, private rooms, kitchen, gym, media, and game rooms. It had been built to keep the pack together, and now it was just a place to conduct business.

The slap of my shoes echoed in the bright, empty hallways as I made my way through the building. I followed along and veered to the left where the old sleeping quarters were. Keeping the captive there was Jade's idea, insisting he be kept comfortable until we could determine if he truly was our enemy.

If I hadn't known where he was, I could have followed the smell of cougar, that odd mix of lemon and birch bark, all the way to where Richard slept. It gave the sterile pack headquarters a weirdly cold feel, smelling the enemy within its walls.

As I stepped out of the hallway and pushed through the doors that led to the rooms, Luken looked up and gave me a bright smile. He leaned against the wall, a phone in his hands, just outside the door to the captive's room.

"I didn't expect to see you here," I said. I knew he'd been planning to talk to Jared, but I figured he would have been shot down.

"Me neither," he admitted, hastily pocketing his phone and straightening as I approached. "Jared said he'd think about it and stuck me on guard duty while they're on the hunt." He shifted from one foot to the other and averted his gaze. "About Jade, sorry I gave her a hard time."

"I'm not the one you need to apologize to, man." The words sounded normal, but my tone was hard and direct. His smile dimmed, no longer looked bright but breakable, and I heaved a sigh. "If you would have talked to her, you wouldn't have to be stuck on guard duty. You'd be on that hunt with them right now. She would have gone to bat for you, and if that didn't work, she would have pestered him until he agreed."

He didn't look like he believed me, or it could have been that he just didn't want to believe me, but it was the truth. Jade would have welcomed the help, and she would have forced the issue until she won.

We stood there in silence; the only sounds were our breathing until he cleared his throat. "I'm guessing you came to see him," he said. He didn't wait for my answer before he turned and stiff-armed the door, letting it swing open.

"Any movement?" I asked as I stepped in and flicked on the light switch.

The room was simple, holding only a bed and dresser. The walls were painted in a pastel blue, and the window coverings were fringed with a pale green lace, the remnants of whichever pack member had once made it their own.

"Nothing yet," he said. "I've been checking every fifteen minutes."

My gaze locked on Richard lying flat on his back in the bed. He had passed out before the team had shown up at Jeff's. I hadn't thought much of it at first. He'd been so torn up and beaten at the time it had made sense that his body would shut down, try to heal. But the wounds were closed now, looking more like old scars than fresh cuts. And he didn't really look asleep. He was too still. His eyes didn't flutter. His muscles didn't twitch. It was almost as if he'd been drugged into a comatose state.

About ten minutes later, I made it back to my office, feeling about fifty different kinds of pissed-off. Not that I hadn't seen it coming, but I was now certain that the little gift from Jade's father was more of a distraction than anything else. The question was: what was he trying to distract me from?

Man, the urge to race out and beat the shit out of Jeff until I had the answers I needed was nearly irresistible. But then, so was the desire to keep Jade happy, and beating her dad wouldn't keep her happy. I seriously never thought loving someone could be this damn confining.

I heaved a sigh and settled in behind my desk. "I'm guessing this meeting is about your report on the team," I said. "What did you find out?"

I expected Tommy to tell me I was wrong and urge me to wait. They'd made it clear in the email that I should hear whatever it was from the team, but from the look he exchanged with Chris, I assumed my guess was right and that waiting was no longer an option.

"None of them are going to talk to you now that Jared's back and breathing down their necks." He collapsed onto the couch across from my desk and stretched his legs out in front of him. A slow, grim smile twisted his mouth, and he said, "The team, all five of them are half brothers. Same father, different mothers. Jared was born here, but the others came along a couple years ago."

I frowned and began tapping the pen in my hand against my desk restlessly. I looked at Dominic and cocked a brow. He was frowning, too, and shrugged as if this was the first he heard about this.

"Who's their father?" I asked as a fast ripple of irritation passed through me.

"That's the interesting part. You killed their father," Chris said, his voice carrying a dark undertone. He leaned forward in his chair, resting his forearms on his knees. "According to Landon, Ray tracked them down and changed them just before he fought and won alpha. He was building a pack that wouldn't think about trying to overthrow him, even before it was his."

I felt Dominic's eyes on me, and I dropped the pen, splaying my hands out on my desk, as I settled a glare on him. "Why doesn't anyone in this damn pack know about this?"

Dominic stared at me for a moment, his expression unreadable, and then said, "Knowing Ray, he probably didn't want anyone to know they were his sons. It explains a lot, though. The team always looked the other way when Ray stepped out of line. It was smart not to let anyone know. Too many gray lines when you have that many blood relatives in power positions. If I'd known, I would have fought it, and I'm sure others would have, too."

His weak explanation didn't improve my mood, even if it did shed some light on why all those pack members had cowered back, clearly afraid to interfere, while Ray had been beating his mate. If the team had always looked the other way, then there was no one to have their back if the alpha abused his power.

I was starting to feel a bit ill. "Should I be worried about Jade out there with them?"

"No." Tommy said it with certainty. "Landon and Mark are loyal to you. Beck is stuck in the middle somewhere, loyal to the pack and to his brothers, but he wouldn't let any of them, not even Jared, touch her. He loves her, even if he isn't sure about you."

"None of them will talk about Jared," Chris added. "They're trying to cover for him. It's pretty obvious he would love to see you dead. And Craig hates you for touching Erika."

I leaned back in my chair. I didn't know what surprised me more ... that two of them were loyal to me or that two of them would be happy to see me dead. I guessed it could have been worse.

"Don't blame yourself," Dominic said after a stretch of silence. "When your mate's ex-whatever-he-was wants you dead, he wants you dead. There's nothing you can really do about it. And besides," he shrugged, "Jared always wants someone dead. He'll get over it."

CHAPTER 25

JADE

I had expected to be taken to the last trail that was uncovered, or at least to the base of the mountain where the cougar tracks were thicker, but instead, the team had turned off and headed straight for a new patch of land that hadn't been searched. And I really didn't like where they were planning on searching. We were heading straight into the hunting camps.

I knew that hunting season wasn't open yet and that even if it was, hunting wolves was illegal, but even knowing that, it still didn't seem like such a hot idea to go running into a place that potentially had men with guns.

But I figured the hunting camps were a good place to look. They had shelter. They had beds. And they were only used a couple weeks of the year.

Jared's deep brown wolf led the way, keeping a muscle-burning pace. The team stayed with him, running in watchful silence. We ran for a solid twenty minutes before he finally slowed to a light jog and cut right, heading down a dirt roadway.

The roadway hadn't been traveled recently. Not a single tire track was pressed into the dirt. Trees hung overhead, and sprigs of weeds and grass had popped up sporadically down the center of the path. The forest was darkening quickly, the sun almost gone for the day, and skeletal shadows crisscrossed along the path in front of us.

Jared slowed again, veering left as he followed a bend in the trail.

And then the first camp came into view.

The building ahead had a rotting sign hanging over the door that read, *Brinkwell.* It was a large rustic-looking cabin made of logs. There wasn't much of a clearing, as if the owners had only cut down enough trees to make way for the structure, a few picnic tables, and a fire pit.

Beck moved in closer to me, hugging my side. He growled when I pulled back and away from him. It was a flat warning to stay close, and he reinforced it by nipping at my shoulder.

I stopped dead, cocking my head to look at him. His eyes stayed on mine as he dipped his head, pressing his muzzle to the ground. His nostrils were flaring with each long breath he took. He nosed at a small pile of leaves, pushing them toward me, and I breathed in the scent.

There was, I realized, a faint trace of cougar on those leaves.

Jared growled, and Craig, Mark, and Landon moved in around him. He pawed at the wooden door of the building, but it didn't budge. His coat began to shudder and ripple. The dry crack of bones sounded loudly in my ears. His fur receded in a quick, clean motion. And then he was human, standing on the rickety-looking deck. "Beck, don't leave her side," he said in a ragged pant, and then he shoved the door open.

AIDAN

"She's not going to like this," Dominic said, but he pushed the door open and hopped out of the car anyway.

I got out of the car and pressed the lock button on my key fob. "Yeah, well, Jade's worried about her, and I need to talk to her."

The Dog Mountain General Hospital didn't look different from a hospital in any other small town. The building was a nondescript brown brick structure. If it weren't for the big *Hospital* sign and even bigger *Emergency Entrance* sign, you wouldn't have even really known it was a hospital. There were two parked ambulances in the lot and a few cars, most likely belonging to the medical staff.

As I walked through the emergency doors, people noticed me. Everyone knew who I was, what I was. I didn't really like it, but I could do nothing about it. No one looked at me directly, but I could feel them watching from the corners of their eyes.

Mrs. Shaw sat behind the desk at the nurses' station, and she looked up as the doors slid shut behind us. She didn't smile as she said, "Hi, Dominic," and then she gave me a curt nod, "Aidan." In her late forties, she was an attractive woman dressed in bright floral scrubs. Her dark brown hair was tied in a tight bun. She looked a lot like her daughter, same big brown eyes, same nose and cheekbones.

"Hey, Mrs. Shaw," Dominic said with a little wave. His tone was light, and he smiled. "Could you maybe spare a minute?"

"Depends," she said. She didn't meet his gaze. Instead, she kept her cool brown eyes locked on me. "Is he here about my daughter or my husband?" Her tone was casual, sweet even, but her face was tight.

I approached the desk and leaned against it. Keeping my voice just as light, I asked, "Would it make any difference which one I'm here to talk to you about?"

"Yes," she said tightly and nodded. "Yes, it would."

"He's here about the team, Mrs. Shaw," Dominic said and smiled again. She didn't smile back, didn't even pretend to. "And about Jared stopping by to see Jeff this morning."

Mrs. Shaw swallowed hard. Her entire body tensed, and then like a rolling wave, she relaxed. "As you can see," she said, nodding toward the waiting room, "I've got work to do."

I glanced over my shoulder at the empty waiting room and frowned. I hadn't expected to get a *no*, at least not right away, and my heart sank a little. "Look, Pam," I said. "We can do it now when your husband isn't here, or I can come by the house later."

"Where's my daughter?" she asked, her voice cracking over the words. There was a subtle change in her scent, the tanginess of fear or paranoia, so light that I almost missed it, but it was there.

"She's out with Jared," I said, watching her closely. I leaned a bit closer, and dropping my voice low, I added, "And his brothers." She stared at me for a long, hard moment. Her fingers were trembling now, and the tanginess increased in the air. "I'm not trying to scare you, Pam," I added, feeling more than a little heartsick. "Really, I just have a couple of questions, and I promise you, your answers will remain confidential."

I was pretty sure she didn't believe me, but she let out a pent-up breath, and her shoulders sagged as she gestured to the closed door of the triage station.

JADE

There were more hunting camps hidden in the woods than I had thought. Big log structures full of bunk beds. We'd found three more in the last two hours, all of them empty, but all of them had the same scent of birch bark and lemon and cat.

But this one was different. This one had been vacated in a rush.

And it hadn't been empty long. The scent was thicker here, and it still clung to the grass and trees in the area.

We were getting closer.

The problem with getting closer, though, was that we learned some truths that I seriously could have done without knowing. One of those truths: they kept the women in cages made of thick barbed wire. We'd found traces of old human blood around the crude structures. And there were thick chains and long leather whips on the ground, the kind of whips you saw in the hands of large animal trainers.

It was best not to look at it. Better to keep going. Stay focused.

Beck stuck close to my side, so did Landon. Tension was running high within the team, and I had a feeling that Aidan and Tommy were right; the tension wasn't just from the hunt. The only one that paid any real attention to Jared was Craig. The others stayed focused on me, and through me, on the hunt.

I put my nose to the ground, searching for the trail. But there wasn't just one trail. There were many. Each one I followed wrapped around, branched off, met back up, and then backtracked. Each loop took me back to the same place. To the cages.

I scanned the grounds again, looking for anything I could have missed the first time. There had to be something. Had. To. Be. It just wasn't possible for a full pack to vanish without a trace.

I trotted toward the base of a towering oak that was roughed with deep gouging marks. Someone barked, Beck nudged at my side, and I growled, snapping out at him to leave me alone.

The gouges looked like claw marks, and they shot up into the low-hanging branches. Could they have climbed the trees? They were big cats. They could climb, right? Leap from tree to tree, hiding their real trail.

Beck nudged me again and growled another warning. I dodged to the left, circling the tree, and backed up to look at the trunk better. I heard the loud snap at the exact moment I was ripped from my feet and tossed into the air like a ragdoll.

And then I was hanging upside down, dangling by a leg about five feet from the ground.

Adrenaline took over. My bones began to remold, breaking and shifting, as I swung, bobbing, back and forth. As I finished the change back to human, sharp pain lanced through my leg as if a fireball had been shot within my body. The rope seemed as if it were tightening with each small movement, cutting deeper into my flesh. I screeched, and my eyes stung with tears, and for a moment, I lost my breath to the skin ripping, muscle tearing pain.

I couldn't hear anything over the loud buzzing in my ears as my blood rushed to my head. Thick warm liquid trickled down my leg, and I fought the panic that began to claw its way through my chest. I started to pull myself up, using my arms and abs. I needed to get the rope off. I needed to get down.

After a few grunts and a lot of muscle burn, I managed to loop my arms around my knees. And then I saw my mangled ankle. The rope had cut deep, hidden in my skin and under the blood, and I lost my balance, falling back to dangle again.

"I tried to warn you," Beck said with a rumbling chuckle. "Next time, don't shift. Your skin and muscles rip more easily while your body is reshaping."

"Glad you find this amusing," I snapped, fighting against the pain. I'd be damned if I was going to let him, one of the tough enforcers, see me cry over a little rope burn and cut.

Beck chuckled again, pacing around and staring up. I tried not to watch him, focusing on anything but his lean naked body or his wide, muscular shoulders. And it was in that second that I realized that I was hanging upside down, stark naked. I felt a blush reach my cheeks, and a whole new panic settled into my belly. My anxiety ratcheted up when the others gathered around him and started to shift. Laughter echoed through the air, hard and loud.

I should have stayed a wolf, I thought bitterly.

"This is so not funny, guys," I hissed, folding my arms over my chest in an attempt to cover my breasts. "And it hurts like hell, so get me down and don't look."

CHAPTER 26

"Well, shit," Dominic said. "I really didn't see that coming."

I glanced over at my beta. He was grinning like a fool as we left the hospital. He walked beside me with restless, twitchy steps as if he were itching to shift and burn off some energy.

"Really?" I asked. "'Cause I thought it was pretty obvious." I dug in my pocket for my keys and unlocked the car. The headlights flashed, lighting up the parking lot.

Dominic laughed. "Yep, that's right. You knew all along that Jared went over there to beg her father to help him get her back. And then when he said no, Jared tried to beat a *yes* out of him because Jared's always been the desperate type, and it's not like I can smell the stench of lies coming off you or anything."

Okay, so yeah, it was a lie. Whatever. At least I was now certain that Jade's mom knew nothing of what her husband was really into. The woman truly believed he worked for my pack. And she also believed he was a good man. Knowing that lifted a little stress, although not enough.

217

I got into the car, slamming the door, and when Dominic jumped in, he was still laughing. I narrowed my eyes at him and wondered if I just kept my mouth shut, if maybe, just maybe, the conversation would end.

When the silence stretched, he laughed. "Come on, Aidan, lighten up."

"How I am supposed to lighten up about this?" I pushed back my hair. "Jade is just a trophy to him. A prize. Something to wave in my face. And she doesn't see it. You heard what Pam said. Jared's using her to get to me. The pain it would cause me was his damn bargaining chip this morning." *Oh, hell.* I was really starting to feel like a failure. As a male. As an alpha. And it was burning away my sense of self-worth.

"Start by picturing Jared begging," he said, chuckling. "Then picture the look on Jade's face when you tell her about this."

I winced and looked away. "I'm picturing the look, Dom, and it burns."

JADE

Beck cut me down — literally — and I fell five feet, butt naked, into Landon's arms. As I landed, all I could think was, thank God Aidan wasn't around for this one. He would have lost his freakin' mind.

Within seconds of landing, Mark had tossed a dirty old wool blanket over me, covering me up, and then Landon carried me inside the hunting camp. He'd put me down on a ratty old couch that had some odd patchwork pattern on it. The thing was faded and worn, but it was ridiculously comfortable, and after thirty minutes of sitting on it, I was ready to take the ugly thing home with me. It was that comfortable.

Having the rope pulled out of my skin was not fun, and yep, I screamed and cussed up a storm. The raw gash it had left behind ran all the way around my ankle and cut through the muscle, almost to the bone. But it was out now, the wound was healing, and the bleeding had stopped.

The guys had found some clothes: bright orange hunting jackets and coveralls. I felt as if I were drowning in them. The jacket was rough against my skin, and so were the stiff jean coveralls. But at least we were all clothed as we waited for my leg to heal enough to make the trek home.

A cold sweat broke out over my skin as I shifted on the couch, placing my foot down flat and putting some pressure on it. Pain shot through my body like fire, and I quickly swallowed the gasp. I'd been testing it almost every five minutes now, but still, it hurt — bad.

"That's going to hurt like hell for a few hours," Landon said. He was hovering, so was Mark. It was getting close to suffocating. And each time Jared moved, they slid closer to me, pinning him with heated glares.

The only reason I pretended to ignore their crazy aggression was because they looked as if they were ready to smack Jared around, and my instinct was telling me that if I called attention to it, it would only make things worse.

"I'm good," I hissed. "We've got to get back. Let Aidan know what we found."

"Jade, you need to heal," Beck said and gave me one of those firm *big brother* kind of looks. He stood under one of the light fixtures, and the way the light hit his face made his cheekbones look hollow and the creases above his brow, harsh.

"No," I said, shaking my head. "I need to get out of here. Seriously, this place creeps me out." I glanced over at Jared and wasn't really surprised to see him still brooding, leaning against the doorframe. "You done searching the area?" I asked him.

He looked me over with cold, harsh eyes, and as he did, I tried to remember a time when he'd ever looked at me with even a sliver of warmth. I couldn't. Jared didn't do warm. His voice might heat a little, but that gaze was pretty much always cold. Right then, all I wanted was to get home and see Aidan. See his warmth. Feel some heat. I forced a smile, trying to show I was good to go, even if I wasn't sure if I actually was.

He didn't answer me, and nobody else spoke up, so I finally said, "Jared, I want to go home now."

Then, without breaking the cold eye contact, he pushed off the doorframe. He stalked toward me with a slow, predator-like grace, his lips lifting into a sly grin. "Your scent draws him to you, but does he love you?" His tone was flat.

I stayed silent for a moment, wondering where the hell his question had come from. A flicker of unease tightened in my chest as he watched me expectantly, waiting. My forced smile faded, and I frowned. "Yes, yes he does."

"Then you don't love him." More coldness. God, I could almost feel it in the air, pulsing out from him.

"I do love him." I said it fiercely, so fiercely that I was pretty sure I shocked the entire team. For a breathless moment, they all turned to stare at me, stunned. The moment didn't last.

Jared took another slow, stalking step and stopped smiling. "Then why haven't you claimed him?" His question cut through me like a knife's blade.

Mark and Landon moved closer to me, their faces as hard as a stone. They growled, low and deadly, their gaze locked on Jared, watching his approach with trained eyes. Craig turned, moving in, flanking Jared. His eyes flared, and his muscles began to tick all along his neck.

"Jared, that's close enough." Beck's voice barely carried over the increasing sound of the growling coming out of Mark and Landon, and it didn't stop Jared from taking another step.

The five of them, Jared and Craig on one side, Mark, Landon, and Beck on the other, stared off. The growls increased as the tension rose. The air crackled with it, and I started to crack.

"What the hell has gotten into you all?" I shouted. My imprint heated, my skin shuddered. I let my scent thicken, hanging like a heavy mist over us, and I focused on calling their attention to my alpha wolf. The echo of growls slowly softened, and then there was only the heavy pumping sound of their breathing.

Jared recovered first as my scent began to recede, and he looked at me with a haze of violence clouding his face. His lips pulled up at the corners again, but his eyes stayed cold and black. "Come on, kitten," he snarled. "We all know why you asked me to come back. And don't think no one has noticed that it's you who's standing in Aidan's way from trying to kill me. It would take a moron not to see it." He took another step toward me.

Beck shoved him back so hard that Jared stumbled. "I said that's close enough." His voice was a low, menacing growl as he faced off with Jared. "Take one more step, and I will kill you."

Dammit! What the hell is going on with my team? I harnessed my scent again and forced their attention. It took a bit longer than the last time, but one by one, they each started to relax, thankfully not fighting the call of my alpha wolf. Jared even bowed a little. The show of respect was a shocker. And then he gripped Craig's arm and dragged him out the door.

AIDAN

Running on the treadmill turned out to be a good relief. It kept me focused and let me think as I waited for Jade to return. My thighs were screaming as I hit the tenth mile, but I wasn't ready to stop. I increased the incline, found my stride, and kept going.

Dominic had finally given up on trying to talk to me and left. I figured that was probably for the best. The more I thought about the information that Tommy and Chris had uncovered, the more I wanted to punch something. And listening to Mrs. Shaw confirm it all plus some, seriously hadn't helped.

I knew the team was a necessary evil to defend my pack, not just from outside threats but from me. But I kept coming to the same conclusion: I needed to disband them and build a new team. Blood was thicker than pack to some, and those boys were a perfect example of that. *Dammit!* Jade had had enough heartbreak. She didn't need this.

At that moment, the gym doors swung open. Jade. Her scent filled the air like a warm breeze through a farmer's fruit field. I glanced up. Landon had a loose arm around her waist, and she leaned into him as she limped into the room. Mark and Beck crowded in behind them. And none of them looked happy.

I hit the emergency stop button and was off the treadmill before the belt stopped rolling. Jade looked pale, and the scent of her pain mingled with her natural fragrance, causing anxiety to spike through my head. My instincts fired up because Jared and Craig weren't with them, and that had to mean something had gone wrong. More wrong than her being hurt. Even if he hated me, Jared wouldn't leave her like this. He wouldn't. My mouth went dry as if my tongue had shriveled up, and a low rumbling sound went through my chest.

Just as I was going to go to her, she said, "Before you get all growly ..." Pain laced her voice, and it showed in the deep lines on her forehead. She sucked in a breath. "I can't walk without his support yet." She wasn't looking at me. Knowing her, she didn't want me to see the pain in her eyes. She probably figured it was a weakness.

I went to her in a rush and gathered her into my arms. As soon as she was settled against me, I felt her soothing hands stroke down my shoulders as if she thought I needed calming. "What happened to you?" I demanded. My voice was too harsh, raw. Maybe I did need calming.

"Hunter's trap," she said. She leaned into me, kissing my cheek at the corner of my mouth. "I was looking at some claw marks on a tree when I got snagged in a trap." Her hand brushed over my chest and drifted up to my cheek. "I'm fine. Really, I'm fine."

I lifted my gaze, fixing it on the boys. "Where are Jared and Craig?"

"Taking a breather," Beck said. He fell into an attack posture, bending his knees, bringing his arms up. "And it's best they take it."

I glared at Beck and let out a bitter laugh. My chest burned so badly with white-hot rage that I thought if Jade wasn't pressed against me, I'd probably let him attack and then kill him for trying it. "Which one of them are you willing to fight me to protect?"

He didn't get a chance to respond. Jade stiffened and dragged in a lungful of air. "Aidan, let this one go," she said, brushing another kiss over my cheek.

She glanced over her shoulder. "Beck, you'd better relax that glare you have fixed on my mate."

I was so pissed off that it took me a moment to see what was happening right in front of me. Without a word, Beck relaxed and whipped his head down, fixing his gaze to the floor, obeying her command.

My jaw dropped on its own, no matter how hard I tried to keep it up. I couldn't believe she had spoken to him with that kind of command. And I really couldn't believe that he had listened. Wait, had she just called me her mate?

I put a hand over my eyes and scrubbed at my face. Okay, this was good, right?

Her scent shifted then, and it confused the hell out of me. I could smell her pain, but there was also a thick flare of sweetness, the same sweetness she'd had in the showers. Her delicate touches were ruining my focus, and when I glanced down at her, it was clear that that was exactly what she was trying to do. Distract me.

Sitting down seemed like a damn good idea right then.

I shook off my fury and sucked in a breath, and then I scooped her up and carried her over a weight bench. I sat her down gently and kneeled in front of her. Once she was settled, I took the foot she'd been favoring into my hands, rolling up her jeans. Her ankle was swollen and raw-looking, with an angry red line encircling it. I looked over my shoulder, glaring. "How the hell did she get so hurt?"

Landon grinned, shaking his head. "She shifted while she was dangling upside down by the rope." He chuckled. "You've been too easy on her. Our girl stays with you for a few days, and she forgets everything we taught her."

"It's not funny," Jade hissed as a rosy flush crept up

her neck. She managed to put the entire definition of embarrassment into it.

And that's when I fully understood her scent and the touches. The entire team had seen my mate naked, dangling by a rope, and she probably assumed I'd lose it. I knew I shouldn't have, but I smirked and chuckled. Seriously, I had never met a werewolf who was as paranoid about being seen naked as she was. It was adorable and incredibly impractical.

She must have seen me realize it because she said, "Not a word, Aidan." Her eyes blazed with fire. Her throat worked hard, and another brilliant flush crept up her neck.

I quickly swallowed my chuckle and put on my best serious expression. I figured it wasn't very good because Jade rolled her eyes and pursed her lips. "Tell him what we found, guys," she snapped.

"Uh-huh, sure," Beck said with a stiff nod and came over to us. He wouldn't look at me, but then that was probably a smart choice on his part because, yep, I was still simmering. "We searched four hunting camps. They'd been in all of them. I'm pretty sure the last one was where the *accident* happened." He looked a little green suddenly, and he swallowed a few times before continuing. "There were barbed wire cages with traces of human blood, whips, chains ..." Another hard swallow. "Jade found claw marks on the trees."

"They're climbing the trees," Landon added. "It's why we keep losing their damn trail." He was still in the doorway, stiff and straight. His tall, long legs were like thick boards, and his arms hung like metal rods, rigid and unbendable. He stared at me with wide, red-rimmed, baby-blue eyes. I could almost taste his anxiety in the air. He looked back at me with an intense focus, and I got the gut-twisting sinking feeling that he knew Tommy and Chris would have told me everything while they were gone.

"The marks were deep, not just one of them scratching, but really cut in," Mark continued. "I think Jade's right about them climbing, but I can't see how they could jump from tree to tree. It's not like they're small cats. You'd think the branches would snap on the landing."

"About Jade ..." Beck started, shoving his hands in his pockets. He glanced down as if he were trying to put some words together in his head but couldn't quite find any he liked.

"Don't worry about it, guys," she said in a low, calm voice. "I'm almost as good as new. Honest." But she wasn't. She started to tremble as she gave me a bright, brittle smile.

"Sorry we didn't take Tommy and Chris with us," Landon said. He looked overly calm, and his glare was still pointed.

Oh, hell. He must know they told me. With a shrinking feeling, I wondered if I should apologize for killing their dad.

Landon smiled then, a sad smile, and before I could think of anything to say, he said, "You should probably take her home. She's exhausted."

CHAPTER 27

JADE

I grabbed a steamy breath of air. My nerves were too tight, too bunched up under my skin, and the blistering shower wasn't helping much.

Aidan had been so quiet on the drive home as if he'd been waiting for me to open up. He hadn't asked anything, and I hadn't either. The words had been on the tip of my tongue, but they hadn't fallen from the safety of my mouth. Why was it so hard to admit that I may have been wrong?

Beck had threatened to kill Jared, hadn't he? And then he'd threatened to attack Aidan, too. Jesus, I'd been so surprised by the menace I saw in those guys tonight. I'd always known they could be scary. I even remembered when I went to all costs to avoid them. But they had always been close with each other. Always.

But they weren't close. Not now. Not anymore. And it was my fault. I didn't have a clue why, but I knew, just knew that it was.

If I hadn't stepped in, harnessing my inner-alpha, well, I wasn't really sure if we all would have made it back. No, I wasn't sure of that at all.

Commanding them the way I had really hadn't left a good taste in my mouth. It was the vicious look that Jared had given me that made me feel sick as if I'd stepped over a line by using my inner-alpha on him and his team. I'd stripped him of his authority without thinking, and I was pretty sure he would never forgive me for that.

Damn, I still felt sick.

My eyes watered, and I leaned my forehead against the tiled wall as the scalding water beat against my skin. I'd been such a fool to bring Jared back into the mix. I should have just let him go.

By the time I'd finally turned off the water, it had started to run cold, but at least I was beginning to feel a little more like myself. I dressed in a rush, pulling on jeans and a sweater, and went straight for the kitchen. My stomach was grumbling, and the house smelled deliciously like *Shake 'N Bake* chicken.

Aidan stood over the sink, elbows deep in suds as he scrubbed at a baking sheet. When he saw me, he grinned. "How's the ankle?" he asked, drying off his hands on his jeans.

"Hurts, but it's getting better," I said. I hobbled over to the table and sat down. It was set, which seemed out of place. Aidan just didn't set the table. He didn't usually eat at it either. Mealtime was more of a *grab-and-go* thing with him, leaving everything on the stove. Normally, we would dish out what we wanted before heading to the couch. But at the table were three lit candles, placed in the center, the flames tall and flickering. "What's all this?" I asked, eyeing the candles suspiciously.

Aidan went to the oven, pulled it open, and with a towel draped over his hands, he pulled out two heaping plates of chicken and vegetables. He placed a steaming plate in front of me. "I'm trying to make up for my crappy growling earlier."

I laughed a full-belly laugh, and darn, it felt good. "By lighting smelly candles?"

He rounded the table, set down his own plate, and took a seat. He gave me one of his lopsided grins and gestured to the plates filled with chicken and vegetables. "And I cooked dinner."

I smirked, trying not to laugh again. "You could also just say sorry, you know."

Aidan looked down at the table, furrowing his brow. "Isn't this better?" he asked. He was absolutely serious.

I blinked, shaking my head. "Nope, saying sorry is always better." I closed my fingers around my fork and scooped up a piece of broccoli. "That way, I get to feel like I was right."

He snorted and rolled his eyes. He looked as if he were about to say something, but he must have thought better of it, and dug into the food instead, which was probably the smart thing to do given the wicked smirk that was playing on his lips.

We ate in silence for a few minutes. The food, like always, was fan-freakin-tastic. One of the things I loved about Aidan, the man knew how to cook. The chicken was juicy; the vegetables warm but still had that nice crunch. Delicious.

I swallowed a mouthful of chicken and looked up. "Something is really wrong with the team," I said. As soon as the words were out of my mouth, I kind of wished I hadn't said them because it was pretty much the last thing I wanted to talk about right then.

Slurping his drink, Aidan leaned back in his chair. His smirk was gone. "Yeah," he said.

Considering what had happened with Beck, I really expected more than just *Yeah*, but it didn't look like I was going to get it. In fact, he was looking at me with a perfectly guarded expression, which was weird. Aidan wasn't much for guarding his feelings, at least not with me. With me, he kind of sucked at it.

I pushed some food around my plate, glanced back up at him, and heard myself ask a question that I wasn't sure I really wanted the answer to. "How did you know I was with Jared earlier?"

"Your Dad," he said, forking a piece of chicken and popping it into his mouth. He chewed it slowly, considering, and then swallowed it down. "Jared beat the shit out of him and then took off when you called."

I was thrown for a minute, and I was sure my eyes went saucer wide. "What was Jared doing with my dad?" I dropped my fork. "Wait. He hit my dad?"

Aidan nodded. His eyes were darkening, a rich brown velvet and some of the guardedness faded as if he had just then decided to tell me what was going through his head. "Jeff said something about people getting hurt when he fights with his brothers."

I stared at him blankly for a few long seconds, trying to understand what Jared's fighting had to do with anything. I puffed out a breath. Pulled one in and said, "He doesn't have any brothers." I was sure of that.

"About that." Aidan set his fork down. He watched me with an intense stare, the kind that he usually reserved for when I was pissing him off or when he was about to tell me something I really didn't want to hear. "He does have brothers, four of them."

And just like that, our nice dinner turned into a long, long evening.

Eventually, Aidan finished telling me about the newest piece of information that Tommy and Chris had found out. He told me about his concerns with everyone in the team being brothers and stressed that he thought we should take apart the team and rebuild it.

He went on to fill me in on how the pack had handled me taking off with the guys, which, as it turned out, was better than I had hoped, and he thought that some of the males were warming up to me. I thought that it was about time we had some good news.

But then he told me about his visit with my mother, and when he was done, I was pretty much numb.

He kept his tone detached and direct through the whole thing, only giving the facts and closing off all emotion. Except, he watched me as if he were assessing just how upset I was about the news, which, on a scale of one to ten, I was sitting somewhere near an eleven.

Given everything he told me, it was a surprisingly short conversation, and when he finished, I tried to tell him about what had happened at the camp, but he cut me off, gave me a kiss, and told me nothing had to be decided tonight, and then, he went to take a shower.

I puttered around the kitchen, washing the last few dishes. I thought about everything. About what I could fix and what was completely out of my control. But mostly, I thought about how this was the first time Aidan had talked to me, really talked to me, about pack stuff without trying to protect me.

I stretched and changed into a pair of boxers and a tank in the bedroom. I pulled my hair back, tying it into a loose knot, and waited for Aidan to finish his shower.

I had every intention of staying awake. I really did. I wanted to talk to him about what had gone down at the hunting camp and about what we found, but as I laid down and my head hit the pillow, sleep took me in a rush.

AIDAN

Jade was a bed hog.

I had an elbow digging into my ribs and a knee in my back. The covers were kicked off the bed, not even a sheet left. I went to roll over a little, but I couldn't. Somehow she'd managed to shove me to the edge of our king-size bed.

The space on the other side of her was loaded with the pillows she'd flung. She had even snagged mine, I noticed, which she was now using as her own.

I held in my laugh and worked to dislodge her knee and elbow without waking her up. She made a contented sound from the back of her throat and wrapped an arm around me, nuzzling her head into my side. She didn't fully wake up, stuck somewhere between sleep and awareness, and when I kissed her forehead, she sighed, and then her breathing deepened and evened out, and she was lost in sleep again.

I probably should have been asleep, too, but sleep was definitely not my friend tonight. My brain was too full of useless little bits of information. The team was all brothers. I killed their father. Jared wanted revenge in the form of taking Jade. The cougars kept their women in cages. They used whips. They used chains. We didn't know where to find them. Jade's mom was innocent and trapped in a house with the devil. The devil was Jade's dad. I loved Jade. Craig wanted me dead. Jade loved the pack. She wanted to protect the team. The information was starting to sound like a record, with a pounding base, playing on instant repeat through my head over and over. There was lots of information, but not enough on any one thing to really do anything with. Utterly useless.

I grabbed my phone from the nightstand, checking to see if there was any news about our sleeping captive.

Nothing. It was just after three in the morning. Beck would have just started his shift with Erika in tow. Erika. I really needed to talk to Craig and Jade about that. She couldn't be babysat forever. Except, I really didn't have a clue how to broach the subject since it kind of was my bad judgment that led to her being stripped of her beta status. Just another thing to add to the *I don't know what to do with it* pile.

I set my phone back down and was about to close my eyes and listen to the god-awful stream of useless information in my head again when a tinkle of keys caught my attention. A lock clicked. A door opened and closed. And then I heard Dominic. "If you're awake, it's just me."

You've got to be kidding me, I thought, and held in the groan, not wanting to wake up Jade. I started to get up, slowly lifting her arm from my chest. She murmured something that sounded a lot like *Move over* and started shoving at me again as I slid off the bed. With a soft chuckle, I grabbed a T-shirt on my way out of the room and tugged it on as I headed downstairs.

I found Dominic sitting on my couch. He was in blue — a dark blue T-shirt, blue jeans, and a light blue jacket zipped halfway up, and he was looking happier than he should for three in the morning.

"What are you doing here, and why do you have a key to my house?" I asked, in a hushed voice, eyeing him from the bottom of the staircase.

"Of course, I have a key," he said cheerfully, flashing me a bright smile. "I'm your second in command. Why wouldn't I have a key?"

I didn't answer that. Over the last month of knowing Dominic, I found it better not to give him a reason to go off on one of his mind-numbing lectures. I sighed, sitting down in my chair. "It's three in the morning, Dom."

He was still smiling a way too sunny smile, and come to think of it, I didn't think I'd ever seen a real smile on him before. He might smirk or grin, but he never really smiled. "If you want it to work, you need to stop holding onto things that will keep you from moving forward."

So it wasn't the boundaries lecture he had in mind. Fantastic. I didn't particularly want to listen to whatever he had to say. Honestly, I wanted to crawl back in bed and wrap my arms around Jade. But it didn't look like that was going to happen. "If you're trying to give me more Jade advice, I don't want to hear it. I almost lost her once because of your advice."

Dominic stretched out on the couch, his arms behind his head, staring up at the ceiling. He was silent for a long moment before he said, "Did you tell her everything?"

"Of course I did," I said, furrowing my brow. "What kind of a stupid question is that?"

Dominic shifted. He steadied his icy blue eyes on me, and his smile turned cold. "She didn't call Mac, figured you were reverting back into that *I'm not going to tell her something that will piss her off* mode."

I hoped I didn't look as annoyed as I felt, but I figured I did, judging by his cool chuckle. "You woke up at three in the morning to come here and ask me if I talked to her," I said dryly.

His eyes narrowed. "Nope," he said. "I was over at the headquarters checking in. The hostage woke up. Oh, and I had to break up a fight between Jared and Beck."

CHAPTER 28

AIDAN

Jade had adorable bed head. Even though her hair was tied up, the indentations by her temples were visible, and stray strands flipped all over the place. Waking her up had been a bit of a challenge. It wasn't until Dominic had come in with a pitcher of ice-cold water threatening to dump it on her that she finally sprung from the bed. By the time I had finally hustled her out the door and into the car, it was closing in on four in the morning.

She walked a few steps ahead of me, her hands continuously running over her hair and then down her wrinkled hoodie and yoga pants, trying to smooth everything out, but she only succeeded in making herself look more rumpled. The hoodie she was wearing was mine, and every few seconds, I noticed her discreetly pressing her nose to her shoulder, pulling in a deep breath of my lingering scent, and each time she did, something in my chest expanded and warmed.

It felt complete. Perfectly whole.

The parking lot was pretty close to deserted, with only a sparse few vehicles, all of them belonging to the team. The air had a bite to it, stuck in that place where any precipitation could easily change from rain to snow in a heartbeat.

Dominic walked along beside me. He still hadn't patched things up with Jade, both of them too stubborn to apologize first, I assumed. Needless to say, the drive over had been on the tense side and painfully quiet.

Jade held the door open long enough for me to catch up and grab it before she took off down the hallway at a determined pace. She was focused, in some kind of zone, so she wasn't really paying attention, and when she reached the doors to the meeting room, and they flung open, she was startled, stumbling back a step.

Jared grinned as he let the door close and stalked toward her. He was in matte-black tonight — black jacket, black T-shirt, black jeans — there wasn't a speck of color except for the sparks of gold in his dark eyes. And he was sporting one hell of a shiner. He locked eyes with me as he closed the distance to Jade. He leaned into her, pulled her into a firm hug, and said, "Hey, little girl."

Clearly, he wasn't done trying to push my buttons.

Jade flinched away from him as if his touch burned and cut me a nervous glance. Her face went tight and still, and for the first time ever, she looked at me with something that resembled real fear. She stayed close to Jared and readjusted her stance, spreading her legs hip-length apart, squaring her shoulders. There was no doubt in my mind that if I made a move, she would place herself between him and me. The look she gave me had a strange intensity about it, as if she knew exactly who she was or who she wanted to be, and she wasn't going to let me change that.

The truth? I loved it. I loved her fire and never wanted it to change.

I swallowed my growl, and I folded my arms over

my chest, hiding my clenched fists under my elbows. I grinned. It took a hell of a lot of effort to do it, too, but I managed a grin that I hoped looked somewhat real.

She arched a perfectly shaped brow and looked at me suspiciously for a second, and then she was suddenly crashing into me, and her hands were in my hair, and her lips were pressed to mine with a quick, warm kiss.

"What was that for?" I asked, wrapping my arms around her waist.

She giggled and grinned up at me. "I love that grin."

And right then, I thought that maybe, just maybe, showing her that I trusted her was a big step in the right direction for us. Hell, if it got me more of her kisses, I would keep the damn grin even if it killed me. I smoothed her hair and stole another kiss. "Let's go see what he can tell us."

Jared crossed his arms and frowned at Jade (she didn't even notice), and then he cut me a vile look. He held it for a long moment before he pivoted and followed Dominic into the room.

Richard had a few new bruises, and so did Beck.

That was the first thing I noticed when we walked into the meeting room. The entire team was there: Jared, Craig, Beck, Landon, Mark. Tommy and Chris stood on either side of Richard, and Erika sat in the far corner, clutching a brown paper bag. The man was maybe nineteen or twenty, with a sharp face and intense smoky gray eyes that didn't stay still, roaming the room in a constant, jittery motion. He was sitting, unrestrained, in a wooden chair, his hands on his thighs and fingers splayed. He wasn't big, not like my wolves, but he wasn't small either, a medium build.

"Shouldn't he be tied up or something?" Jade sounded anxious, but she walked toward him with a sure purpose, even if she was.

"Come on, kitten," Jared said. "You know we don't need to tie him up." He was watching her in a far too personal way, and she didn't even glance at him when he spoke. From the way he was gritting his teeth, I could tell that he really hated that she ignored him. I, on the other hand, kind of loved it. She kept walking as if he weren't even there, as if she hadn't just protected him in the hallway.

"Jared," Landon snapped and shoved him back a step when he tried to follow her. "Show her and her mate some respect. She's the only reason you're here and still breathing."

"Which one of them hit you?" she asked. I wasn't even sure if she knew what was going on around her. She was focused in a way that I'd never seen in her before. She sounded concerned. She looked it, too, as she crouched down in front of him, inspecting his split lip.

Richard looked confused, leaning back in his chair, away from her. His eyes darted around, and he started to shake when Dominic moved closer. I gripped Dominic's shoulder, pulling him to a quick stop. I wanted to see what she did, how she handled him. And Tommy and Chris were close. They wouldn't let the cougar touch her. I locked stares with Tommy. He smirked and nodded, stepping in closer to Jade and Richard.

"It's okay," Jade said in a sweet, soothing tone. "I won't let them touch you again."

It seemed to take forever. Richard took a few hard breaths, searched her face, and then sighed. "Look, I already told them what I know." His voice was hoarse. "I already showed your boys where they are on this map. I was never involved in the decisions. I don't know why my pack is all male. I'm not important enough in the ranks. Women came in, they were used, and then they were gone, replaced by new ones. My mate was in the last batch, so I took her and ran. All I know is Dog Mountain used to be our town, our territory until you wolves came along."

"You're lying," she said. There was no malice in her voice, still soothing and calm. She stayed crouched in front of him, her eyes never straying from his. "Why are you really here?"

He let out a strangled sigh, and if I had to guess, I thought he looked relieved to be caught in the lie. "Because you'll kill me fast, Jeff would have made me suffer." His voice held so much anger, so much pain, and he was speaking the truth. He really believed we wouldn't torture him. He attempted a smile, but it wasn't quite right. It was shaky, and the look in his eyes made it clear he had regrets.

"What did you do to earn your death sentence?" she asked, clenching her fists, gritting her teeth. Richard paled, and he started to tremble as her skin darkened with hair.

"Jade," I said, calling her attention. She rocked back and lifted to her feet in a fast motion. She shook out her hands as if she were trying to shake away the adrenaline that I was certain was burning through her veins.

Jade took in a few sharp breaths and paced a few steps as she got herself under control. It would have scared me how close she was to shifting. She looked as if she were ready to kill him for his lies and we needed him, except the team wasn't concerned at all. They watched her, but it wasn't because they were worried she'd lose it. It was because of the man that sat in front of her.

"You're Jeff's daughter," Richard said and made a startling kind of sound which could have been a laugh but sounded more like a gasp.

Jade's eyes flared as she turned back to him and nodded. "I am."

Richard made that startling laughing gasp sound again. "How did you wind up a wolf?"

"Long story, involving that hardheaded, pain in my ass alpha over there," she said. "If you lie to me again, you'll wish you had stayed with my father." She crouched down again and met his eyes squarely. "Why do you have a death sentence?"

He shifted his gaze away from Jade and frowned. "Same reason you all are going to kill me." He looked back up then, fixing his eyes on me. "I'm the one that killed the girls."

CHAPTER 29

Some days lasted a lifetime. This was one of those days, and as the sun set, there was still no end in sight.

My stomach was a little queasy, flipping over and over. The team stood around, looking as if they were more than capable of brutal violence and completely willing to inflict pain. Except the violence and pain were directed at each other.

The team, a strong group of werewolves with a single-minded purpose of upholding the alpha's laws and protecting the pack, slowly drifted apart. It was almost tragic witnessing it. Even when I hated them, I always had kind of respected the bond they'd had. I wasn't really certain what had changed, but I knew it had something to do with Jared. Whatever ridiculous ideas he was holding onto was driving a wedge between them all.

We spent the entire day questioning Richard. After he finished explaining the real reason as to why my father was intent on killing him, Aidan had taken over with the questions because, well, I'd come close to attacking the bastard. He had executed the women. It hadn't been an accident. They were murdered after three months of being held captive simply because he thought they were no longer *fun* to play with.

Tommy and Chris finally took him to the cells about half an hour ago and had agreed to stand guard. It was either lock him up out of our sight, or one of us would have killed him.

But he had given us a piece of useful information. Ray had killed Bruce when he first took over the pack in a drunken bar fight, and it was because of that fight that there had been a deal struck with my dad. It was Ray's way of apologizing for taking out their leader. He would look the other way as long as they stayed off of his land. With Ray gone, so was the deal he'd had with my father.

"So, what do we do now?" I asked. I was still trembling with white-hot fury, and Aidan reached out to pat my shoulder, stroking my cheek as he pulled back. He smiled, his eyes growing warm as he released a little trickle of his scent to soothe me. He took a seat and stretched out a hand to me. There was no trace of the possessive, jealous edge usually there when Jared was around. It was simply a hand, an invitation. And I took it, settling myself on his lap.

"He'll confess his crimes to the team and us with the pack standing as witnesses," Beck answered.

I craned my neck, looking back at Aidan. "And then?"

His dark gaze turned serious, and his smile faded, and then it was just too much. "He'll be put down, Jade," he said.

I stirred in his lap, trying to hold back a shiver. He must have felt my unease because he started rubbing my back. I pulled in a deep breath and shut my eyes for a second. I wasn't sure why hearing it out loud was getting to me. I'd wanted to kill Richard myself not too long ago. I still did, but handing down his death sentence as if I were the judge seemed a bit too real.

But it had to be done. The longer we had questioned him, the more certain I was of it. He would kill again, whether it was with his pack or alone. The truth had been in his scent, in his eyes. Hell, he had even stated it bluntly.

And it wasn't as if we could hand him over to the police. Most people didn't even know about werewolves. Our town was special in that way. We lived in the open here, but it wasn't the norm.

When it all came down to it, shifters dealt with shifters.

"Why is what they're doing our problem?" Jared asked.

My eyes popped open at his cool tone, and I looked at him. He was straight-faced, as if he really didn't get why we had to do something. "Are you kidding me?" I said. "Of course, it's our problem."

Jared didn't respond immediately. He was staring at me. I didn't need to wonder what he was thinking. The detachment was clear on his face. He really believed we should look the other way. "It's really not," he said finally. "We've done just fine in protecting this town from them. They haven't threatened us outright."

My fury got a thorough kick start, and I growled, "Tiffany ..."

"Is dead," Jared said, cutting me off. "You killed her, Jade, and her deal died when you ripped out her throat." There was no emotion in his remark. He was stating a fact.

"We're dealing with it because it's wrong," Beck said with a frustrated growl, and I got a clear impression that this was not the first time the guys had had this conversation.

"People do wrong shit all the time," Jared said

blandly. "I don't see us running out to stop it, so why now?"

"Because we know who's responsible," I shouted. "We can stop them. We can stop my father." I sounded desperate, and I hated it. "Don't make me regret saving your ass, Jared. I won't do it again."

Jared chuckled, a cold, raw sound. "You didn't save me, little girl, and I've got to say, I'm a bit hurt that you think he would actually win against me."

I bristled and sat a little straighter in Aidan's lap. A growl tore from my throat, and my inner-wolf flipped in my stomach. No one spoke about my mate like that. No one. "Watch yourself, Jared," I snarled. "I'll rip you apart if you come near him."

Aidan chuckled and pressed his lips to my ear. "Easy now," he whispered for my ears only. He brushed a kiss across my neck, and then he rose, bringing me up with him. He started toward Jared, approaching slowly. "You know, I think it's time we clear the air between us," he said to Jared.

Aidan's scent started to thicken in the air, a forceful punch of power and greens. That was never a good sign when Jared was around. My inner-wolf pressed against my skin, ready to break free and defend what was ours. I reached out for him, acutely aware that Landon, Mark, and Beck were moving in closer, their golden eyes fixed on him, but he stepped away from my hand.

"Nothing to clear, alpha," Jared said. He sounded calm, but his jaw ticked, and he stood a bit straighter, rolling his shoulders back.

"You sure about that?" Aidan asked, stopping a few feet away from him. "Because I heard something that's pretty damn interesting yesterday."

Crap! My body temperature dropped to freezing.

This was not the time. Everyone was too strung out. "Aidan, not now," I said.

"No, Jade," Beck said. He looked at me gravely. "It needs to be out in the open. My brother needs to learn his place."

Jared blinked and looked at Beck in question. They held each other's eyes for a long moment as if they were having a silent conversation. Slowly, Jared's face went red with fury. He shifted his gaze to each one of his brothers. Disgust passed across his face in a quick flash before he forced a blank stare on Aidan. "Don't look at me like you regret killing my father."

"I don't regret it," Aidan said. It sounded harsh, but it was the truth. "I regret not knowing he had kids. I regret not giving him a service so you could have closure. If I'd known, I wouldn't have covered up his death. I would have given you guys time to mourn."

That was a little too much truth for Jared, I thought. He looked shaken and then angry. When he glanced at me, I immediately felt bad, bad enough to look away.

The silence stretched thin as Aidan waited for some kind of response from Jared, and as the seconds turned into minutes, I thought I was going to burst from the tension. But then Landon stepped forward. He looked weirdly calm. He took a knee in front of Aidan and bowed his head. Beck joined him, so did Mark, and then, after another long second, Craig took a knee, too.

"Our father failed this pack," Landon said. "Thank you for saving the pack from him."

"Don't bow to him," Jared shouted. I winced and brought my hands to my ears because when he yelled, it was so loud that it felt as if my eardrums were going to pop from the sound. "He doesn't deserve your respect. He doesn't deserve to be the alpha."

"You want to settle this now?" Aidan growled. "If

you don't think I'm fit to be alpha of this pack, then I'll welcome your challenge."

They stared off for a long moment, Jared's scent was thick in the air, but Aidan held his at bay. I didn't really get it until he glanced at me, studying my expression, which was probably a little freaked out. His nostrils flared, looking for any trace of a reaction from my inner-wolf, and then he laughed, a shock and thrilled sound. When he shifted his focus back on Jared, a strong wave of leafy greens and power and sweetness filled the air. My heart started banging in my chest, and Jared, although he fought it so hard that the blood vessels along his cheeks looked as if they were about to burst, bowed his head.

"That's what I thought," Aidan said dryly. "Pretty sure if you actually believed you could take me, it would have happened already."

Jared met my eyes for a brief second before heading for the door. "I'm out," he said. I went after him, reaching out for his hand, but Aidan stopped me, snaking an arm around my waist. Jared gave us a one-fingered salute, and without looking back, he went out the door.

CHAPTER 30

The team didn't want to talk. I figured it was a guy thing. They grunted a few *S'okays*, and *We don't blame yous* to Aidan.There were some awkward back slaps and a few rough-sounding chuckles. And no one said a word about Jared's freak out. I felt like an outsider watching them, not part of the alpha pair and not part of the team, just a bystander peeking in on a scene that made absolutely no sense to me.

Within five minutes, it was over, and so was our meeting. They set up a new watch rotation to guard the cougar, and then the guys trailed out with their heads hanging a bit lower than usual.

I shot Aidan a hard questioning stare once they were gone, but all he did was shake his head, and then he slipped a hand into mine. He squeezed, a reassuring press of his fingertips, and without a word, he led me out of the building.

The car ride home was a silent one. Aidan's scent was calm and relaxed, and his expression was similar. He held my hand the entire way, rubbing small circles on my palm.

When we got home, he gave me a distracted kiss and

mumbled something about taking a shower. I wanted to say something, but I couldn't. My throat felt tight, as if hands were choking me.

Day from hell, I thought, as he disappeared up the stairs. I considered calling Marcy and Dominic but decided that even though I wanted to talk about everything that had happened with the team and the cougar, I didn't want to talk to them about it.

I went into the kitchen to grab something to eat, but I realized I wasn't really hungry once I opened the fridge. I paced around the house some. I wanted to call the guys, make sure they were okay, and then I wanted to find Jared and knock some sense into him. I knew he was hurting, but if he kept this crap up, he would find himself thrown out of the pack or worse. Alphas die. It sucked, but it happened. He couldn't blame Aidan, not for this. *It was the way of the pack.* The thought made me laugh, a harsh sound. How could I rationalize a death like that when I fought everything else?

Aidan was just turning off the shower as I padded up the stairs, and I headed for the bedroom, figuring I should get changed before he came in. I quickly kicked off my jeans and hoodie and tugged on a pair of boxers and a yellow tank, and then I crawled into bed, ready for the day to be over with.

Aidan pushed the door open a few moments later. He glanced at me and his sexy lips lifted in a crooked smile. His hair was a carefree mess and damp from his shower. He smelled so good. Fresh and clean. He was wearing nothing more than a pair of boxers. My eyes drifted over him, completely on their own, and settled on the raised scar of his alpha imprint on his right pec, a jagged letter "A," which matched my own. His carved face had a contented look to it as he moved toward me.

He crawled onto the bed, and as soon as he was settled, I snuggled in against his warm body. "Are you okay?" My hands were shaking, my lips tight, as I looked up at him, hoping for some kind of insight on what had happened between him and the guys.

"I'm fine, sweetheart," he said. The answer made me want to scream. How was he fine? I just didn't get it. I figured he noticed my confusion because he leaned down, pressed a kiss to my forehead, and said, "Did you just expect us to shed some tears and hug it out?"

"Yeah, kind of," I said, nuzzling my head against his bare chest. "Or at least show some kind of darn emotion."

He laughed as his hand drifted along my back and teased the hem of my tank top, and I shivered in delight as his warm fingertips brushed along the base of my spine. "What about you?" he asked. "Are you okay?"

I held my breath for a long moment. Was I fine? No, not really. My life had been one hell of a ride since I met Aidan, and it didn't seem to be stopping anytime soon. My father, the pack, the team, Aidan, they all seemed like problems, and I had no idea how to solve them. I let out my breath in a slow hiss and said, "Yeah, fine."

"Jade, look at me," his voice was full of command, and before I knew it, my body had complied. I twisted my head, resting my chin on his chest. His handsome face was hard. "Don't lie to me. We're past that shit."

"It's nothing." Another lie, but the thing was I really didn't know how to tell him I felt like I was being pulled in a million different directions. I didn't know how to say that I wanted the team to stay together, especially since he'd made it clear last night that we should take it apart and rebuild. I didn't want to talk about the fact that I wasn't okay with sentencing the cougar to death even if I knew he needed to die, and I really didn't want to talk about my dad.

"Still trying to protect him." It wasn't a question. His eyes hardened further, and his jaw started to tick.

I lowered my lips to his chest, littering it with teasing kisses and little nips. It was a distraction; I knew it, he did, too, but even so, a whole new tension tightened his muscles, and he let out a soft groan. "I don't want to fight," I whispered between kisses.

"I'm not picking a fight, are you?" His voice was husky, and his hand slipped under my tank, rubbing a tingling trail up my spine.

I sighed and shivered. "It has nothing to do with me protecting Jared." I lifted my head, meeting him square in the eyes. "Sometimes, the best move a leader can make is to step back from a battle when the potential loss is too high. Losing the head of the enforcers is a pretty big loss, don't you think?"

He didn't answer, and I continued the soft trail of nips and licks up to his neck. Another soft groan left his lips. "If you keep that up, I might not be able to behave myself."

"Who said I wanted you to behave?" I asked, nipping at his earlobe.

Aidan put a hand under my chin in a blink, lifting my head up. He kissed me, a dominant, thorough kiss, invading my mouth with smooth, powerful moves of his tongue. I really wasn't one-hundred percent sure how I came to my conclusion, but as his tongue tangled with mine and his hands ran along my skin, I knew one thing: I was sick of being sensible.

Funny, when it came right down to it, the decision was an easy one. Or maybe I was just completely and utterly overwhelmed with everything else that was going on, and that one thing was the only thing that made an ounce of sense. Either way, it didn't matter.

My body swayed closer to him, and I pushed on his chest to break the contact. He eased back, but only slightly. His warm brown eyes met mine, and I knew what he was thinking as he laid his head back on the pillow. He thought I was stopping him before anything unchangeable happened, and before he completely closed off the ideas that were burning in his eyes, I whispered, "I'm ready."

"Uh ..." He looked down at me, utterly confused for a moment. His nostrils flared then, searching my scent. His gaze darkened with desire, but there was something else, too, uncertainty, hesitation. I was a bit — a lot — terrified of that small spark in his eye. The one that pushed past everything else, showing me what I'd seen before. I was slowly losing his inner wolf. I could see it, God, I could even smell it.

I pulled in a shuddering breath. My nerves skittered and jumped. I pushed away from him, sitting back on my heels. "I mean, if you haven't changed your mind, that is." My voice (thankfully) was cool, not giving way to my jittery nerves, although I was pretty sure he could smell them anyway.

He shook his head in a violent shake against the pillow. "No, no, I haven't. You just kind of caught me off guard there. I figured ... well, I thought ..."

"You don't sound too sure," I said, knotting my hands in the hem of my tank.

Aidan scrubbed at his face and groaned. "I just don't want you rushing into this if you're still not sure, and I don't want this to happen if it's just to fix things with the pack or with me."

My inner-wolf was a traitor. I was trying, man, was I trying, to play it cool, but thanks to her, my body was burning wickedly hot. She wanted to fix that fading look in his eyes. I did, too, but that wasn't the only reason I wanted this. My mind, my body, my inner-wolf just knew it was time to stop being afraid of losing myself to him because the truth was, I'd been lost since the first time I met him. "This is for me," I said. "If it helps to fix the pack, that's an added bonus, but this is for me."

Aidan was ... nervous, like really nervous. It was kind of sweet and seriously unexpected. That deadly, predatory guard of his was gone. "This is forever, Jade. It can't be undone."

"Good," I said and smiled. "I want forever with you. I love you."

Aidan didn't seem sure, not even a little. He eyed me with doubt that pierced like a hot needle through my heart. And suddenly I couldn't breathe. His eyes narrowed, but not unkindly. It was as if he were trying to decide if he should take me seriously or brush me off.

After a painfully long moment, he said, "Come here."

And my body (or it could have been my inner-wolf) obeyed the command. Before I realized I was moving, I leaned into him again.

He sat up and caressed my cheek, a steaming brush of fingertips trailing along my jaw and dipping down my neck. "You sure?" he asked.

I nodded. I lifted my hands, pressing them against the hard lines of his chest. He continued caressing my skin, a slow trail back up my neck and my lips parted when his fingertips touched them, and he paused, slowly tracing their edges.

He kissed me, but it wasn't demanding. It was soft, testing, and he tasted sweet and minty. Warmth spread through my entire body right down to my toes, and suddenly I didn't want the sweet, soft kiss. I wanted more. I needed more.

Everything poured out of me. All the desire I'd been holding back since I first met him made me feel as if I were on fire. I leaned back from him, breaking the kiss, and stripped off my tank. I wanted to feel his skin against mine so badly it physically hurt.

Aidan watched me for an excruciatingly long minute. His eyes flared golden, his inner-wolf coming out. He let out a low growl of approval and licked his lips. And then his hands were on me, and mine on him. Our lips met. Gone were the sweet testing kisses. He didn't hold back, and neither did I. The world around us began to tilt and fade until all that was left was him and me, lost in scorching touches and feverish kisses.

CHAPTER 31

AIDAN

"Can this wait?" I asked. Okay, it was more like a demand into the phone. I tried not to look at Jade as she crawled back into bed, but not looking wasn't really an option. My gaze drifted back to hers, and I met her hooded eyes. With her long brown hair, still damp from her shower, hanging over her shoulders, and her perfect creamy skin, my blood was already running hot just looking at her. But then she gave me a seductive, hot as hell smile and wagged her finger at me, calling me back to bed, and my entire body went up in flames.

"No, kid, it can't." Tommy's voice, perpetually rough, held a lot more gravel than usual. "I'm bringing the boys to you now. We're ten minutes out."

I rubbed at my face and let out a frustrated growl. The sun was just barely up, and Jade was lying in my bed with nothing more than a towel on. Damn, all I wanted to do was get back in there with her, but of course, I couldn't. There was something else that needed my attention. "I need thirty," I said, watching her wind a strand of hair around her finger. I breathed in a deep lungful of air, catching her new scent, and a growl started to build in my throat. "No, make that sixty."

"Ah, hell, it happened, didn't it?" Tommy muttered. He paused for a second, letting out a long breath that crackled over the phone line. "Shit, kid, this really can't wait. It's about Jared. I'm so ..."

"Don't say you're sorry," I snapped before he could get the word out, and I forced myself to turn away from Jade. "I'm liable to kick your ass when you get here if you do."

"But I am." He paused for another long breath and then said, "Ten minutes."

I hung up the phone with a curse and walked over to the bed. I leaned over Jade, gave her a long and more than a little possessive kiss, and then as much as I hated to do it, I pulled away from her and said, "Time to get dressed, sweetheart. The guys will be here in ten."

Her reply was a purr that came close to undoing me. "We still have ten minutes."

JADE

Aidan laughed. I didn't think I had ever heard him laugh like that before. It was real and full of cheery energy. He was happy, and I loved it. He caressed my cheek and kissed my forehead, and then he pulled away again. "Ten minutes isn't long enough," he said, his voice low and husky. He backed up a step and smirked. "I'm going to jump in the shower, and you better have your cute butt dressed when I'm done." Aidan didn't wait for my protests before he turned around and headed out of the room. A second later, I heard the rush of the shower as he turned it on.

With a long sigh, I pulled myself out of bed

grudgingly. I went to the dresser, tugging open a drawer, and began to riffle through the minimal clothing I had here at the house.

I had only just gotten out of the shower when Aidan's phone had gone off. I knew it was freakin' horrible to be annoyed at the interruption, but I couldn't help it. Really, was it too much to ask for just a few more uninterrupted hours with my new mate?

Then again, it wasn't as if they knew we had taken that step yet, so I figured I really couldn't blame them.

Letting my towel drop to the floor, I pulled on a pair of panties and then fastened my bra. Even annoyed, I was still grinning. Last night had been more than I had expected. So much more. It had been a slow, blissful hour, full of sensual exploration, discovering each other in an entirely different way. I had expected to be nervous, but after the first few minutes, my nerves had vanished. Being with Aidan was comfortable and exciting, and breathtaking. I had let myself go, and so had he.

I pulled in an idyllic breath, catching the change in my scent. I pressed my palm to my nose, grinning. I could actually smell the difference on my skin, a layer of leafy greens coating my natural aroma.

I'm really his, I thought, as I stepped into a pair of jeans. *And oh, God, he's actually officially mine.* My grin widened into a painfully big smile. My chest felt so full; I felt so complete. It was utterly amazing.

Banging, like someone was hitting the front door with a baseball bat, wiped the grin from my face. With a quick glance at the clock, I snagged a T-shirt and tugged it on, thinking ten minutes couldn't have possibly passed yet, but yep, it had.

I rushed out of the bedroom, and as I passed the bathroom, I heard the shower still going. "Hurry up, they're here," I called out, and then I hit the stairs at a jog.

The thudding at the door didn't stop until I yanked it open. I blinked against the bright sun, once, twice, and then my eyes went wide, and my lips parted with horror.

Craig stood in front of me, his left eye black and swollen shut. There was a blood-crusted gash running down his right cheek, stopping at the base of his chin. His neck was covered in bruises, and Jesus, I could actually see individual fingermarks there. Beck and Landon were behind him. They didn't look as bad, but each of them was sporting a nice shiner, and Mark, who stood off to the side, had a purplish bruise on his cheek.

"Where's Aidan?" Tommy asked, his voice all rough edges. He didn't wait for me to move out of the way before he started to shove the guys into the house, not too gently.

I blinked and cleared my throat. "He's upstairs," I said, backing up as everyone crowded into the living room. "In the shower." I chewed on my bottom lip, scanning the guys over. "I don't think I want to know what happened." I swallowed down the dread that was climbing up my throat. "Do you want some ice? Or something for the pain? Or ... Or ... What the hell did Jared do this time?" God, it had to have been Jared. I just knew it. He'd been so pissed yesterday. He'd been ...

"They're fine," Chris said in a lazy drawl, closing the front door. He flexed his arms, his biceps curling up thick, as he fixed a steady glare on the team. He was giving off a clear-cut vibe of a guy who didn't tolerate any crap. With the way he carried his tall, bulky frame, I didn't doubt for a second he wasn't opposed to using his fists to make sure everyone understood it. "Start talking, boys. You've got a better chance of making it out of this alive if you talk to her before Aidan." He smiled at me then, or at least I thought the rough curve of his lips was supposed to be a smile, and said, "She seems to have a soft spot for you boys."

The four of them exchanged tight-lipped looks. Landon started to shake — literally — and it was all wrong when he tried to smile at me. My inner-wolf shifted and stirred, and I growled. It came out before I could swallow it, fierce and all animal. "What have you done?" I demanded. My imprint heated, my scent flared, and all four of them dipped their chins, casting their eyes to the ground.

Tommy's shiny head took on a pinkish-red hue. "Please," he started and then cleared his throat. "Jade, control yourself, please. You're mated now, Aidan's scent mixed with yours is ..." He cleared his throat again and rubbed at it hard as if he were trying to massage away a lump that was blocking his voice.

I pulled in a deep breath, forcing my inner-wolf to stand down, which was, as it turned out, a crazy amount of work. Sweat beaded along my spine, and my hands trembled. But I managed to rein it in if only a little.

Tommy sucked in a noisy breath, and he shoved at Craig, growling, "Tell her."

Craig stumbled and fell to his knees. He wouldn't look at me, and I didn't know if it was because he physically couldn't look up or if it was that he didn't want to. "Jared," he croaked and winced. His voice sounded raw as if he'd swallowed a handful of broken glass. "He knew where the bastards were, Jade. He's known for a week."

Heavy footsteps coming down the staircase and a deadly growl told me that Aidan had heard what had just been said. I wanted to turn away. I wanted to go to him, but I couldn't move.

Craig might as well have punched me. It probably would have felt better. His accusations gutted me and left me raw and exposed and empty. "No." I shook my head. "No, he would have told me. You're lying. Jared's a dick, but he loves this pack. He wouldn't hide something like that. He wouldn't."

"You would scent that, Jade," Beck said, giving me one of those crappy reasoning looks. "You know he's telling you the truth."

Oh, God, I thought. Was this really how the rest of my life was going to be? Lies and betrayal? Aidan was behind me, close enough that I could feel his breath teasing the hair on the top of my head. I could hear his steady breathing and the rhythmic thumping of his heart. His scent was calm, and he was deathly quiet. It scared me a bit. As dread choked me, the only thing I could get out was, "Why?"

"Aidan took our father from us," Mark said. His eyes were dull when he looked up as if he had checked out and his mind was somewhere else entirely. "We wanted him to feel the same pain we felt when he died. Jared thought if he spent enough time with you, you'd mate with him. Aidan took something from us, he was going to take something back. He stalled on the hunt. We all did. We knew if you found them, you'd walk away from Jared. He just wanted more time to win you over."

Craig cleared his throat. "We didn't know he'd found them until this morning," he said. The smell of his desperation left a bitter taste in the air. "I swear it. We didn't know. He went ape-shit crazy when we told him we were done."

"You helped him." I was shaking all over. "You all stood by and helped him try to ruin my mate. You ...

you ..." I growled. They all plotted against my mate. My mate. The people I trusted, my friends, my team. "How didn't I smell the lies?"

"You never asked," Beck said, again with that reasoning tone. "We never had to lie to you."

Landon lifted his chin a little and looked over my head. "Aidan, I thought she wanted him," he said, and damn him, he actually looked ashamed. "All of us did. Her inner-wolf reacted like Jared was to be her mate. She was throwing off her scent for him. If we'd known she wasn't into him, that it was just her wolf sensing his dominance, we wouldn't have helped stall things. We wouldn't have helped keep you from her." He swallowed a few hard swallows, and his face drained of color. "We stopped helping him when she submitted to you when you took her from Jeff's."

There was dead silence for a long breath. It was violent and cold, and when Aidan finally spoke, I found it hard to breathe. "You know I'm going to hunt him down, right?" Aidan's voice was a lethal toned whisper behind me. I turned to him and looked up. His expression was both striking and brutal. He looked me in the eyes and said, "And when I find him, I'm going to kill him. You are not saving his ass this time."

I knew I was probably supposed to reason with him, do the devil's advocate thing, but I couldn't. I wanted blood, too, so bad that my body lurched as my inner-wolf tried to break free. I'd always known Jared was loyal to a fault. I just never thought that loyalty could have been for Ray.

CHAPTER 32

AIDAN

It would have been better if Jade had defended him.

Jade didn't say a word. Instead, she gave me a terrible blank look and stood perfectly still. Her heart was slamming fast against her ribs. I could hear it so clearly. I could smell her bloodlust, too, a thick bitter-sweet aroma that had my inner-wolf pressing against my skin.

It struck me then, I was finally going to get my chance to kill Jared, and she was going to let me. Damn, by the look of her, she wasn't just going to let me. She wanted to do it herself. I really didn't know how I felt about that.

"You won't need to hunt him, kid," Tommy said. "He's challenging you for alpha. The pack has already gathered to witness."

The laugh that came out of my mouth was cold. "He thinks he can challenge me," I said and shook my head. "He lost his right to do that when he put his needs before the pack." I looked at the team. Their desperation, their fear, it all hung in the air like a pungent cloud of smoke. "But what should I do with you four," I said, stepping around Jade. "I find myself stuck here. I get revenge, and I can smell that you didn't know what Jared was hiding, but you helped him. You knew the cougars wanted our females and you helped delay the hunt."

Across the room, Beck shuffled his feet. "We meant what we said to you yesterday. You saved us from our father; I'm just sorry we didn't see that sooner." He raised his chin and stoned his face as he looked at me. "We will stand behind you if you allow it, and if you won't, we will accept your punishment without a fight."

"You knew she didn't want him, didn't you?" I laughed coolly. "Yeah, you did. You were always with them training, weren't you? You stuck close."

Beck nodded. "Because Jared wanted to force her, and I wasn't going to let him do that. No matter what, it was always her choice."

I rocked back on my heels a little bit as a punch of adrenaline shot through me. *Force her.* Another blast of steamy adrenaline rushed to my head.

"Easy," Chris said in a calm, low voice. "Easy there, kid, you need to think this one out. They came forward. They're giving up their own flesh and blood for you, for your mate."

I didn't want to hear that. I didn't care who they were giving up. *Force her.* He'd known. Beck had known that Jared was willing to force her. And he'd let the bastard sleep in her house, in her room. My inner wolf's savage nature took over. There was no logic to it. I was taken over by a possessive instinct.

At the sound of the first pop of bone, I heard a soft rasp, and I glanced over my shoulder. "Aidan, stop," Jade said. She reached out a hand to me, and I ignored it.

A series of pops and snaps broke out. My clothes tore and fell, my body remolded. And then I was a wolf. My lips peeled back, and I growled as I pivoted and stalked toward Beck.

Jade cut in front of me and said, "Aidan, remember what I told you last night. Sometimes the best move a leader can make is to step back from a battle when the potential loss is too high."

I heard a rustling and then a series of soft thumps. I glanced away from Jade, curled my lips further, and growled at the team. All four of them were on their knees, their necks craned out, their eyes closed. The silent offer reaffirmed what Beck had said. They would not fight me no matter what action I took.

"You are not this person," Jade said softly. "Your fight isn't with them."

JADE

Jared had called me soft once, and yeah, maybe I was soft. By pack law, I shouldn't have stopped Aidan, shouldn't have stopped his inner-wolf from killing the guys. By pack law, death was what they deserved. But I just couldn't let him do it. Not when they had willingly come forward. It may have been delayed, but they had done the right thing in the end. And I knew he would regret it afterward. I knew he was already bleeding inside from taking their father from them, even if he refused to show it.

It took thirty long minutes for everyone to get their heads back together and another ten after the guys told Aidan exactly where the cougars were for him to calm down enough to leave the house. I thought it was probably cold outside, there was a heavy wind, but I didn't notice the temperature. I couldn't feel it. I couldn't feel anything but the ice that shifted through my veins.

My werewolves were all gathered at the edge of the clearing, standing back — cowering — from Jared. He looked worse than the team had when they'd shown up on our doorstep. He was cut and bruised, and his right elbow was bending the entirely wrong way. His eyes were on me, though. They were so black, like bottomless pits. His pain and outrage rose up around him, hanging like acid in the air.

In front of him, discarded like a piece of trash, was Richard. He was dead. His blood no longer pumped through his veins, his heart no longer beat in his chest, and no breath would ever be pulled into his lungs again. A primal and territorial rage filled me. What struck me as odd, though, was that I was not angry that the man was dead, but because his sentence had been taken from me, even if I had dreaded having to issue his death sentence, it was my right to do it. This was my pack.

Luken was there, too, Richard's last guard. He was on his knees, although not because he wanted to be. He didn't look as if he could have gotten up even if he wanted to.

As I scanned the scene in front of me, there were, I realized, different shades of hatred, and until now, I had only ever felt a ghostly shadow of that emotion before. I hadn't really hated Dominic when he left me for the pack, although at the time, I thought I had. I hadn't truly hated Aidan for all his lies and manipulation or Marcy and Dominic for helping him. And I hadn't hated my father when I found out he was the devil. I'd been disappointed and hurt and angry and lost.

But, no, I hadn't hated them at all.

That had been a tingling sensation with a pinch, like getting a needle at the doctor or a blister. It was annoying, and it burned a little when poked at, but it hadn't been anything like what I felt at that moment.

Funny, but I never thought hatred would hurt so badly. It was like scorching heat, burning me up from the inside out, but at the same time, from the outside pushing in; I was cold as ice. My heart pounded so hard that it felt as if at any moment it would just stop beating as if it were about to give out on me. And God, did it hurt.

My mouth went dry, and I pressed closer to Aidan. His body was hot, solid, and strong against me. The silence in the clearing was voluminous. Aidan hadn't said anything yet. He was too calm. And right then, calm was, well, calm was scary. I thought I would have preferred to see the outrage he'd shown at home. At least that I could understand. But he just stared at Jared, an intense kind of stare that would have made pretty much anyone queasy.

"Who do you think you are?" Aidan finally asked. His tone was freakishly composed. "You are not the judge and executioner for this pack."

When Jared didn't answer, Aidan paced forward, leaving my side. He clasped his hand behind him. He wasn't looking at the dead body strewn out on the brittle grass. His eyes were fixed on Jared, a controlled stare that gave nothing away.

Aidan was only a few feet away when Jared gave a reaction. He shrugged and then winced from the movement. "Head enforcer is the executioner," he said dryly as if he were bored by the question. "And soon enough, I'll be alpha."

Aidan barked out a laugh. "You really think you can challenge for alpha with what you've done."

Jared's face grew red and furious. "Thanks to my brothers," he said with a venomous glare at them, "you will kill me if I don't."

Aidan seemed to consider Jared's words as he visibly measured the distance between them with a darting, calculating shift of his eyes. "You'll die either way, Jared."

Jared shifted his weight to the balls of his feet as if he were readying himself for a collision, but Aidan didn't move.

This was cruel, I thought. Really cruel.

Aidan flicked a small glance in my direction, and as if reading my thoughts, his eyes narrowed in warning. I knew then that I had to say something, even if I didn't want to.

Planting my hands on my hips, I stepped forward, and I said, "Last night, I told my mate that losing you would be a big loss to this pack. I defended you to him, again. I'm always defending you, Jared. You hid the cougars' location from me. You wanted to force me to mate with you. Have you told everyone how you plotted against us? That you betrayed us to get even for Ray's death? You tried to kill your own brother when he wanted to come forward. How am I supposed to defend you now? How? Give me a reason!" It all spilled out in a desperate tumbled mess, and I realized I actually wanted a reason to keep him alive. Maybe that was why the hatred hurt so badly; I honestly didn't want to hate him because he could be a good person somewhere under that cocky, jerk facade. I had seen it. I knew it was there.

Jared groaned and rolled his eyes. Not the response I had expected and definitely not the one I wanted. "They don't have to like me, Jade. They only have to fear me. And he's not your mate." He said it with a smile and a cocky wave of his hand.

I stepped closer, trying to not let my boiling hatred consume me. "Are you sure about that?"

CHAPTER 33

Jared's first mistake was striking Jade. His second was shifting.

The second she moved in closer, Jared's nostrils flared, catching the change in her scent, which was growing stronger with every passing second. He sagged, and his demeanor went from cocky to seething in a split second.

Jade was trying to give him a way out. She wanted him to live. I could hear it in her voice, that hint of desperation. Jared knew it, too. His eyes flared, and for a quick second, he even smiled a sad tilt of his lips.

But then, he moved and got in her face. He lifted his hand and backhanded Jade, hard enough that she stumbled. And then he shifted.

If he had stayed human, he might have had a chance.

Jade may have given him a way out of this, but she wasn't stupid. *Thank God she wasn't stupid.* She was out of her clothes a second later. She didn't hesitate in her shift, letting her inner-wolf out in a breath. And I was right there with her, my bones breaking and snapping. Hair sprouted over my skin, my canines lengthened.

It only took seconds, and then we were both wolves,

big and snarling, black beasts. We moved like killers, stalking around him, waiting and ready for the strike. We moved together perfectly, Jade and me, completely in sync.

Jared shifted back and forth, pivoting to keep us both in his sights. He looked for his opening. He waited. He even backed up a step. And we stayed on him, stalking him like the predators we were.

Jade's breath was a constant growl, each inhale and exhale carrying the sound. At least until Jared looked her straight on, and she froze stiffly.

And that was the opening he had been waiting for. Jared launched at Jade, his lips curled, teeth sharp, and jaw open for the bite. That was his third mistake. It was also the mistake that solidified his death.

Males did not attack females. Especially not the alpha female.

My thirst for blood rose up, but I wasn't the only one who felt it. Growls erupted all around us, and wolves sprung forward from the sidelines.

Jade tensed, and a quick burst of her fear tingled at my nose. But her fear didn't last. She dodged his lunge just as I launched forward, tackling him to the ground. There wasn't time for anything fancy. I pinned his neck into the grass with a hard press of my teeth. With a graceful leap, Jade was on him, too, planting her front paws on his chest, snarling down at him.

Jared thrashed beneath us, growling and snapping. I saw the pack circling from the corner of my eyes, watching with hunger. Growls pierced through the air. The team had shifted, too, and closed in on us, but they did not attack, did not try to save their brother.

The pack moved in closer, snarling viciously. And I knew right then that if I didn't kill him, they would. The scent of savagery and bloodthirstiness clung all around them. Jared was not walking out of this clearing. The pack wasn't going to let him walk after attacking Jade. But then, neither was I.

Jared bucked hard, fighting with everything he had. Just like his father. But this time, I did not wait for his submission. I knew it would never come. No, this time, I ended it fast, burying my teeth in his neck, and biting down until he laid still. Until he was gone.

JADE

When Jared took his last breath, I backed up in a rush. Aidan let go of his neck as soon as I moved and looked up at me. It was a slow, searching look, and he didn't break it, not once, as he shifted back to human.

Wolves were howling all around me. The pack who had hated me had shifted to protect me. I'd seen them do it and rush in when Jared launched at me. And now they howled, a sad, pain-filled song. My insides shriveled and twisted listening to it.

Aidan rose up, and his eyes were still on me. He moved slowly as if he was scared I would run. He found his pants, tugged them on, and then he was standing over me. He dropped down to his knees. His hand trembled ever so slightly as he reached out and ran it along my fur. He pulled me to him, wrapping his arms around my neck, and he hugged me close. His murmurs were soothing sounds, not really words, and I almost missed it when the words actually came out. "I'm sorry." His voice was raw.

I ached for him. I knew he really was sorry.

But it wasn't his fault. Jared could have made a graceful retreat. I would have let him bow out of town. I would have made Aidan let him, too, no matter what his crimes were against the pack or against us — the alpha pair. For that one desperate moment, I would have let him go. But he hadn't wanted that. He had wanted revenge.

I shifted in Aidan's arms, and he didn't let go, not even as my bones snapped and moved under my skin. I didn't respond right away when I returned to my human form. I simply gazed at him, hoping he would see that I understood.

"Thank you for making it quick for him," I whispered after a long moment. "I'm not sure the rest of them would have."

His gaze fell, and he nodded. His throat bobbed with a few quick swallows, and he released me from his arms. As he rose from my side, the pack began to shift back to human, and as they did, cheers rose up loud and quick. I took to my feet and swallowed down the bile that rocketed up my throat. My insides were twisting and clenching with pain.

They were cheering over his dead body.

"How can they be happy about this?" My voice was a whisper. I didn't expect an answer. I didn't really want one.

"They're not cheering because he's dead, Jade," Beck whispered from behind me as a windbreaker wrapped over my shoulders. "They cheer because the alpha pair is together. They cheer for your union. They cheer that you fought for them. That you didn't let them fall into the hands of Jared. They cheer for you, not for him. Never confuse that. It'll kill you if you do." The heartbreak in his voice made me ache for him. He slid in front of me and pulled the jacket closed.

Landon drew close, and he touched my arm. "Jared was already dead, Jade," he said. "My brother died the same night my father did."

I nodded because, really, I couldn't do anything else. Craig came forward, and so did Mark. The four of them surrounded me, and then I was in their arms. I don't know how long we stood there, finding support in each other's embrace, but by the time we let go, the cheering had dried up.

The pack had circled us, dressed once more. There was no malice in their movement, and I had the distinct impression that the circle they formed was one of protection.

I slid away from the guys and looked for Aidan. He hadn't gone far, just a few steps away. When my eyes landed on him, he smiled, although it didn't look real at all. I couldn't guess what he was feeling. Most likely because I was choking on my own emotions, and he had that calm fearless expression back in place.

He came to me, his warm weight settling in behind me, and his arms went around my waist. He squeezed me and pressed a kiss to my cheek, and then, he addressed our pack.

"Thank you, my friends," he said, his voice loud and strong. "Today, you've shown me that despite our differences, we can truly be a pack. You all didn't hesitate to rush forward when my mate was threatened, even though not all of you felt she was worthy of alpha, and I thank you for that. I will not forget it."

I looked out over the pack standing around us. I searched inside myself for a connection to them, that little thread of feeling that I had come to depend on. I found it in Dominic's hazel eyes and Marcy's sorrow-filled gaze. I felt it in Trevor's protective arms that encircled his human mate. I saw it in Erika as she looked at me with regret and admiration. I found it in all of them, that little piece of me. That sense of belonging, of possession, and of unyielding protectiveness. It swelled in my chest expanded my heart. We may have been splintered, but we were a pack. We were together, and we would support the cracks while they healed.

As a unit, the pack lowered to the ground, kneeling and bowing — a sign of their loyalty to Aidan. I found myself wondering if it might have been for both of us. Whether it was for him or for us, I felt the resolve tighten in my chest. This time, no matter what, I would not fail them.

As I looked out over the sea of bowed heads, I said, "Thank you." My voice was weak, very weak. I cleared my throat and blinked away the sting of tears. "Go now and rest. Grieve the loss of our brother, and comfort the ones he left behind." My voice still trembled, and Aidan's arm tightened around me, supporting me. My heart was pounding hard against my chest, and I strengthened my grip on my emotions. "But be ready. We know where the cougars are. The time is coming to take out our enemy."

As soon as they started moving, heading for the woods, I turned to those who had stayed behind. My friends: Marcy and Trevor, Tommy and Chris, the team, Dominic, even Erika, waited before Aidan and I. Waited for the words I figured neither of us wanted to say.

Marcy managed to whisper the question on all of our minds. "What happens now?"

"We bury our brother," Aidan said with compassion, choosing to ignore the real question behind her words.

A string of faint but heart-filled, *thank-yous* spilled from the guys, and a tension that I hadn't noticed was there until it lifted, dispersed into the air. And then the waiting started once more.

I swallowed hard, pulled in a breath, and said, "And then we tell my father I'm mated and watch for the next play of his game to drop."

Note from the Author

Thank you for reading *Deadly Mates*. If you enjoyed this book (or even if you didn't) please consider leaving a review on the site where you purchased it. Word-of-mouth is crucial for any author to succeed and your review, even if it's only a sentence or two, makes a huge difference in helping new readers make the decision to read my books. Many thanks for your support.

XOXO,
Ashley Stoyanoff

Acknowledgments

An enormous thank you goes to my family and friends. When I think of your unwavering support, words fail to capture how truly grateful I am. I love you all.

To my husband, Jordan, thank you for talking to me about the characters as if they were real people. You make me laugh, you keep me challenged, and I love you for it.

And to my editor, Kathryn, your enthusiasm and insight makes me glad you are on my team.

Last, but not least, a big, huge thank you to all of my fabulous readers. You guys are the best and I couldn't have done it without you all!

About the Author

Romance author Ashley Stoyanoff is the recipient of two Royal Dragonfly Book Awards for young adult and newbie fiction. Her first book, *The Soul's Mark: FOUND*, came out in 2012. Her other passions include reading and shopping for the latest fashions. Learn more about Ashley and her work at ashleystoyanoff.com.

Further Reading: Deadly Pack

Did you love *Deadly Mates*? Then you should read *Deadly Pack* by Ashley Stoyanoff!

Since becoming the alpha female of the Dog Mountain pack, Jade certainly has had her share of challenges. She's had to prove herself to a bunch of werewolves that she spent years hating; forgive her mate who'd done nothing but lie to her, and face the grueling fact that her father leads a pack of werecougars, who are responsible for tormenting her werewolves for many years.

On the upside, the Dog Mountain pack is finally coming together—now that Jade and Aidan's mate status is official. And now that they know where her father's been hiding his nasty pack of beasts, Jade and Aidan can concentrate on stopping them once and for all.

But when Jade's dad finds out that she's become Aidan's official mate, all hell breaks loose, and Jade and Aidan soon learn that his plans for their werewolves are bigger than anyone could have ever suspected.